Bruno Beaches is a mature, retired police officer who has had a lot of life experience from work, business, and family life. He started writing seriously after two failed marriages where he used the creation of stories to explore the dynamics of marital relationships. Those two initial novels whet his appetite, and he carried on writing and has written four more works of fiction, all heavily influenced by his understanding of the human psyche. He has a large family to whom he is very close, and he enjoys gardening, DIY, dancing and keeping fit. He is a compassionate 'people person', and has always taken a keen interest in behavioural psychology and relationships and currently works in the care industry.

Bruno Beaches

ROTTEN LITTLE DEVILS

AUSTIN MACAULEY PUBLISHERS™

LONDON * CAMBRIDGE * NEW YORK * SHARJAH

A CIP catalogue record for this title is available from the British Library.

ISBN 9781035830350 (Paperback)
ISBN 9781035830367 (ePub e-book)

www.austinmacauley.com

First Published 2024
Austin Macauley Publishers Ltd®
1 Canada Square
Canary Wharf
London
E14 5AA

I wish to express my hearty thanks to Cynthia. She is a practicing humanistic psychologist who very kindly agreed to give me her professional input as to how the counselling sessions in the story between Charlotte and a counsellor like her might have gone. She was a pleasure to work with and the only reward she wanted was to know that her wise words might be of some constructive use to some of the readers of this book, and to help provide awareness that there are always skilful capable counsellors out there ready to help people who are only too willing to assist people struggling with any kind of life issues. I am very grateful for being allowed to introduce her voice into parts of the story. Her particular discipline goes beyond the behaviourist and psychodynamic approach of psychology and looks at free will and the individual as a whole and emphasises the importance of the individual striving towards personal growth and fulfilment.

For we wrestle not against flesh and blood, but against principalities, against powers, against the rulers of the darkness of this age, and against spiritual hosts of wickedness in the heavenly places.

Ephesians chapter 6 verse 2

Chapter 1

The angel Emmanuel stood in front of the arch-devil Gronoff and demon Munther. He had entered the devil's very own chambers hidden in the earth and he would never be allowed back into heaven again. He trembled, such was his consternation and his discomfort was exacerbated by the awful, pungent smell of the place. It was causing him to gag. This was a life-changing process, but he had finally made this decision following many years of indecision and uncertainty. Gronoff displayed a confusing mix of expressions that morphed repeatedly from disdain to excitement and back again.

"What made you come over?" He asked tersely, his rasping gravelly voice seeping through his yellow teeth on a raft of strikingly noisome breath.

"I want to be on the winning team."

Emmanuel did his best to sound sincere and trustworthy, but he knew his answer probably sounded comical, naive and childish. He wasn't trying to be humorous, but Gronoff laughed loudly, pleased that this freshly fallen angel believed that the darkness was winning.

"You think we're winning, after so many millennia of battle?"

Emmanuel realised that his voice had come across as uncertain and weak. He couldn't help it. Now that he had made his move, he was feeling very nervous and vulnerable. He was at their mercy, and devils were not well known for their kindness and mercy.

"Definitely."

"You know there's no going back don't you? Now you are now a fallen angel just like the rest of us!"

Emmanuel didn't like the mocking tone in his voice. Hadn't they done the same thing, only many thousands of years earlier? Gronoff was still curious, mocking and searching. He had the power to reject this rebel angel. If he did that, Emmanuel would be cast out, simply to become a lone, lost, abandoned spirit, destined to exist meaninglessly, forevermore, in perdition. He had to convince Gronoff that he would make good devil material.

Gronoff sneered. "How are we winning?"

Emmanuel answered with more conviction. "It seems to me that people have turned their backs on God and that they have adopted 'science' as their new idol."

Gronoff mulled this over for a few moments. He knew that people were treating science as the new God and that his fellow devils were fully exploiting such erroneous preoccupation, but he wanted to know more. He was suspicious and sceptical of this newly-fallen angel.

"Be more specific. What do you mean by science?"

"I realise that most people haven't actually got a clue about science, but it's a modern notion sold to them by their leaders, and they accept that."

He paused to see how he was coming across. Gronoff told him to carry on. He firmed himself up some more and tried to sound more confident. He spoke more loudly, more boldly, and determined not to be so distracted by the smell.

"The last straw for me was recently, when politicians ordered the churches to stop meeting together and to stop singing praises to their God, in the name of science, and all the churches bowed the knee meekly to their new lords without hesitation. In fact, they were more obedient to their earthly rulers than the so-called non-believers. Then, after they were eventually allowed to meet up again, they were given ridiculous instructions about when they could stand up or sit down, how closely they got to sit together, whether they could actually sing or just mime. It made my insides squirm; it was so hollow and pathetic. Clearly none of them had any real faith in the god they professed to follow. That was it. That was when I realised that the church on Earth was over. It had no backbone. It revealed a total lack of proper conviction and belief. It was finished, beyond redemption."

Gronoff beamed a wide enthusiastic yellow-toothed smile. "Yes, that was so gratifying. We laughed at them so much."

Emmanuel seemed to have said enough to convince Gronoff who removed his clasped hands away from his chin, nodding sagely.

"At first, you will struggle to take the opposing viewpoint with any conviction, but don't worry; our work will grow on you."

His smile was malicious now.

"To start with, just remember that we do the opposite of everything you have been used to, up there. If you always remember that, you will do ok. Do everything to undermine all of the Ten Commandments and remember that everything we do is to bring about the destruction of the human race."

Emmanuel had nothing in particular against the human race, but quite simply, like he had genuinely explained already, he just wanted to be on the winning team, simply a matter of survival. They all had an eternity to think about.

"Yes, Gronoff."

"You will be assigned to specific people in due course, but for now, until you have settled in and learned the ropes, you will accompany Munther here. He will show you the work that we do."

"Yes, Gronoff."

"What did you say your name was again?"

"Emmanuel."

Gronoff's countenance became angry at the sound of that name, and he answered fiercely.

"You will never utter that name again. Ever! You will be known henceforth as Quithel."

"Yes, Gronoff. Quithel!"

"Oh, and one other thing. You'll get used to the smell!"

Both he and Munther laughed raucously.

**

Samuel Sheppard tucked his baby girl up into her bed and kissed her goodnight. They had just finished a story. She was so pleased to finally have her own room now that she was seven, and had some privacy from her older brother Bronson.

Munther whispered in Sam's ear, "You are such a good father, getting on with your family chores as soon as you get in from work. You deserve more recognition from your wife. She doesn't value you enough."

He popped his head around Bronson's bedroom door.

"You've got another fifteen minutes on that thing before it goes off and you can start getting ready for bed!"

"Ow, Dad, don't be so fucking mean!"

"Bronson! How many times do I have to ask you not to use that kind of language in this house?"

"But Dad, everyone at school uses it all the time. We're encouraged to express ourselves naturally. To be ourselves and to be inclusive. To say and think whatever we want."

"Well, not in this house. We're not that kind of inclusive and we still have standards about the kind of language that is tolerated. Now you have ten minutes!"

"Fucking hell, Dad!"

Samuel went downstairs to see how dinner was coming along. He was disappointed to find the kitchen in a redundant state. He found his wife, Abi, in the lounge. He gave her his well-practiced tired look, flavoured with a hint of exasperation.

"Abi, you haven't started dinner yet!"

She looked disgruntled that his expectations were too demanding and continued sorting out her books.

"I just had a bit of marking to do and I wanted to get that out of the way first."

Munther whispered in her ear.

"He really doesn't appreciate you, does he? He just wants what he can get. You give in to him too quickly. Most of the time, you're just his sex-toy and cook and nothing else."

She looked at Sam fiercely wondering whether to have an argument, but really, she was too tired for that. She ameliorated.

"I'll start it in a minute, dear. It won't take long. We've got stir-fry."

Munther whispered in Sam's ear, "You were better off when you were just dating. You fucked her far more often, the food was better, and now she just takes you for granted. You just pay most of the bills and you're no longer her priority. The kids are."

Samuel sat down grumpily and put the news on. He hadn't checked the news since listening to it in the car on the way home from work about an hour earlier, and he felt the pressing need for a misery-fix.

**

Munther took Quithel to the top of a church roof to give him his first lesson. They lay on the grainy tiles looking vacantly into the sky as Munther began to proudly impart his wisdom.

"We work subtly, chipping away to undermine. Obviously, they can't see us, and sometimes I wonder if they can actually even hear us. Half the time they seem quite deaf! But they do have many characteristics that work in our favour. You can't just sit on someone's shoulder all day long just constantly spouting bad stuff. It won't work. They would just tune you out. We have to be very sensitive and subtle. We can't hear their actual thoughts, but you learn to interpret the tone of their language and their expressions pretty quickly, and then you can often work out what they are thinking. That's what we work on. We build on their own insecurities and bad tendencies. You got that?"

"Yes, Munther. I already know a lot about human nature."

Munther looked at him momentarily, sceptically. "What would an angel know?"

Quithel got the feeling that it was best not to answer that question, and Munther carried on.

"Remember these three things about people and you'll do well; one-they all possess an innate need to worship something or someone—mostly, its film stars and sports stars, but these days we somehow seem to be able to dredge up all sorts of dross and make them into celebrities or what they call influencers. Any kind of human worship is good for our purposes."

"Yes, Munther."

"Two-a belief that somewhere along the line they have been wronged, and the world owes them."

"Yes, Munther."

"Three, they have a never-ending thirst for pleasure. Remember these three things and it will make your job easier."

"Yes, Munther."

"And also remember that the Dark One hates marriage and families because the light one instigated them for the propagation of the species, so we must work to undermine them at every opportunity."

"Of course."

Then Quithel had a question. "If we're all about the destruction of the human race, why can't we just do more to actually harm people directly?"

Munther looked annoyed. "We are not allowed to. We can only influence. People must bring harm upon themselves. It's all about choice unfortunately and we can only help them make the worst choices, but as you'll see, that's not so hard to achieve."

He laughed almost feverishly, with such relish. Quithel thought about asking who put this restriction on them, but that would be a stupid question. It must have been God. God was big on free will, and he guessed that Munther would not want to talk about that. On reflection, Munther wondered if he had made devils seem rather impotent, so he added something more positive.

"We do have a few nice weapons at our disposal, such as disease and natural catastrophes, but we'll talk about them another time. You have to learn to walk before you can run."

"Yes, Munther," he answered meekly.

"Earlier on with Samuel and Abi, all I was doing was trying to make them feel hard done by. Half the time it's just about sowing seeds. Humans love to dwell on stuff. Brooding on a problem always makes it seem far worse, and most people in relationships feel taken for granted. Come along. We've got other people to visit. We can't be everywhere at once like some beings, so we keep on the move, drip-feeding here, there and everywhere, constantly drip-feeding. Quithel, be a drip. The world needs drips!"

He laughed at his feeble attempt to be comical and Munther just looked at him blankly.

**

Charlotte was a favourite of Munther's because he had been grooming her for years, and now he felt that she was close to taking her own life, and he was excited. Helping to bring about a suicide was almost as good as helping to orchestrate some kind of disaster. They found her alone at home as usual, slumped on her sofa watching a popular comedy soap. It was really depressing her. The humour was predictable and silly, and the characters were too outlandish, and the content was blatantly riven with liberal dogma that was designed to direct the way she thought, and she was well aware of all this, and it annoyed her so. She was not an unintelligent woman, and she saw through the way these kinds of programmes set out to subtly influence people's perceptions and to mould their thinking. She was quite the cynic. It just made her feel even more that she didn't fit in. TV was just a distraction from real life, but she felt that she didn't want the life or the distraction, but it was company, and she was so lonely. She craved company. Munther spoke to her.

"Seriously, what is the point of this shit life? Nobody cares about you. You'd be better off just ending it and escaping all the bad feelings. You've never got any money to do anything interesting. They give you enough money to barely keep you alive, and you always struggle to pay all your bills. It's just an on-going never-ending torment. If you ended it all today, people would realise just how badly they've treated you."

The dull sadness in Charlotte's eyes grew even denser. She picked up the remote and started flicking channels and tucked into another jumbo packet of crisps.

Quithel had a question for Munther. "How come you've been working on her for so long? Isn't she a lost cause for you if she hasn't killed herself by now?"

Munther laughed, reminiscing and mulling this over.

"I've been that close so many times, but each time, at the crucial point I had to depart."

Quithel looked puzzled. Munther noted his quizzical look and explained, "She must have someone praying for her. Probably some old long-lost aunt, granny or something. Fucking grannies!"

"What, and an angel suddenly appeared?"

Munther looked at him fiercely. "You can't use that word anymore, not now that you're on our side. We refer to them as light-reps or light-agents."

Quithel looked a little bit annoyed about the semantics, but he quietly waited for an answer to his question.

"We don't actually see them, just like people can't see us, but we feel their presence and we have to go."

"Why?"

Munther looked cross. This was clearly an awkward subject for him.

"It's difficult to explain. You'll know what I mean when it happens to you."

Quithel looked a bit nonplussed, but Munther had a question for him.

"When you were a light-rep, you must have been sent out on missions?"

"Not me personally. We spent most of our time worshipping the highest in heaven."

Munther laughed at the thought. "Didn't you get bored of all that ecclesiastical bullshit?"

Quithel took a few moments to reflect. "Not really. I used to actually find it inspirational and uplifting. It was kind of trance-like."

An angry look came over Munther's face. "Well, that's all gone now. You mustn't speak of such things again."

"But I was just answering your question."

Munther answered abruptly. "You've got to stop thinking like a light-rep, you tosser, and start thinking like a devil. Constantly, all the time. There's no room for reflection. You're supposed to be transitioning! Don't forget that! Please don't take forever!"

"Okay," he replied quietly, surprised at Munther's vehemence. He considered Munther to be a very frustrating being to converse with and realised that he would have to keep his responses to him carefully measured if he didn't want to be constantly chastised. They focussed back on Charlotte. She looked so drained and enervated. Not only did she live alone, she had no close friends or family. Munther whispered in her ear.

"You've got loads of pills in the bathroom. Why don't you just take enough to end all this pain? It would be so easy. Just go quietly to sleep, a really satisfying, peaceful sleep."

She looked seriously contemplative and went to get up. Just then the phone rang.

"Fuck those interfering bastards!" Munther cursed.

"Is there a light-rep here now?"

"No, but those old people who keep praying for her and others like her, they are such a pain in the arse. I hate them! They are the bane of our work. Come on, let's go."

**

Alexander sat down floppily on the settee which almost abutted his mother's armchair. She glanced over from the television and looked at him pointedly through her thick black glasses, her fingers still working away automatically, rapidly adding stitch after stitch.

"And to what do I owe the privilege of your company, may I ask?"

"Don't be mean, Mum. I often sit down here with you."

She looked surprised. "Not since you were a little boy as far as I can remember."

He gave a little chortle. "Oh, you are funny, Mum. Do you fancy a cuppa? I'm going to make one."

"Well, as you're offering, yes please, that would be nice. That spicy scene in Emmerdale has rather dried out my throat."

Alex contorted his face. "Emmerdale? Spicy scenes? I didn't think those words could be put in the same sentence."

"You obviously haven't been keeping up with the times. The soaps of today are very different to the soaps of yesteryear my dear."

"Thank God, I don't watch them then."

He got up and went into the kitchen. Everything was the same as when he had been a boy, except that now he was a fifty-five-year-old man and had last lived in this house thirty-seven years earlier. Colours had faded, but little had needed replacing over the years. A few new mod-cons had arrived such as that new-fangled air-fryer. She had bought one because a friend had convinced her that they were the new indispensable gadget that everyone had to have, but nevertheless, she never used it. It looked rather out of place, like an afterthought that nobody knew where to put. It would probably look cumbersome in any kitchen. It was big and a funny, awkward shape.

He had returned to his family home following his divorce a few months earlier. His wife of twenty-six years, Prescilla, had decided that they had grown apart over the years, and she wanted a fresh start whilst she still had 'the chance'. *Of course,* she still loved him, she just wasn't *in love* with him, and apparently that was enough to terminate a marriage of twenty-six years. Their modest family home got duly sold in the 'process' and he got his half of the equity, but he wouldn't be able to buy another home of his own without taking out a new huge mortgage, and he simply wasn't prepared to do that. His mum seemed very happy to have him back home, and so, for the foreseeable future, that was that, a done deal, and it seemed to be working out very well. He would comfortably nap mid-afternoon for an hour after returning from his early-start postman job, and his bedroom was a decent enough size to quite happily double up as his office. Of course, there was no rent to pay. She was his mum!

His passion was making reels for the internet exploring the wonders of how the human body works. He would spend a great deal of time trawling through written information and illustrations either from books or online, and then using some high-tech computer programmes, with which he demonstrated a good deal of expertise, he would create easy-to-understand animated videos for the layman. This fascination had started five years earlier when he realised that he knew so little about health and his own body and it still consumed and excited him so many years later. The more he learned, the more he realised how little he knew.

He took for his mum a mug of strong tea and sat again on the sofa before excitedly asking her, "Mum, did you know that the liver is involved in over five hundred different metabolic processes?"

Without taking her eyes off the TV, her fingers constantly twitching rhythmically over the needles, she answered evenly "No, I didn't know that, love."

"Every part of the human body is astonishing," he confirmed with a broad smile on his face. "Particularly the way that hundreds if not thousands of processes all work together to exactly complement each other. It's like every single cell in your body has its own little brain orchestrating everything in precise detail. If it didn't happen like that, each cell would die. Then we would die."

"Lovely, dear. I suppose it all works amazingly well until it doesn't."

He thought about that for a moment. "Yes, very deep, Mum. And how is your angina today?"

"Not too bad, dear. Must not complain, the pills seem to still be working, until they don't."

He was always rather stumped by her phlegm. It was strange that he, her only son, became so easily animated by contrast.

Munther whispered in his ear. "You could do very well out of this, Alex. House all paid for, and she has money in the bank that she has no real use for. What might happen if she forgot to take her blessed pills?"

He shook those ridiculous and pointless thoughts out of his head as his mother asked him a question.

"Are you still happy being a postman, dear? Have you thought about going back into computers?"

"Mum, you know why I left computing. Five years ago, I had two colleagues die of heart attacks in less than a year. They weren't old. It was just their lifestyle, and much as I liked them, I didn't want to join them in the next world, not yet anyway. I decided to do something physical that was good for my body. Something that would help keeps me alive for a bit longer."

"I've made a ripe old age, and I didn't become a postman."

"That's just obtuse, Mum."

She glanced at him over the top of her glasses quizzically. "Anyway, I didn't think you believed in the next world?"

"I don't. It's just an expression, and anyway, I am still using my computer skills. You know I am, on my very own platform on new tube."

"Yes, but that's not a proper job, is it?"

He stared vacantly at the TV screen; two people arguing sternly with each other across a pub table. They looked cross and miserable. He thought to himself, *this is what they call entertainment?* He answered Dawn without looking at her.

"Mum, I have a proper job, *and* I make extra money from my website."

She looked at him quizzically again. "Oh yes. You've mentioned money from advertising, but that doesn't add up to much, does it?"

Now he looked at her rather excitedly. "It depends entirely on how big your following is, and I've just broken the one hundred thousand barriers, and that's pretty good."

"That's nice, dear. So long as you're happy."

She gave him a heart-warming smile before looking back down at her knitting.

Chapter 2

Charlotte was well aware of the bridge between two rocky hills. She had crossed it on the bus many times. On a clear day, from the top deck, one could clearly see the stream at the bottom of the gorge about one hundred feet down, flanked by large rocks and scrub. It was well known locally as a place where desperate, sad people occasionally threw themselves to their bloody, smashing death. It was on a fairly rural route about two miles outside of town, just a relatively quiet road with a pedestrian and cycle path on one side. A wire fence had been added alongside the footpath to deter jumpers, but it was a half-hearted affair which might help prevent accidents but did nothing to deter determined jumpers.

She wondered what to wear. The fact that she was about to kill herself didn't distract her from the present awareness that other strange people would be closely examining and then handling her pulped body, and she wanted to appear as dignified as she could be, even in death. That meant that she would certainly need to wear trousers, preferably jeans, and a substantial tight-fitting top. She wondered about jewellery. Yes, she'd like something to give her extra dignity, but nothing ostentatious. She racked her brain. She had no jewellery that was of sentimental value. It would be nice to be accompanied by a meaningful heirloom, or something that formed a connection with another person, but she had nothing, so she just went with a fake pearl necklace she'd got from a charity shop a few years earlier. She liked that one. Before finishing dressing, she emptied her bladder. She didn't like the idea of leaking urine even if she was just a corpse.

Outside in the early evening, it was drizzly and cool. She would wear a coat. Her favourite coat was a dark red woollen one. Not ideal for rain, but hey, what difference would it make tonight? She didn't need to stay dry for anything. She was feeling so nervous. Should she have one last conversation with anyone? And if so, who? She couldn't think of anyone, and anyway, how would that work? What would she want to talk about? Might she not give her game away and then be drawn into a painful unwinnable argument about the messy subject of suicide?

No. It was too late for conversations now. She had made her mind up. She couldn't take the risk of being distracted, and grabbed her handbag and made for the door. She understood that a lot of women possessed several handbags, each one preferred for different occasions, but she only had one, and she wanted to take it with her because its contents would quickly identify her. She visualised in her mind newsreel footage of women jumping to their deaths from towering infernos, and they always clutched their handbags. She used to wonder why on earth they would have grabbed their handbags, but in time she realised that it was to avoid the ignominy of not being identified. Within her bag was her purse, complete with bank cards and her mobile phone. That was who she was, just the unremarkable possessor of a few bank cards. She might lose her life, but not her identity.

Before she strode outside, she conscientiously turned off the lights and locked the front door. *Why did that matter*? She asked herself. It didn't matter, but it was just a habit and keeping up the pretence of normality until the last minute. She trudged the five minutes to the bus stop, her head fogging up with wild thoughts. *Would it hurt? What if she actually didn't die but only broke her back? How long would it be before someone spotted her mangled body strewn messily over the jagged rocks? If enroute her phone rang, should she answer it?* Despite the cool drizzle she felt warm tears dripping down her cheeks. She defiantly wiped them away and instantly regretted putting on make-up for this special day. She had already smeared her cheap mascara. She wasn't even used to wearing make-up and now her face was beginning to look a mess even before she smashed it on the rocks.

The bus arrived. It was half empty, and for that she was grateful. It meant that she could sit on a seat on her own. This was no time for small talk with an over-friendly stranger, unlikely as that was. As the bus trundled onwards, she looked through the window. There wasn't much sign of normal life outside apart from the traffic. Everything looked rather dull and grey in the constant drizzle and she was beginning to feel dreamlike. She felt like she was already letting go. At the next stop, a large man in his fifties, wearing a heavy overcoat sat directly across the aisle from her. She felt him looking at her. She pressed her hands down hard on her bag on her lap and stole a glance towards him. Momentarily, her eyes caught his. She immediately looked down. He knew something. She was sure of it. After a minute or so, she couldn't resist checking on him again, and she found that he was still looking at her. His hair was immaculate, but his expression was rather fixed and intense. He had terrible scarring on his face. As soon as she noticed that, she stopped looking. He made her feel nervous. He definitely knew something. She could feel it.

A few minutes later, she pressed the stop button and alighted just a few hundred yards short of the bridge. She stood and watched the bus move off. The scarred man hadn't gotten off the bus with her, but she couldn't see him inside. Her mind was playing tricks, probably because of the state it was in. If he had alighted with her, she would have gotten back on because he definitely spooked her. As the bus slowly disappeared off into the distance, she felt grateful to it in a peculiar way. It had played an important part in the last moments of her life. It had kindly transported her to her final and ultimate appointment. She actually gave it a little wave goodbye, as if there were people on board whom she actually knew, and maybe they would miss her. Then she walked slowly, but purposely towards the bridge. She would have to get to the middle of it where the drop was at its deepest. The further away from that point, either before or beyond, the more quickly the ground climbed up towards the bridge and the scrubbier and less rocky it became, and at these places, one was far less likely to be killed outright, and that really wouldn't do. The path was rarely used by pedestrians. Normally, cyclists were quite common, with just an occasional dog walker, but it seemed that in this weather, she might not see anyone.

She walked steadily towards the centre and as she did so, gradually the form of another person took shape half way along, just standing quietly by the fence. The closer she got to this person, the slower she walked, wondering who this was and what they were doing. When she got within about eight feet of them, she stopped and took stock. A man about five feet ten inches tall, early forties, dressed in a rather scruffy dark grey suit. Despite the suit, he had a slightly bohemian appearance because she could clearly make out that his hair was long and dreaded. He hadn't looked at her yet. She wondered if he was even aware of her presence, despite the fact that she was so close. He was staring down across the gorge, seemingly lost in thought. She was nervous about his presence but she felt compelled to make a connection with him. She sensed that he was desperate. In a strange and inexplicable way, she knew what was on his mind and it made her feel desperately sad for him. She coughed. No response.

"Excuse me, are you ok?"

She surprised herself by actually addressing him, and for a moment wondered what had possessed her to do so, but then it dawned on her that she instinctively felt deep compassion for him, and her humanity made her reach out to him. He still failed to acknowledge her and so she moved a few feet closer.

"Excuse me?" She exclaimed more loudly.

He suddenly turned towards her with a stark look of embarrassment on his sullen face.

"I'm sorry. I didn't mean to startle you," she explained a little more quietly.

Her eyes searched his face in the dim street light. He didn't say anything, but he started to cry, and buried his tightly shut eyes in one clasping hand. His shoulders jerked up and down in time with his sobs. Her heart swelled in empathy. Normally, she would be very wary of strangers, but hey, she was about to kill herself, so did it matter if just for once, she threw caution to the wind? She moved closer, within touching distance and placed a hand on his shoulder. She felt like saying that she knew what he was going through, but that would have sounded so stupid. She actually knew absolutely nothing about this man, so she just tried to reassure him.

"Please, don't cry. It can't be that bad."

That didn't sound a lot less stupid, because what did she know about how bad it was? But she was just responding to an overwhelming urge to help him. It was an atavism she couldn't resist. She had no idea what the right words were in this scenario.

"Can we talk about it? I'm more than happy to help if I possibly can?"

This was weird. She never put herself out for people, yet here she was almost forcing herself upon this stranger, and this compulsion to help him wasn't fading. It was actually giving her a sense of purpose she couldn't remember having had for a long time.

The man started to abate his crying, and then he spoke. He had a nice soft gentle voice that made her think that he himself was a caring gentle man.

"Thank you, that is very kind of you."

She was none the wiser as to what he was doing there, but she boldly ventured her thoughts.

"You were thinking of jumping, weren't you?"

He held his eyes again and cried some more. Hearing someone else vocalise it re-aroused his emotions. He was an honest man and answered truly.

"Yes."

"Do you want to talk about it?"

"No."

She stood quietly for a moment wondering what on earth she should say next, and to her surprise, she found herself announcing boldly.

"Well, I'm not going to let you!"

He gave a little sharp laugh, but said nothing. He wondered how she thought she might be able to stop him if he was determined. He stopped crying. He looked at her piercingly for the first time. He saw in her eyes and face intuition, discernment and compassion.

"You're an angel," he said quietly, fixing his gaze on her now. She laughed.

"I am far from being an angel, I can assure you, but I don't mind pretending, just for one night."

She returned his gaze. This was no time to be coy. She wanted him to see that she meant what she had said about not letting him jump and she stood firm.

"You're not going to let me?" He queried.

"Definitely not!" she said, smiling bizarrely.

He was deep in thought for a few quiet moments, then, "Well then, there's no point in hanging around here then, is there?"

She felt delighted. "No, definitely not."

She turned slightly to indicate walking away but paused for him. She was worried that he was just playing with her and would lunge over the fence at any moment, but he moved in her direction and she placed one hand around the upper arm nearest her to gently lead him. As they started to walk slowly and silently in the direction of town, and with each lumbering, laboured step, she felt slightly more confident that he just might not launch himself into the abyss.

When they were a reasonable distance away from the centre of the bridge, she wondered if she might tempt some information out of him.

"Have you lost a loved one?"

He gave a short laugh. "No, nothing like that."

She noticed the wedding ring on his finger. "Wife left you?"

He looked a little horrified. "No, she's fine."

"You could leave her in other ways you know, without hurting yourself."

He shook his head. "No, really, it's not her. I don't want to leave her, well, not in that sense."

"Do you want to tell me what it is then?"

She knew that she was chancing his patience, but she also felt like it would be great for him to get things off his chest. They were still walking side by side along a deserted pavement. She had let go of his arm now, and the lights of town ahead were glowing ever more brightly. He was quietly thoughtful and then he stopped to look at her.

"Not now," he explained. "I am too upset."

"When then?"

He looked at her, searching her eyes. She was sincere.

"I don't know."

"Shall we meet tomorrow for a chat maybe?"

"Do you think that would be a good idea?"

"Most definitely."

They resumed their slow walk in silence as he pondered. She was the first to speak.

"Look, if we don't meet for a chat, I'll be worried about you all day long tomorrow. I might even take up a vigil on the bridge to make sure you don't come back. You're not going to put me through that are you?"

He chuckled a little then asked, "Do you know Billie's Bistro?"

"Vaguely."

"Shall we meet there tomorrow for coffee?"

"Great. What time?"

"Is eleven ok?"

"That's fine. Do you think I should have your mobile in case you don't show up?"

"I don't think that's a good idea. Don't worry. I will be there. I'm good at keeping appointments."

Munther was livid. "What kind of bad luck do you call that? Them both arriving here at the same time? I'm so fucking angry, I wish I'd pushed them both over the top myself."

"But you're not allowed, right?"

Munther gave Quithel a really dirty look. Often, he really hated his impotence.

"Correct, but I wish. All my sterling efforts coming to nought, again! Fuck those interfering light-agents!"

Quithel watched his subjects disappearing towards town.

"Damn, damn and damn some more!" Munther spat out a string of expletives before telling Quithel that he was totally fed up with this shit, and that it was time for them to leave. He wanted to go to a rowdy pub and cause a big pub fight.

With a bit of luck, someone would get knocked unconscious and smash their head so hard on the ground that it would kill them.

Charlotte and the man carried on walking in more silence. Any conversation was probably best left for the following day. Eventually, they came close to her road.

"I need to go that way," she explained.

They stopped on the street corner.

"Ok," he said as he pondered what was the right way to thank some stranger, who had just probably saved your life?

"Listen, thanks for being here tonight. I don't know what to say. It's been weird."

"Yes it has, but you can tell me more tomorrow, ok?"

"Yes. Ok. What's your name by the way?"

"Charlotte."

She held out her hand, and he shook it.

"Peter," he announced.

"Pleased to meet you, Peter," she said very politely. "I'll see you tomorrow."

He nodded, and with that she turned away, heading towards home, her own thoughts of suicide completely non-existent right now. She turned again and saw him walking back towards the bridge. She called out as she walked quickly back towards him.

"Hey, where are you going?"

"To get my car."

She looked confused. "Where is it?"

"I left it near the bridge."

Her mind was racing. She couldn't possibly allow him to go back there alone. He might jump.

"I'm coming with you."

"Are you sure, you've only just walked all the way back here."

"Definitely."

As they strolled quietly back she asked him. "Why did you walk back with me and not get your car then?"

"I don't know. It just seemed like the right thing to do."

They did indeed find his car near the bridge, and they stopped at it.

"Can I give you a lift home now?" He asked politely.

She pondered the possibilities. The safest thing was for him to drive off and for her to slowly walk back and make sure he didn't come back to the bridge again.

"No, I'm fine. I'm going to walk back."

He looked puzzled. "Are you sure?"

"Definitely. I want to."

"Okay. I'll see you tomorrow then."

She watched him get in his car and drive back towards town. She was back near the bridge, alone with her thoughts. She was tired from all the walking, and damp from the drizzle, but really, any thoughts of self-harm seemed a lifetime away. Then she started walking home, feeling absolutely knackered but somehow so much lighter.

**

Munther and Quithel were having some down time, resting on a church roof in the pale moonlight. Munther had a predilection for church roofs, partly because he liked the height of them, and partly because it made him feel superior to sit on them. This one overlooked a huge cemetery.

"There are quite a few graves down there which I contributed to," he announced unexpectedly. A wry smile crossed his pale face as he reminisced silently. Quithel was often reluctant to ask Munther questions because he wasn't usually in the mood to answer them, and they made him terse, grumpy and objectionable. However, Quithel couldn't easily dampen down his inquisitive nature, and he felt that as Munther was mulling over some of his achievements this was as good a time as any to pick his brain.

"Munther, is there a reward system for devils that are particularly good at their work?"

He was thinking that God was big on rewarding effort and devotion, and he wondered if it was similar on the dark side. Munther answered knowledgeably, tapping into his many thousands of years of knowledge and experience.

"The most amazing strategy ever introduced was by Traxodyl, and not very long ago either. He started sowing the seeds of doubt about creation. He went about whispering to scientists that everything came from nothing, and that there was no God of creation. Of course, none of us thought he would have a hope in a dark place of making that stick. I mean, why would human beings ignore the evidence of their own eyes? Humans have worshipped a God of some description since the beginning of time after all."

He paused. This was a good time to reflect some more upon the human condition. He spoke earnestly, "Quithel, there are three things you must remember about people; one-they are completely illogical compared to us; two-they are often completely unpredictable; three-they associate new-fangled belief systems with higher intelligence and superiority."

Quithel looked at him silently, wondering how many sets of three things there were, but he moved on to another question.

"How does this relate to a reward system?"

"There aren't many positions of authority within our organisation, but I'll give you the best example. Since the overwhelming success of his evolutionary strategy Traxodyl was placed at the left hand side of the Dark One, and he has been there ever since, dishing out his orders to his minions. He's a self-important, sanctimonious bastard. However, recently another devil called Malin challenged him for that position after the runaway success of his equally crazy notion."

Munther shook his head in quiet disbelief, only whetting Quithel's curiosity.

"Which was?"

Munther looked at him seriously.

"It was another completely hair-brained notion that he could get people to destroy babies in the womb. I mean that sort of thing has gone on a small scale since time immemorial. It always used to be that if a man didn't want an offspring, he would just kill the mother before she gave birth, but times have changed, but never before had anyone conceived the idea of destroying babies in the womb on an industrial scale, and like it was a virtuous thing. Again, none of us thought that this notion had a leg to stand on, given a mother's normal fierce protective love for her child and all that, but we were wrong and it took off like a plague, across the whole world. Like I said, humans can be completely unpredictable. Before you knew it, Malin and his agents were instigating this new process more and more over the entire world. Religious opposition crumbled before them like melting ice. Humans love power, and this gave them power in an area they never had power before. Then, following the runaway success of his programme he approached the Dark One stating that his influence had achieved much more damage than Traxodyl's had ever done, because it had led to the direct destruction of millions of lives, but the Dark One didn't see it that way. He maintained that the damage done by removing people's belief in a

God was far bigger, and that without that, Malin's own notion of killing babies in the womb would never have even got started. He stated that the undermining of people's belief in a God had rendered them unspiritual, and as such they were unlikely to believe in an afterlife, which was very advantageous for us devils. They were less likely to embrace a proper moral code, as opposed to a merely political one, and were less likely to be anal about the sanctity of life itself. As a result of all these things, our leading them along all sorts of paths of destruction became so very much easier and had a resoundingly positive effect on our mission."

He smiled broadly, but his smile quickly vanished as he warned Quithel. "Don't you ever get between Malin and Traxodyl. They hate each other."

Then, as he contemplated their hatred for each other, he laughed an amused, joyous laugh. Quithel was mulling over the implications, and then poignantly asked.

"What about the devils who cause wars? Don't they get rewarded? I mean, they cause the most deaths, don't they?"

Munther looked sternly at him.

"Quithel, devils don't cause wars. Humans do. We only put certain thoughts into their heads. Remember what I told you about being sensitive and subtle? We just exploit their emotions, you know. Greed, hate, prejudice, envy and outrage. All the usual stuff that makes them want to fight and destroy each other. That's all we do. They are a bloodthirsty lot and only need a little encouragement. The real challenge for us is to find those rare devious individuals who have evil hearts but charismatic and attractive personalities. They have an amazing ability to get everyone else on their side and to fight their battles for them. They're the ones at the top of the tree, the really cunning ones. They never go to war themselves. They hide away in their cosy whiskey-sodden, bomb-proof bunkers with corteges of whores and sycophants, and they send their stupidly loyal serfs to die for them by the million. Like I said, humans are incredibly illogical."

Quithel mulled this over. "So, there are no rewards for instigating wars in which millions die?"

"Nope. Wars are not unusual. There are always wars. Don't get me wrong. They are great for us. Very many lives are dispatched, but there are no accolades for individuals like us, I'm afraid. Anyway, we have a dedicated war council who work behind the scenes on relevant individuals. They seek out the movers and shakers who have the ability to start wars, and they permeate them with the kind of ideas and philosophies to get the destruction started. Councils do a great deal of work behind the scenes which greatly aids the work of those on the coal-face like you and me."

Quithel looked puzzled. "What councils? How do they work?"

Munther shot him a cold stare. His generosity had run out. "Not now, dense one. You ask too many questions. Come on, we have much work to do, you slacker."

With that, they left the roof in search of their prey.

Chapter 3

Later that night Munther and Quithel visited Pete the Preach as he slept next to his wife Elsie. Munther leaned closely besides one ear.

"How can you be so useless? For a short while you were brave and strong enough to take charge of your life, but you let some strange, meaningless, insignificant woman deter you. Where was your backbone? How could you have been so easily deterred? Why are you so weak?"

Quithel was curious. "Can he hear you when he's asleep?"

"Yes, absolutely. In fact, I sometimes think it's the best time to try to influence them. They are not so distracted. Apparently, they dream during the night which is where stories are going on inside their heads, but in a weird disjointed way. I know this because they often talk about their dreams when they are awake, and I know they usually remember at least bits of what I tell them in the night. Also, even though they don't seem to understand their dreams, they attach a great deal of significance to them if they actually remember them, like they really mean something, or are messages from the universe or something."

This still seemed strange to Quithel. "Does this ever wake them up?"

"Not usually. Some devils specialise in giving them nightmares which are so scary that they wake them up in terror. Children are particularly susceptible, but that's not my forte."

He then got back to Peter. "What is the point of carrying on? You are wise and educated. You know how terrifying the future will be. Very few people know what you have discovered. You know that you can escape those terrors now, before they happen. That's got to be the best way forward. You need to man up and have the balls to do what you've got to do and finish it! Stop being a wimp! Escape the tribulation!"

After several minutes of cramming Peter's head with his suicidal encouragement, he said to Quithel. "That's enough food for thought for him for the time being. Let's go and work on Charlotte now. She's also such a failure."

The next morning Peter entered Billie's Bistro nervously. He felt guilty visiting a strange woman behind his wife's back. He had thought about just not turning up. He wasn't feeling too good after all. His head was muddled. His sleep had been very disturbed by a troubled mind, overthinking and going round and round in circles, but to fail to show up would be dishonourable. How could he even think about standing up a kind person who had possibly saved his life, at least for the time being? She had shown him unwarranted, undeserved kindness and compassion. He didn't lie to Elsie. He just obfuscated, mumbling something about having to visit parishioners who were facing hard emotional times and who sought his biblical advice. He did have another home visit lined up after Charlotte, so later on, he could freely talk to Elsie about that one.

It was a grey drizzly day again, but at least he had managed to park his car fairly close by so his Mac wasn't too wet. He pushed the door and missed hearing the old-fashioned bell tinkle as he did so. Years earlier it was still in operation, but perhaps as the cafe became busier and more popular, the bell's regular tinkling became something of an annoyance, or a new owner didn't like its antiquity, and it had been duly removed, but he still remembered it as a rather whimsical and pleasantly quaint welcoming. He entered in silence, with nothing to trumpet or tinkle his arrival. He immediately saw that the place was almost full up and there was a fairly loud muffled din of voices. He scoured the faces to see if he could see Charlotte. He couldn't, and then he wondered if he would properly be able to recognise her. He had after all only seen her in relatively poor lighting in the dullness of a grey wet evening, and he hadn't exactly stared at her in order to remember her features. He had barely looked her in the eye because of his embarrassment. He scoured a second time, this time just focussing on people who appeared to be on their own, and there weren't many of them. She didn't appear to be anywhere, so he looked for somewhere to sit where they might have the best privacy. A table for two near the front door seemed to have the most space around it, so he planted himself there, and removed his damp Mac before studying the menu. A few minutes later, the waitress arrived to smile at him and ask if he was ready to order.

"I'm actually waiting to meet someone, but I'll order a flat white coffee with toast please to be getting on with."

She smiled at him as if she knew something, something discreet and personal, and he immediately wished that he hadn't mentioned meeting someone. She confirmed that it was ok to bring him his order before the other person arrived and he agreed that it was. Now that he was actually waiting for this strange woman to show up, he began to feel that it was unlikely she would even show up at all, so when his coffee and toast arrived, he quickly delved into it. He was halfway through it when Charlotte did in fact clumsily make her way through the door, almost falling onto his table. She immediately recognised him.

"Sorry I'm late. I woke up late, and then I managed to drop a bowl of cereal on the living room carpet. I had to do my best to get that cleaned up. You know what stale milk smells like? Fuckin' awful!"

She suddenly remembered that she knew nothing about this man, and maybe swearing would offend him. She looked nervously at him and said quietly, "Excuse my French."

She studied his features to measure his reaction. He smiled.

"Please, you don't need to be coy around me. Nothing much surprises me," and he stood to indicate that she took a seat near him. She sat and commented.

"I see you've started without me." She gave a little nervous laugh and added, "Oh, that phrase reminds me of a joke about sex." Now she wished she hadn't said that. "I'm sorry. I'm just blurting out any old rubbish. I must be nervous."

"Please. Just relax. I'm very impressed that you have bothered to show up. I half didn't expect you to."

She smiled, feeling like it was nice that somebody appreciated something that she was actually doing, but he wondered if that remark could be taken as rather insulting. They were both feeling nervous. He qualified it.

"I didn't mean that I didn't think that you're a person of your word, I just thought that this being such a weird situation it might have seemed quite sensible of you not to show up. That's all."

"It's okay. I get where you're coming from, really. You're right—it is weird—but I said that I would be here and I am a woman of my word."

He looked at her thoughtfully. "You don't mind referring to yourself as a woman then?"

She gave him a very confused look. Was he being rude about her? He quickly qualified his remark.

"I mean, there's so much controversy these days about identifying a person by their apparent gender, you know."

She laughed some more and gave him reassurance. "Oh, I'm not into all that PC bollocks I can assure you. I've got all the correct accoutrements of a proper woman I can assure you."

He smiled at her and tried to avoid automatically giving her the once-over. They were both quiet for a few moments, taking stock of the situation. There was no music in the cafe today, but the general buzz of various conversations created quite a backdrop of noise. The waitress, who seemed to have eyes in the back of her head, swanned over.

"Can I get you anything, love?"

Charlotte looked at Peter's plate and quite fancied his buttered toast.

"May I have a large cappuccino and some toast please? Brown."

"Of course."

There were little portions of butter, jam, marmalade and Marmite in a wicker bowl on each table. Alongside that was a rather charming small vase with three gerbera flowers in it. Each table had one. Peter picked one up.

"I say, aren't these gerberas beautiful? Such vibrant colours! I don't think I've ever seen such strong yellows and oranges."

As he spoke, he beamed at the flowers as if he'd never seen such beauty before.

"Yes, they are very cheerful, I must say. You know your flowers then?"

Peter chortled a little, as if to shrug off the compliment. "Not as much as I would like."

A slightly awkward pause followed. Charlotte didn't entirely trust herself to say the right thing so it was up to Peter to break the ice, which he did with the obvious question.

"If you don't mind me asking, Charlotte, but why were you on that bridge last night?"

She had already decided that she was going to lie about this. She just didn't want him knowing that she was feeling just as desperate as he was. What good would she be to him if he knew that she too was on the verge of giving in to her inner demons as well?

"I often go for long walks. It's the only exercise I take."

He accepted her explanation at face value. After all, generally, lots of people were serious about taking exercise.

"Oh, that's good. I was afraid I'd interfered with your plans, that's all."

"Oh no. I was just killing time and getting some fresh air."

"Oh that's good. I can see that walking is a nice straightforward way of keeping healthy. No gym memberships or having to drive somewhere. No costs etcetera, not that I know if you're a member of a gym or anything."

She felt guilty that he believed her so readily, and she wanted to change the focus to him so that she could stop lying. "So, are you going to tell me why you got to the point where you got to yesterday?"

He chuckled. "It's a long story."

"I've got the time. I take ages drinking a nice hot coffee." He pondered her situation. Before revealing intimacies to her, he wanted to know more about her.

"What do you do for a living?"

She looked a little sad. "Nothing, I'm on the long-term sick."

He was surprised. Because of the way she had dealt with him yesterday, he expected her to have a decent job, or be some kind of professional maybe.

"Oh that's a shame," he mused thoughtfully. "May I be so rude as to enquire why?"

Just then the waitress arrived with her coffee and toast.

"Thank you," Charlotte responded appreciatively before turning her attention back to Peter.

"Depression, I used to work in a supermarket, you know, on the checkouts, but I used to go sick too often, usually with depression, and eventually, they laid me off, and I've been on the sick ever since."

She looked sad at the explanation and he looked concerned.

"Have you ever received counselling for it?"

Charlotte laughed. "You're joking! All I ever get are pills, pills and more pills."

She didn't look satisfied about the situation.

"Oh, I'm sorry. That must be so tedious."

"Yes it is, but hey, I'm not here to talk about me!"

They both chuckled a bit, and then Peter bravely got ready to start talking about himself.

"I'm not sure how much I will tell you, but you will treat this in total confidence, won't you?"

"Cross my heart and hope to die." She did the actions, but looked a bit embarrassed about the 'hope to die' bit and said no more, not knowing how to unsay it.

"Well, the first thing I should say about myself is that I am a minister."

She couldn't stop herself looking aghast. "What, you mean like a vicar, or a priest?"

"Yes, exactly like that, except in the Baptist church, we're called ministers."

"Well, I'll be fu…"

She stopped herself just in time. "I mean, you do surprise me. A man of the cloth thinking of, well, you know…"

They were both trying to keep their voices down. They may have been in a public place, but this was a very private conversation.

"Yes I know. It's shocking, isn't it?"

He looked very displeased with himself.

"Yes. I presumed you were going to be some kind of villain on the run or a bankrupt embezzler or maybe a kiddy-fiddler awaiting trial or something like that."

He looked at her, quietly shocked. She carried on gayly without realising perhaps the gravity of what she had just said.

"So, what happened? Aren't you supposed to be filled with hope, faith and praise for the Lord?"

He looked at her sadly, feeling the condemnation. She qualified herself.

"Sorry. That might have sounded a bit like I'm taking the piss. I'm not. I'm just processing my surprise in my own inimitable, highly annoying way. Sorry."

"Please. There's no need to apologise. I understand. We come from very different places."

He thought about that remark and then added.

"Sorry, I really didn't mean that remark to sound condescending or judgemental."

"It's okay. I know you weren't putting me down. I can tell that you're a nice man. You have a good heart, but it's true we come from very different places. You have a responsible calling in life, and I have none."

He blushed a little and remonstrated with her low self-esteem. "Please, don't put yourself down. There's so much more to people than whatever occupation they might or might not have. I mean, look at last night. You did a wonderful thing, as a person."

She laughed a little in acknowledgement. "Yes, but believe me, that was a one-off. Most of the time I am just wasting myself, my time and any talents I might have, although to be honest, I haven't found any yet."

The focus seemed to be coming around to her again, and she didn't want that, so she asked, "Please, tell me a little more about yourself and your situation?"

She leaned in, genuinely deeply curious. He felt that this was strange—thinking about opening his heart up to a total stranger—but it was also relatively

36

easy. She didn't know him. She wouldn't judge him, and of all the people he could talk to, she seemed most appropriate just because she had been there for him in those crucial moments.

"I've been in the ministry for twelve years, but each year, it gets harder and harder. It wasn't that long ago that we could readily talk about all kinds of subjects, like sin, chastity, the sanctity of life, judgement, even basic concepts relating to men and women—binary concepts—but nowadays, these subjects are all off-limits. Too judgemental, non-inclusive, or just plain offensive. Things that used to be sins aren't sins any more. In fact, 'sin' itself is a dirty word. Things are changing so fast that my head is spinning. As a preacher of the word of almighty God, I'm supposed to stick to biblical principles, but as society moves further and further away from them, I feel increasingly that my hands are tied, especially in the pulpit, because you don't know who's there listening, judging, and just getting their ammunition for making horribly woke accusations against you later. I find it depressing that I am expected to water down my sermons and to dilute God's truth so that I don't offend new, modern, secular conventions. It's been the case for a very long time that the media feeds us only what suits them. They stick to whatever narrow bandwidth they've been given by their agenda-driven masters, to help achieve the goals of their oligarch sponsors. We kind of understand that, and accept it as the way of the world, but it shouldn't be like that in the pulpit too."

"Yes, I can see that, but surely that's no reason to, well, you know, take it out on yourself."

"Oh yes, I quite agree. No, that was just the background that I'm giving you. What's really got to me is the future."

Charlotte looked quite confused. "Have you been looking into your crystal ball?"

He laughed. "You don't know how close to the truth you are with that remark, Charlotte."

She didn't understand. "You're going to have to explain."

"Well, as the topics which I can happily preach on are diminishing by the week, I've been looking for subjects which I am still allowed to be honest about, you know, without fear of offending current sensibilities, so I started to study the book of Revelation. I think it is okay to talk about that subject because it's all about the future. But it's a book which preachers tend to shy away from because it seems full of riddles, and it's full of prophecies about the end times, so it has always seemed rather untopical. I mean, who honestly believes that their generation is going to be the last one?"

Charlotte mused on that thought for a few moments before replying.

"Actually, I think a lot of people today are incredibly worried about the future right now. You know, climate change, pollution, cutting down all the rainforests, pandemics, chemtrails poisoning the air we breathe, fluoride poisoning our water, 5G frying our brains, chemicals seeping into everything we eat or put on our skin, doctors getting us to take all kinds of poisons that turn our brains and organs into mush, just so that they and their big-pharma bosses can make loads of money, whilst the rich get richer and the poor get poorer, and sicker."

He looked at her quite gobsmacked by her concise summary.

"You're trying to cheer me up, right?"

She let out a conciliatory, nervous laugh.

"Sorry. I'm meant to be encouraging you, aren't I? I'm not very good at getting things right am I? Sorry."

"No, please, don't apologise for being astute and aware. Those are really good things. Well done. I wish the people in my congregation were more circumspect. Maybe I am barking up the right tree by looking into Revelation. Maybe people are ready for a little introspection about the future, if that's not a contradiction of terms."

"So, you thought you could get your teeth into that one without offending anyone because nobody would think it would be relevant to them, and they would just sit there pretending to be listening but really with their minds switched off?"

He laughed. "You certainly have a way with words, Charlotte."

"Sorry. I wasn't *trying* to be rude. It just comes naturally. Sorry."

"Please, don't keep apologising. You're entitled to your opinion, and in all honesty, I find your frankness refreshing. Very few people these days speak their truth openly."

She smiled at him, relieved that she wasn't apparently offending him. He continued, undaunted.

"I like to think it would be relevant, and it certainly would challenge their comfortable settled attitudes and their apathy, but to be honest, I've never really studied it myself, not in any great depth, so recently, I've been delving into it properly for the first time. But the more I studied it, the more terrified I became for our future, well, to the point where I felt that I really couldn't face it."

"This book is that bad?"

She looked shocked, but the look of consternation and fear that came over his face easily trumped her expression. "Yes, really."

"But is it meant to be sort of, what's the word, allegorical? You know, not to be taken literally, just like the rest of the stories in the Bible?"

He looked at her with a slight hint of disbelief. Clearly, she wasn't a believer.

"Well, that all depends on what exactly you believe, doesn't it? For example, do you believe in evolution?"

She laughed. "Of course, I do."

He stayed very level-headed. "You see, that to me is just a meaningless, unsubstantiated fairy tale."

Her eyes grew noticeably bigger as she expressed her amazement and raised her voice. "You don't believe in evolution?"

He just looked at her, waiting for her astonishment to subside. Then she carried on, more quietly.

"Oh, I see. So, you take the Bible literally, about creation and Adam and Eve and the talking snake in the garden?"

"Yes."

He looked at her resolutely. She pondered quietly for a moment, hiding as best she could her surprise at his naivety and then asked, "So, what's so scary about Revelation then?"

He looked at her thoughtfully, wondering if he should really share his dark thoughts with her. "Are you sure you want to know? It's quite horrific."

Now he had seriously got her curiosity up and she answered enthusiastically and brightly. "Yes, really, I do. I love horror films."

He went on, rather comically. "Well then, if you are seated comfortably, I shall begin…"

Chapter 4

Alexander was in his room admiring his latest work of art on the screen. After six long months of devising it, he was finally happy with the graphics. It had taken a long time to even get around to the immune system, but when he finally did so, he found it to be such a massive subject. Considering how vital it was for human health and how hard it worked, he felt that it was probably the most ignored part of the human body. He used to think that people just took it for granted, without really knowing how it worked or how to keep it in good shape, but at least they believed in its existence. Then the pandemic was alleged and it became obvious by the way the populous was so easily catastrophised that they actually didn't believe in its effectiveness at all.

True, there were already lots of videos on the internet allegedly covering how it worked, but in his opinion, they were all too simplistic and cartoon-like and totally failed to convey the magnitude and momentousness of this incredible wonder. The graphics in these other reels were usually like doodles, simplistic blobs representing viruses or cells, conveying mere academic knowledge and names, whereas he wanted to capture something of the apocalyptic nature of infection and the essence of massive internal warfare as the body fights off invader after invader. Rather than something reminiscent of 'Finding Nemo', he wanted it to be like 'Lord of the Rings' meets 'Jurassic Park', filled with commensurate bloody and astonishing fight scenes. These were real battles that were being silently fought minute by minute, twenty-four hours a day within the amazing human body, and mostly, without the host even feeling any side-effects. He intended for his own rendition to inspire the awe, amazement and respect that the immune system deserved.

Of course, computer-generated-imagery was such a boon to any film maker these days. He was fascinated by what he could do with it, and it was the CGI which would really impress the viewer. Sound effects of the battle had already been added. Lots of noisy munching, scrunching and squishing; elephants blowing their trumpets; the buzz of insects; the flapping of wings; snakes hissing and the sound of walls crashing to the ground to name but a few.

The final touch was the narration and that was what he hadn't finished yet. He was unsure that his voice carried sufficient poise and calibre to do the complex graphics justice, but it would have to. The viewers would have to go without the silky smooth voice of some highly-paid actor. He had used animals to represent the various compositions of the human and invading cells because he thought that the viewer would find them so much more memorable. He scrolled the video back to the start, triple-checked that the recording device was primed, took a few gulps of water, and prepared to narrate. He had the sheet of words on the computer desk in front of him, but he had already run through them and amended them so many times, that he knew them by heart now. He focussed on the screen and pressed play.

Battle commenced, with huge armour-clad elephants with huge wooden chests strapped to their backs, trumpeting and raising their huge trunks. They were animated, ferocious, and were charging at an invading army of snakes. When they were within striking distance, the elephants trampled them, grabbing them in their powerful trunks and literally ate them.

He narrated in a dulcet tone. "The elephants represent macrophages, the first and most powerful line of defence within the human body once the outer protective layer of the skin or mucous membrane has been breached by invading pathogens. They recognise the snakes as alien entities by the Pathogen-Associated-Molecular-Patterns on their surfaces, otherwise known as PAMPS."

He tried to give his voice an even and authoritative edge. Inside his head he was hearing David Attenborough and he was attempting to mimic his pace and authoritative tone, which had proved so unassailably popular since the dawn of television.

"These are just one of several types of white blood cells known collectively as leukocytes. We'll have a brief look at them all over the next few bloody minutes."

The battle scene was open and dusty to emphasise the relatively miniscule size of the combatants. They would be microscopic elephants. The marauding, trumpeting elephants already at the scene of the battle were soon joined by a host of others, trundling in from nearby passageways, which in reality would be arteries and veins. There was much noise and vibration to alert them. They stood in front of a huge grey stone wall. The invading snakes were slithering quickly along the dusty floor instinctively trying to get to the wall. They somehow knew that they would be able to burrow into that wall, reproduce, and destroy it block by block.

Alexander continued with his pseudo-Attenborough impression. "The snakes represent viruses or bacteria or some other type of pathogen, and if they can get into the wall blocks, they will destroy them from the inside and use them to rapidly reproduce themselves, to emerge from the debris in greater numbers to destroy more of the wall. This wall is symbolic of any human body tissue."

At this point in the proceedings, a troop of ninja monkeys appeared in a rather frenetic manner, also attacking the snakes, frantically wielding their knives to slash away at them.

Alexander expounded their behaviour. "These monkeys aren't particularly careful about not slashing body cells in the process of attacking the snakes. They are effective at inflicting damage but because of their somewhat indiscriminate hacking, they are also something of a liability. If the snakes are not too large, they like the elephants will eat them. These crazed monkeys represent neutrophils, another type of leukocyte or white blood cell. In fact, they are the most common of the white blood cells. They are not nearly as large as macrophages, and they are not nearly as deadly, but there are lots of them. As they also occasionally engulf and digest the incoming pathogen just like the macrophages do, a process known as phagocytosis, they can also be referred to as phagocytes."

Hoards of different coloured mice arrive on the scene. There about twenty five variations of them but they all do the same thing. They attach to the snakes and bite holes in their skin. This doesn't kill them, but it does weaken them, and their presence on the snakes helps the elephants spot the snakes and therefore enhances the battle response.

Alexander continues to narrate. "For the purposes of this video, despite their power and apparent superiority, the elephants and ninja monkeys are not getting the upper hand. Too many snakes are slipping past their defences and are getting to the wall, and once in the wall, they multiply quickly. For the elephants and monkeys, their one job in life is to protect the human tissue all around them. They are always on guard at all points inside the human body, ready to put a rapid end to any lucky, or not-so-lucky, invaders, but on this occasion they are being overrun by the sheer quantity of invading snakes. Huge wall blocks are crumbling around them, piece by piece as snakes enter them and corrupt them.

The elephants instinctively know that they need help to defeat this capable foe. Fortunately, they are only the first part of a comprehensive defence system, known as the innate immune system, and they know how to summon help from the secondary part of the immune system known as the adaptive response. Just to confuse matters, the mice are kind of stand-alone, known as the compliment system."

At this point in the proceeding, all the elephants can be seen raising their huge trunks over their backs and releasing the lids on the chests. A host of screeching colourful parrots suddenly emerge dramatically from the chests, flying off in all directions away from the battlefield. Alerted by the screeching of the parrots, an army of spiders begins to appear on the scene, large hairy ones of course. They come out of nowhere and start to climb all over the snakes. They appear to be picking things off the snake's bodies without actually harming them, and then they run off to the nearest passageway out of there.

Alexander explained. "The parrots represent cytokines and interleukins which are chemical messengers released by the macrophages when they need back-up. These will quickly find their way into the bloodstream and travel to the brain where they will trigger a major response. This will be the start of the adaptive side of the immune system coming into play."

Apart from the dramatic visuals, Alexander had added a juicy soundtrack. One could hear the thud of elephant feet stamping the ground, monkeys whooping loudly, snakes being squelched underfoot and the loud cracking of wall blocks breaking apart. The elephants and monkeys relentlessly and valiantly fought on, to the death.

"Most of them will fight to the death through exhaustion, but they will be rapidly replaced by others, as the body's resources are diverted away from other functions such as metabolism and any activities requiring a lot of energy, in order to focus on producing all the immune response cells in vast quantities."

After the parrots had rapidly left the scene to faithfully carry their message to the brain, a cloud of butterflies emerged from the same chests on the elephants' backs. They flew around randomly, like butterflies do, mostly staying over the battlefield with smaller numbers drifting off into all adjoining chambers. At this point, behind the charging elephants and slashing monkeys, komodo dragons sauntered onto the scene. They didn't seem interested directly in the snakes. Instead they were carefully examining the wall blocks, their long tongues flicking in and out rapidly, tasting the air. They looked inquisitive and serious.

Certain blocks would captivate their attention and then these dragons would sink their teeth into the block before casually moving off to examine the next one.

Alexander explained further. "Of course, realistically, I should have made this battle scene underwater with marine life representing the various warring factions because the insides of your body is all bathed in one liquid or another, but I'm sorry, I just found it easier to work with animals rather than fish. You'll just have to imagine the blood flowing, the body fluids, and all the animals not actually drowning. So, the butterflies represent a chemical trail if you will, that will help steer the reinforcements rapidly to the scene of the battle, and the spiders are dendritic cells, another form of white blood cell that is always ready to do its duty. They go over to the pathogens, which helpfully always have 'antibody generating molecules' on their surfaces, abbreviated to 'antigens', and they pick them off and then head off to the nearest lymphatic vessels as quickly as they can. They are creatures that collect a piece of a puzzle from the invader, and then dash off with it to find the other part of the puzzle. They travel up the lymphatic vessels to take the antigens to the lymph nodes where the lymphocytes constantly await just such an event. These lymphocytes are yet more white blood cells known as B, and T Cells. They are called lymphocytes because they mainly reside in the lymph system, particularly inside the lymph nodes."

He leaves his narration there. Something else is happening on the screen—the ground of the battle field bevels. The walls seemed to get bigger. The colours get brighter. These changes are dramatic and exaggerated.

"The effect you can see happening now represents the eventual effect of all those parrots flying off to the brain. The sheer quantity of parrots will influence how much the brain responds. What it does is to cause the body to raise its temperature and stimulate swelling. Invading pathogens often can't cope with the increased heat. The swelling is caused to allow reinforcements to get to the scene of the attack as quickly as possible. The brain is influencing other functions of the body to give the immune system its best possible fighting chance. It is an unfortunate side effect that the pain sensors near the site of inflammation are triggered by the swelling and the heat, but that's a small price to pay for a rapid, effective immune response."

The parrots have all left the battle scene but the butterflies continue to flutter around ceaselessly at the scene and in nearby passageways, signalling the way for immune cells to get to the battle site. Then there is another arrival in the air.

Bats! They flutter around as close to the fighting as they can get. Alexander explains simultaneously.

"The bats arrive in order to reinforce what the brain is doing. They are another type of white blood cell known as basophils and they release chemicals called histamines and heparin. The first chemical dilates blood vessels, again to aid the fast arrival of immune cells, and the second actually thins the blood so that it flows more quickly. I suppose you could say that when the body is under attack, time is of the essence and urgency is facilitated."

The dragons are lumbering around in the background; some actually are climbing up the walls, examining the higher blocks. It is time for Alexander to explain them.

"The komodo dragons represent a third type of lymphocyte white blood cells. The other two, the B and the T cells are still in the lymph nodes, but these dragons are actually known as natural killer cells. They are not summoned as a part of the adaptive immune system. They are always on patrol just like the macrophages and phagocytes. Their job is to find damaged cells and to destroy them before they can multiply into a significant problem, so they are actually one of the many natural defences against cancers and tumours. Basically, the block or human cell that the dragon inspects has to give a chemical password that everything is okay. If the dragon doesn't receive that password, it presumes that something has gone wrong and it injects a chemical which destroys that cell. In our video, if the dragon bites a block it perishes, and any snakes reproducing themselves inside it will also die."

Just as he finishes explaining about bats and dragons, another type of creature scurries onto the scene. Ferrets! They are far fewer in number than all the other animals. They scurry around spitting at snakes, which in turn begin to writhe around in their death throes. Whatever they are spitting is deadly to the snakes.

Alexander introduces them too. "The ferrets represent yet another white blood cell, perhaps the least most important, the eosinophils. To be fair, their speciality is parasites, but that doesn't mean they won't enter into the spirit of things and have a go at viruses, bacteria and fungi too."

The battle scene remains dynamic and animated. Meanwhile, the spiders at the lymph nodes are performing a rushed but mundane task. The video cuts from the battle scene to a large room where lots of spiders are holding the antigens which they have taken from the invaders and they are trying to match them to patterns on the spikes of porcupines. There are several columns where porcupines march in an orderly line past the spiders, and not only porcupines. Badgers too. Every spider is laboriously trying to find a jigsaw match.

Alexander explains. "Each animal has a unique pattern on it, and there are literally billions of different patterns to go through, just like each human fingerprint is different. All the lymph nodes in the body are taken up with this same task, but nevertheless, it still takes time to sift through all the different patterns, usually a few days. It is during this period that the host's body is most vulnerable if the first line of defence is not managing too well. Finally, there comes a eureka moment. A match! Hallelujah! Eventually, somewhere in the system, a match is found on both a badger and a porcupine. It is believed that there are about two billion different types of badgers and porcupines. All the unmatching badgers and porcupines trundle back into storage within the lymph nodes to patiently await their day for battle and triumph. The matching animals self-reproduce at an impressive rate inside the nodes, and as they are produced, they migrate from the lymph system into the bloodstream for rapid transmission to the battle scene, where they are sorely needed. The more butterflies they see on their rapid journey, the closer they know they are getting to their intended destination."

The video cuts back to the site of the battle. There is considerable damage to the building blocks behind the elephants and ninja monkeys. Many dead bodies litter the bloodied ground, and the serpents are everywhere. The first of the porcupines arrive. They dash up to the snakes and fire their quills at them. The quills readily pierce the skin of the snakes. The porcupines magically and rapidly regrow their quills, and they fire them off repeatedly. These quills mark the snakes for destruction. The badgers more easily see the snakes because of all the porcupine quills in them. They brush up against them and a toxin in their fur enters and kills them. All this activity also attracts the komodo dragons that also bite and administer their poisons directly into the snakes.

Alexander adds still more detail. "The porcupines represent one of the lymphocyte white blood cells known as B cells because they originate in the bone marrow. Their quills represent antibodies which bind with specific invading pathogens. They don't kill the snakes, but if enough antibodies attach to the receptors on the snakes skin, they are rendered useless, because it is these receptors that enable the snakes to gain entry to the human cells. At this point, they become useless sitting-ducks, simply awaiting their fate at the hands of the ravenous macrophages, neutrophils and T killer cells. The badgers are another type of lymphocyte white blood cell known as a T helper cell because they are mainly developed in the thymus gland. When a porcupine is in full swing, having been energised by both the spiders and badgers, it can individually produce two thousand new quills per second! The badgers simply roam around orchestrating defences. Somehow their presence re-energises the tiring elephants who now go into overdrive with renewed vigour. "

Now the video clearly shows that the snakes are being rapidly destroyed, and Alexander provides his conclusion.

"The invasion is coming to an end, and the animals are eating up or removing the messy remains. Post-battle, the threat is infection from the dead matter, and the system works in concert to transfer the debris via the lymphatic system and veins to the lymph nodes, kidneys and spleen for them to be ejected from the human body. Some matter, such as dead white blood cells, might end up being ejected as pus through the skin, and the damaged human cells will rapidly be repaired by the body's miraculous healing system."

This sounds like the end of the action, but yet another type of creature suddenly appears, now that the battle has been won. Menacing growling black panthers. They wander around the battle scene snapping at the porcupines and badgers which hurriedly exit the scene and find their way back to the safety of the lymph nodes where the panthers don't patrol.

Alexander explains. "These panthers rid the damaged site of the badgers and porcupines because there is a chance that in their excited state and now that there are no viruses to contend with, they might start attacking healthy human cells, so it is the panthers' job to stand them down. They effectively give the tired, worn out elephants permission to die, a process called apoptosis. In reality, the panthers are known as regulatory T cells, and they help to prevent auto-immune diseases. They don't have to worry too much about the monkeys because their lifespan is merely hours or days at most any way, and the body produces new ones at the rate of a million per second. Fresh elephants will enter the scene to clear up the carnage, but they won't be a threat to the body's cells, because they haven't been weaponised by invaders and the badgers. The Komodo dragons, the natural killer cells, are not targeted as they will carry on searching constantly for damaged human cells to destroy in order to protect the healthy cells."

He clicked off the recording and sat back into his plush office chair. That had gone well and he had that unusual fleeting feeling if actually having completed a project. This called for celebration. He went downstairs and sat on the sofa.

His mother was in her armchair to his right, clicking away with her knitting needles. She looked momentarily away from the television.

"You look pleased with yourself, dear. What have you been up to?"

He couldn't help himself smiling proudly. "Just put the finishing touches to my epic battle of the immune system, Mum."

"That's nice, dear. Did the good guys win?"

"Yes. I don't think it would have the same impact if the body had succumbed to the virus and the host died a slow painful death."

"But isn't that always the end result in life, dear?"

He pondered that for a moment. "Yes, true, but that's only in the very last stage of one's life. All the rest of the time, the good guys win."

She hummed.

"But you've given me an idea. I think my next video should show what happens if you get acquired-immune-deficiency syndrome, and the immune system can no longer cope with attack."

"That sounds nice, dear."

"Mum, did you know that in just one cubic millimetre of blood, there are between five and eleven thousand white blood cells?"

"No, I didn't know that, dear," she answered nonchalantly.

"And that there are at least eight types of white blood cells?"

"That's nice, dear. Are they named after the days of the week dear, with one spare?"

"Not exactly Mum."

He smiled, still absolutely fascinated by the human body.

Munther sat closely beside him and whispered in his ear, "You're full of shit. Not even your own mother is interested in what you do."

The smile on his face slowly faded.

Chapter 5

Munther and Quithel were relaxing, sitting atop another church roof. This time they were looking over bustling streets, with cars rushing from place to place. They were taking time out from tempting and discouraging people to simply chew the cud. Munther didn't often relish having to explain things to his protege, but occasionally the mood took him, and it fed his feeling of superiority. He was in that sort of mood now.

He engaged Quithel. "Do you remember the first day we met you, and Gronoff explained how we must do everything to undermine all of the ten commandment objectives and constantly work at bringing about the destruction of the human race?"

"Of course."

"Well, we undermine everything in the Bible if at all possible, not just the Ten Commandments."

"You mean like mocking miracles and things like that?"

"Yes, that's a good example. We ridicule the things that are easy to ridicule, like miracles, creation, the resurrection, everlasting life, etcetera, but there are more subtle things too. Let me give you one of my favourite examples. I love the subtle, you know. It suits my complicated nature."

Quithel sat quietly, somehow not expecting this to be ground-breaking stuff as Munther continued in his pompous and effected style.

"You remember when God flooded the world and killed off almost the entire human race?"

Quithel chortled. "Yes, he was really pissed off."

He elaborated thoughtfully. "The people that he had actually created to be his friends and family were basically just sticking their fingers up at him. Only Noah and his family showed him any respect, so he showed Noah how to build the Ark to be able to save himself and his family and then drowned the rest of the bastards off with torrential rain!"

"Yes, and all the animals."

"Yeah, and all the animals, well almost all of them."

"Well, afterwards, God must have realised that maybe he had overstepped the mark a little bit with that righteous anger malarky, and so he then made a promise to the few surviving people. Do you remember that?"

Quithel racked his brains. It was a very long time ago. Many thousands of years in fact. Suddenly, he remembered.

"You mean the one about resisting the urge to kill off all the people in the entire world again, even if they did piss him off?"

"Yeah, that one."

Munther cleared his throat and spat out a little dull yellow phlegm before rather grandly quoting from the Bible itself.

"I will not curse the ground anymore for man's sake; neither will I again smite anymore every living thing as I have done. While the earth remaineth, seedtime and harvest, and cold and heat, summer and winter, and day and night shall not cease. And I will establish my covenant with you. Neither shall all flesh be cut off anymore by the waters of a flood, nor shall there anymore be a flood to destroy the earth. And this is the token of the covenant which I make between me and you and every living creature for perpetual generations. I do set my bow in the clouds and it shall be a token of a covenant between me and all the earth. When I bring a cloud over the earth, the bow shall be seen in the cloud, and I will remember my covenant and the waters shall no more become a flood to destroy all flesh."

Quithel looked at him in stunned disbelief. "How do you know all those verses?"

Munther smiled in a conceited manner. "I am rather fond of poetry, you know. I don't spend all of my time just going around causing pain, loss, death and destruction. I am interested in beautiful things too. I like the contrast."

Quithel was a bit confused. "Are we allowed to learn about the Bible?"

Munther looked at him as if that was a somewhat stupid question. "Of course. Knowledge is power. We have to know what we're up against. We have to know what we are undermining. How can we attack a belief system if we don't know the details of what they believe?"

Quithel looked thoughtful. "Yes. That makes sense."

Munther quickly added a proviso, "Not Revelation though. The Dark One forbids that one."

Quithel looked perplexed. "Why not that one?"

"I don't know, but he's very strict about it."

"So, what happens if you learn about that one?"

"I've heard rumours that if you do and he finds out, he'll personally cast you into the lake of fire. Forever!"

Quithel didn't like the sound of that and he had suddenly lost his appetite for questions about the Bible, and he would make quite sure he never learned about the book of Revelation. He got back to the subject in hand.

"So, what's your point about the great flood?"

"My point, my good Quithel, is that the Light One introduced the rainbow as a reminder of his promise not to flood the world again. Quite a significant message, don't you think?"

Quithel mulled this over trying to anticipate the eventual point. "Yes, I suppose so."

"But what does it mean to people today?"

Quithel looked a bit blank and Munther chided him. "You're a bit behind the times, my dear fellow. The rainbow is now associated with diversity, sexual freedom, and non-binaryness. Over the centuries, we have always encouraged people to adopt it for some purpose or other and to forget its original purpose. Its significance changes from century to century, but what's important is that we shroud its intended significance with anything else that suits at the time. We can't have people wondering what rainbows really mean."

He looked at Quithel searchingly to see if he got the point yet. Quithel was not slow on the uptake and he was going to demonstrate it.

"So, your point is that we have disassociated the rainbow from its original purpose by subtly assigning it with new significances at different times, thereby totally undermining its original spiritual meaning?"

"Exactly, my dear chap. My point to you is this; don't get one-tracked with just encouraging people to do bad things and to harm themselves. There's a whole world of opportunity in distortion or suppression of truth, deception, misrepresentation, doubt, fear, perversion, delusion, hubris, betrayal, disinformation, etcetera, etcetera. The list is endless. Even the destruction of one small smile is an achievement," he concluded gleefully.

Quithel contemplated this and said quietly, "Yes, I like the breadth and scope of opportunity that there is."

He smiled at Munther. His smile was definitely becoming more twisted. "Maybe now you could tell me about the councils," he added hopefully.

Munther's mood had changed already, and he was feeling surly. "Not now, you fool. I don't think you can take in too much in one go. You really are quite dense."

**

Charlotte sipped her cappuccino. The way she held it gently to her lips with both hands and keeping her back most upright gave her the air of having some class. Peter by comparison leaned over with slumped shoulders as he sipped his. He was about to give her his overview of the dreaded book of Revelation in between sips of coffee and mouthfuls of toast, and it was as if he was already cowering in fear.

"Well, it was written by one of the apostles called John. He had been imprisoned on an island because of his faith."

Charlotte was already confused and she interjected.

"Excuse me for interrupting, but what is an apostle and why was he imprisoned?"

"An apostle was one of Christ's original twelve disciples, the ones who were commissioned to preach the gospel of Christ after his crucifixion. John was a contemporary of Jesus. He was one of those twelve disciples, and he also wrote one of the gospels in the New Testament, so we're going back two thousand years to the time of the Roman Empire. You must know what the Romans did to people who stood in their way?"

"I know bits about it, I suppose. 'Gladiator' is one of my all-time favourite films."

"Yes, that's a great example. Have you watched 'Ben Hur' too?"

"You mean the sequel?"

He chuckled. "No, just the original. I don't think there was a sequel. It's a very old film."

She looked a little confused. "No, I don't think I know that one."

"Yes, it was way before your time, even before you were born in fact. That's a shame. It depicts Jesus's era with the Romans perfectly. Anyway, in those days, it was quite likely that you'd be imprisoned or be thrown to the lions or burnt at the stake if you believed the wrong things."

"Charming!"

"Yes, exactly, although I do wonder if those practices will soon be back, given the way things are changing so rapidly."

She looked at him a little unsure to see if he was joking, but he seemed deadly serious. He continued.

"John was actually the lucky one. Most of the other apostles had been crucified by now. The Romans were a very bloodthirsty lot, but he was only imprisoned to prevent him from preaching the gospel about Jesus, which the Romans didn't like. He was in his prison cell and was in the spirit when he heard a loud voice like a trumpet…"

She looked a bit lost and interrupted him. "Excuse me, in the spirit?"

"Yes. It means that he was in a very spiritual state. Do you ever meditate?"

"No."

"Okay. I thought we might draw some parallels, but anyway, getting back to John, he was in a state of deep meditation if you like, and he turned to see where the voice was coming from, and he saw seven candlesticks, which incidentally represented the even churches in his day, and in the middle of them was the son of God who shone like the sun, with hair as white as snow, eyes like fire, and a two edged sword coming out of his mouth."

"Yuk! That sounds a bit vile."

She pulled a face like she had just realised that she had stepped in excrement. He ignored her remark and carried on, "He was about to be given messages for each of the seven churches and was instructed to write down messages for them."

"Can spirits write things down? I mean, surely they haven't got hands, have they?"

"He was seeing things in his spirit, but he was still in his body. He could still write things down."

"Okay." She didn't sound very convinced. Then she asked another obvious question. "What did he write on?"

He hadn't thought about that before and he was initially lost for words.

"I mean, he was in a prison cell. They didn't have home comforts in roman prison cells did they?"

He wanted to move on, so he gave her his best quick answer. "If the son of almighty God, the man of miracles, was actually visiting him to give him messages, I don't suppose it would have been beyond the realms of his possibilities to provide something to write on?"

"Hmmmm."

"Maybe he provided him with parchment and quills."

"And ink."

"Yes and ink."

She noticed his frustration. "Sorry. I didn't mean to interrupt you. I suppose I was just thinking out loud."

Without looking much less frustrated, he continued, "Well, after a few polite preliminaries, like the son of God reminding him that he was the alpha and the omega, and that he lived for evermore, and that he had the keys of hell and death, you know, just to put things into some kind of context regarding his absolute majesty, he delivered his seven messages for the seven churches. They included encouragement and also some admonishment because some of them were falling into idolatry or fornication and things like that, you know the sort of thing."

"Of course, idolatry and fornication," she said blandly.

By this time, they were getting some funny looks from other diners who were only managing to pick up tiny snippets of their conversation and a few odd words, very odd words. He continued, unaware and unconcerned if anyone else was listening because he was becoming engrossed in his subject.

"Yes, but what was consistent for every single church was the message to *overcome,* with a promise of a reward if they managed to *overcome.*"

She looked nonplussed. "*Overcome* what?"

"Well, that's what the rest of the book goes on to explain, and that's the really scary bit."

"You certainly know how to keep your listeners in suspense, don't you? Isn't that rather unusual for a preacher?"

"I'm not preaching. I'm just relating a story, a terrifying story but I think it's important that I put it in context."

"I'm not sure it's going to make any sense to me whether you put it in context or not."

She smiled politely. He continued.

"The rewards were all phrased in sentences that would resurface at the end of the book when the salvation of those who overcame was explained."

She looked at him curiously. "Such as?"

"Well, I don't think that they will make much sense to you at this point, but things like 'eating from the tree of life'. Being given 'hidden manna to eat'. 'Having power over all nations'."

"Oh, I quite like that one, but what does manna taste like?"

"That's a reference to the Old Testament when God provided miraculously for his people stranded in the desert, providing them with manna from heaven to keep them alive for forty days and nights."

"Okay," she said uncertainly. "Got anything that I might like?"

"Being clothed in white raiments, having the crown of life, sitting at God's throne, being made a pillar of God's temple?"

She didn't look impressed. "Is that the scary bit?"

"No! That's the good bit."

"Oh." She sounded disappointed.

"Essentially, what he was told was that only the faithful who *overcame* would qualify for salvation in the end."

"You are going to get to the *overcoming* bit, aren't you?"

"Yes, hear me out. *He that hath an ear let him hear!*"

He said that quite loudly, like an announcement, and got quite a lot more odd looks. He smiled, looking a bit pleased with himself, but she looked at him very quizzically.

He clarified. "Sorry, I was just actually quoting from Revelation. That phrase crops up a lot. It seemed appropriate. Anyway, I shall continue, in my own words."

"Good idea," she agreed, "and more quietly."

She tilted her head and eyes towards nearby tables. She didn't particularly want to be the centre of attention.

"Oh, yes, of course," he agreed. He lowered his head. "So after John was told all the messages for the churches, something amazing happened. A door was opened up in heaven, and a trumpet-like voice invited him up into heaven itself to be shown the things that were to come. Immediately, he found himself in the spirit and he saw a throne in heaven."

"Was this an out-of-body experience?"

"Most definitely, so now he wouldn't be able to write things down, but he was no longer being told to write things down, he was being shown unforgettable visions which he would remember and write down later, when he was back in his body."

She looked at him very curiously. "Does your spirit ever leave your body?"

He laughed. "No. It's a very unusual occurrence, like a miracle. Perhaps the best thing for you to liken it to is a vision or a vivid dream."

"Actually, I've got a great uncle who swears that he had an out-of-body experience in hospital when he nearly died. He reckons that he was floating around the room looking down on his own body as the medics resuscitated him."

"Well, there you go then. You know of an example for yourself."

"I think he was just imagining it. Probably the drugs he was on. Hallucinating."

He was a little dismayed by her casual dismissal of such a dramatic event and he side-tracked a little. "I bet he could relate things that he couldn't have possibly known, like who entered or left the room, for how long and in what order?"

He looked at her searchingly. She looked surprised.

"How did you know that?"

"These stories are not that uncommon, and those are the details that people always seem to remember which can't be explained away."

She looked at him with a puzzled expression and whispered, "Hallucination."

He got back onto the topic of John. "The Bible teaches that man was made in the image of God, namely with a body, a soul and a spirit. These days people are preoccupied only with their bodies and souls and don't acknowledge the spirit, which is actually the most important part, because it's eternal. Anyway, John's spirit left his body, and was taken up into heaven. He saw the one seated on the throne clothed in precious stones and there was a rainbow around the throne. He saw twenty-four elders sitting around the throne with crowns of gold, and there was thunder and lightning. There were seven lamps which represented the seven spirits of God and there were four huge unearthly beasts with eyes all over them, and thousands and thousands of angels surrounding them all, and they were all worshipping God, and in the midst of the elders and beasts was the slain lamb of God, but he was no longer slain and dead but alive of course."

"Of course."

"Only the lamb was worthy to open the seven seals in the book in God's hand to discover what they hid, and as he did so there was thunder and lightning and voices like trumpets."

"God likes his trumpets and thunder and lightning, doesn't he?"

"Yes, it does seem so. I think we get our sense of pomp and ceremony directly from God even though we can't call up thunder claps and lightning at will like he can."

He pondered momentarily and then added, "And maybe our love of precious stones too, and bright colours. Anyway, John describes seeing loads of crowns, precious metals and stones, magnificent beasts and lots of music and singing."

"Naturally," she said quietly. She had no idea what he was talking about.

"All these things have scriptural significance, but I haven't got time to explain them all to you now."

"What a shame," she said, rather relieved.

"There are references elsewhere in the Bible to the great tribulation, and John was about to see the actual terms of the tribulation, which would happen at some undisclosed time in the future, in great detail."

"Lucky him."

"It was like he was looking into the future, when God's wrath would be dished out to the earth in the end times."

"That doesn't sound very nice."

"It wasn't. I mean it won't be."

"Hmmm."

"Okay, so first of all, there were seven seals, then seven trumpets, and finally seven bowls. Each one represented a new tribulation. Are you sure you want to hear about them? They are rather terrifying."

"Can't wait!"

She sat forwards, her eyes brightening up. Just then the alarm on his mobile went off and rather embarrassed at the noise it was making, he quickly recovered it from his pocket and turned it off.

"I'm sorry, Charlotte. That was to remind me about my next appointment. I'm afraid that I have to go now."

She looked at him in a very disheartened manner. "You may have finished your toast but you haven't started any tribulations yet."

"Yes, I'm sorry. My introduction was rather long, wasn't it?"

"Well, you're a preacher. That's how they talk, isn't it? Dragging things out into long sermons? I wouldn't expect you to break the habit of a lifetime."

He took stock of her carefully. She seemed to be simple and honest, but he wasn't sure if there was a hint of sarcasm too. He wasn't sure how to proceed now that he had to leave, but she spoke first.

"Well, you can't leave me hanging just like other men are prone to. You'll have to fill me in another time."

She had a little twinkle in her eye, but he was being very careful not to take her the wrong way. He verified what she meant.

"You mean you'd like to hear the rest of the story another time?"

"Of course, what did you think I meant? It would be rude of you not to describe your terrors now that you have introduced them to me."

"Oh, okay. Listen. I just want to thank you again for yesterday. God used you; you know?"

He said that most solemnly, but she laughed.

"Hardly. I don't even believe in God. I just happened to be the one walking there at that time. If it wasn't me, it might have been someone else, or it might have been no one, and you might not still be here."

They both contemplated that thought solemnly. He looked at her with sincerity in his eyes. "Yes, but it wasn't someone else, was it? It was you. God used you."

She felt rather embarrassed by this proposition and changed the subject.

"So, when are you going to tell me the rest of this story then?"

He thought for a few moments. "I've got to work on a sermon tomorrow. How about the next day?"

"Fine," she replied solidly, "but can you make sure we've got a bit more time then? I don't want you breaking off halfway through again and leaving me in suspense about how I'm going to die."

He looked at her quizzically again, wondering if she was getting what he was talking about at all.

"Yes, I suppose so. Same time, same place?"

"Why not?"

"Great! See you on Thursday, eleven o'clock, here."

With that, he got up and left. He was running a little late. She smiled. He had forgotten to pay his bill, but no matter. She would settle up for both of them and maybe later on he would realise that he had left without paying, and that might give him a little extra incentive to show up next time. She was worried that he might not make it.

Chapter 6

Samuel had his own plush office on the sixth floor of a glass-clad, modern, trendy office block overlooking a majestic river and the subservient buildings beyond. His employer, Everyday Bank, leased all of three whole floors, five to seven, and he dreamt of the day when he would be moved up to the seventh floor. He'd made it to six and middle management and he was still only in his mid-thirties. Things were looking good. His particular field was 'compliance'. Compliance had been increasingly forced onto the financial industry by government legislation over many decades, simply because left to its own devices; the financial industry had overwhelmingly proved that it couldn't be trusted to keep its own house in order. Clients had been deceived and exploited at every turn in order that the institution itself could turn in a quick profit. The ethos had been to hide fees and to exploit the client whenever possible. The government itself had happily turned a blind eye to this kind of activity, which bordered on the criminal, as many of its own members benefited enormously from their connections with the banking sector, but in time, public backlash grew too big to ignore.

So, legislation had to be passed, and then these institutions were obliged to show that a particular product was actually suitable and useful for a client, and that the costs and risks had been made transparently clear instead of being hidden or disguised. The financial institutions were tamed and forced to some extent to be moral. The irony, now that these institutions had developed such large compliance departments, complete with sophisticated software and knowledgeable staff, all at their own cost, was that the government itself had begun exploiting them for its own ends. Samuel was regularly finding himself having meetings with clients to explain to them why the bank was unable to release their own money for a particular purpose, because it would transgress a particular pillar of sustainability, as imposed by an all-encompassing government whose ESG guidelines had become a stranglehold throughout all commerce.

He resented the way it made him feel. It was as though he had personally been hijacked by the government to do their dirty work. It would always be about sustainability of course; that word that had wormed itself pervasively into every area of decision making, that carried a solid presumption of respectability and duty, but was really no more than a thin veil of undefined moral bullying. The heavy burden of regulation was wrapped in a warm cosy blanket called 'saving the planet', an honourable and chaste pursuit that nobody would be churlish enough to balk at, no matter how suffocating the effect. However, he had his own secret special way of exploiting the system too.

As a teenager, he had been prodigious. He was one of those extremely gifted, spotty, young hackers who seemed able to get into any system, no matter how well it was protected. Of course, in time, he got caught with his digital hands in the digital till as it were, sifting through and exposing highly confidential documents or information of some big corporation or other. He had no ulterior motive as such. He was doing it just for the thrill, the challenge and to prove himself. Because of his young age and relative innocence, but mainly to save embarrassment to the organisation concerned, no criminal charges were brought, but his parents were put under extreme pressure. They were threatened with jail as accessories and aiders and abettors if he was caught transgressing in similar fashion again. They truly had the fear of God put into them, as a result of which they bent over backwards to channel their dear son's talents into legitimate enterprise.

After years of proper training and proving himself in legitimate fields, Samuel became poacher turned gamekeeper, and he started working for the banks as an online security expert. This morphed over time to something less demanding at compliance where he had now toiled monotonously for some years. At least he had become head of department. Perhaps because of the drudgery of his work or the difficulty of keeping financially afloat in the modern world, or because of the resentment he felt towards the government, he had given in to that part of his nature which was bold, cocky and devious enough to exploit the system.

With much encouragement from Munther of course, who constantly reminded him of the venality of politicians, and the ease with which the super-rich avoided paying any meaningful amounts of taxation themselves, he had devised a simple but beautifully invisible scheme to build up his very own private nest-egg in an untraceable bank account in the Cayman Islands. One day he would be able to escape the hamster wheel and have proper financial independence. His programme intercepted the process of managing charitable donations made by his bank's customers when they added them to online purchases. Because vendors asked purchasers to make donations as a percentage of the purchase price, the amounts donated always included a quantity of pennies. His invisible programme shaved off any odd pennies up to fifty pence and hived them off to his own secret account, which of course he had set up with false details in an even more morally-bankrupt foreign bank, the likes of which had mushroomed over the past century in order to facilitate the hiding the obscenely huge sums of money squirrelled away by the super-rich, and politicians who had no obvious way of legitimately becoming multi-millionaires. Donors were barely aware of what they had actually contributed in the first place, and he felt that none would be aware of a few pennies missing, and that if indeed they did check up on any particular transaction, it would just look like the amount had rounded up or down to avoid expressing fractions of a pound. And so far, he was right, and his fund was swelling steadily, inconspicuously and rather wonderfully.

He wanted to confide in Abi about his scheme, to let her know that he was going to look after her well, and that they would have a secure financial future to look forward to, but he was pretty sure that even though his motivation was so commendable, she might fail to see the sense in it. She might even see it as some kind of transgression. In his opinion, women couldn't automatically be relied upon to make logical decisions. They were often too emotional, or morally ambivalent, and so he chose to bear the responsibility and the worry alone.

**

Quithel had been thinking again about the bigger picture and he wondered if he could come up with a generic attack which might impress the corporate branch. He queried his mentor about an idea.

"Munther, you know that humans are stupid enough to cut down the rainforests even though they know that they are the lungs of the world?"

Munther looked a bit worried. Was Quithel going to come up with a good idea which might make him look cleverer than himself?

"Yes," he answered cautiously.

"And yet they've become obsessed with reducing carbon?"

"Yes."

"Well, as I understand it, trees need carbon dioxide and give off oxygen and people are the opposite. Is that right?"

Munther was getting impatient to learn where this was going.

"We all know this. What is your point?"

"Well, as there is plenty of oxygen in the air on earth, but only a tiny fraction of the atmosphere is carbon dioxide, can't we come up with a plan to reduce the carbon dioxide even further so that there is not enough to sustain the trees. Then, if the trees die, so will humans, but it will be their own fault."

Munther became defensive. "We're not allowed to change things like that. Life on earth hangs in so many fine balances with relation to physics and chemistry. There are hundreds of them, no, thousands, but we don't have the authority to alter any of them unfortunately."

He chuckled as he considered how easy it would be to bring about the destruction of the human race. "We would only need to change one of those fine balances, my friend, and then it would be game over. The measure of gravity, the distance of earth from the sun, the balance of negative and positive ions, the constitution of light and water, the tilt of the earth. The speed of its rotation, the list is endless."

Quithel interrupted him, "Yes I realise that, but what if we came up with a plan to get humans to do it? You know, you said that they're completely illogical."

Munther thought about this very carefully, wondering if there might be some glory in this for him, but he didn't think that there was any mileage in this particular notion because it was already being done.

"Good idea, Quithel, but someone else got there first. Humans are already hell bent on dangerously reducing carbon dioxide."

Quithel looked crest-fallen, and Munther carried on happily squashing his crest.

"We've convinced them that if they don't eliminate more carbon, their planet will incinerate, so they are already doing it, no matter what the consequences. If they carry on at this rate, in fifty years' time, we'll be out of a job."

He laughed maliciously. Quithel felt a little downcast, but he was determined to use his mind to contemplate potentially devastating strategies. He knew that humans had become incredibly clever lately and that each new marvellous invention would have the capacity for as much evil as good. One just had to look out for the opportunities. Humans had discovered the power of splitting the atom and had used that knowledge to make both useful cheap energy, but also nuclear bombs capable of destroying their own planet. They had developed technology to generate a multitude of new chemicals, some of which were used for beneficial purposes, but the best brains in the industry were working on how to make the most potent chemical and biological weapons. He just had to keep his eyes open and spot one new potential before any other devil did so, and he was determined.

**

It was nearly home time, and Samuel was actually just standing at his floor to ceiling window looking out contemplatively over the stunning rooftop views when there was a knock at the door. He turned to see the vice chairman instantly letting himself in. He almost stuttered in surprise. Such visits were most unusual.

"Mr Mainwaring. How nice to see you. To what do I owe the pleasure?"

"Sit down, Samuel. I have something very confidential to share with you."

Mr Mainwaring sat on one side of Samuel's desk, but leaned across it as much as he could with several folds of belly fat perched on the lip of the desktop. Samuel moved his computer screen to one side so that the two men could whisper, face to face. He felt obliged to lean in too, invited by Mr Mainwaring's stance and whispering voice. With barely inches between them, Samuel struggled to disguise the contempt he felt for being this close to a man he had grown to loathe.

"We've been made aware, in total confidence of course, that politicians are going to make a dramatic announcement in the next few days about diesel which will have a very negative impact on the major oil companies. I want you, here in compliance, to be especially vigilant for any unusual trading in oil shares. We don't want to get caught missing any insider dealing. You know how bad that would look for us and compliance in particular?"

"Yes, sir. I understand."

Mr Mainwaring leaned away from Samuel as if to take stock of him. He gave him a hard stare. "Very well," he concluded and left the office as smartly as he had entered, like he had been on a secret mission of some sort, which he was obliged to keep as brief as possible.

Later, when at home, Samuel found Abi in the kitchen, washing up. He stood behind her, embraced her and gently kissed her neck.

"Hello, darling," she said appreciatively in a relaxed warm tone. "Good day at the office?"

"Up until that obnoxious, feeble, pathetic excuse of a man slithered into my personal space and spouted his vile bad breath all over me as he tried to draw me into his latest trap, like the contemptible, slimy creature that he is."

"To what did you owe the honour of a visit from one of your bosses?" She enquired knowingly. Samuel was too preoccupied with his invective to answer just yet.

"I felt like punching him in the face, but all I could do was smile obsequiously and clench my buttocks in order to distract myself from actual physical violence."

She turned towards him and returned his embrace with her wet hands.

"You don't particularly like him, do you?"

"Like him? He's one of the few people I know that gives me a glimpse of how Africans get to the point with someone where they have to entomb them in old tyres and set fire to them."

"Mr Womble?"

"No, not that imbecile. He only makes me wretch. The vice-chair. Fucking Mainwaring. I could resort to actual violence with him."

"So, why would he want to see you?"

He looked at her slightly accusingly. "I've told you before what his game is. It's always the same thing."

"What? Where there's an opportunity to make shed-loads from insider trading, and he warns you off thinking that he's tempting you to get your hands dirty?"

"Yes, the bastard. I know his game. He warns me ostensibly so that I can be vigilant on behalf of the company, but he thinks I'm going to use the opportunity to do a bit of secret trading so that if I catch him doing exactly the same thing, I can't point the finger at him."

"Do you think that maybe you're being just a tad too cynical?"

Samuel let out a brief laugh. "If you saw the look in his eyes, a kind of devious scheming look, and the insincerity in his face, you'd know. He is such a vile two-faced bastard. One day I'm either going to catch him out insider trading, and if not, I'm going to encase him in old tyres and make a burnt offering to the god Plutus."

She laughed. "Yes, well, be that as it may, don't forget he's your boss, and that he pays your bloated wages and our mortgage, so when you feel like setting fire to him, or chucking him out of a sixth floor window, just don't! Maybe you should have a walnut or two on your desk and if he comes in you place a walnut between your buttocks and try to crack it."

He looked at her with a puzzled expression. "Don't you think he might wonder why I'm putting a walnut down my trousers when he comes in?"

"He'll probably just think it's one of your weird fetishes."

She smiled teasingly.

"Only you know my weird fetishes," he replied, as he put on his coy innocent look and gently caressed her shoulders. She smiled more.

"Well, on a more pragmatic note. The kids have had their tea, and it's my turn to cook for us, so it's your turn to read to Sky."

"Fine, we'll carry on this conversation later."

"You mean this conversation about your boss, or this conversation between our bodies?"

He smiled lustfully and caressed her buttocks as she turned to face him.

"I think you know which one."

He pecked her on the lips and moved away. He poured a glass of wine before heading for the stairs.

She reminded him. "We've started *Watership Down* again."

"Again? She knows the story word for word."

"True, but kids love familiarity, and she likes the way you tell it."

Chapter 7

On Thursday morning, Peter arrived promptly at Billie's Bistro and edged through the door in understated fashion. He glanced around, firstly noticing that all the tables near the front were taken, and on walking further in, his eye caught Charlotte waving vigorously at him from a table at the far end. He sauntered over trying not to look particularly pleased to see her. This was a kind of business arrangement after all, something to do with working out how not to kill oneself. Maybe! As he arrived at the table, she stood and greeted him quite enthusiastically. It had been a long time since anyone had shown any interest in her, and it was energising her. She shook his hand politely before they both sat facing each other.

"I thought I'd make up for being late last time, so I got here ten minutes early today."

She smiled broadly, looking very pleased with herself. She was wearing a rather pretty cotton dress with a light cream cardigan over it, and her hair looked much nicer than the last time they had met. She had made an effort to look nice, and he had noticed.

"Oh, that's good. You're looking very well today, I must say."

"Thank you. It's very nice of you to say so."

She felt a little embarrassed, and then carried on.

"I've not ordered anything yet. I didn't know if you'd show up after all."

He looked a little offended that she might expect him not to keep his word. She monitored his expression accurately and explained further.

"It's not that I thought you might let me down or anything like that, I mean, not deliberately, but well you know, after the other evening, anything could happen couldn't it? And you didn't pay your bill!"

He looked shocked. "I didn't pay my bill?"

"Don't worry, I settled it for you. I didn't want you getting arrested. It was only a few quid."

"Oh, I'm so sorry. Well, as you know my mind was elsewhere. Heaven, hell and everything in between. Thanks for covering for me. My reputation could have gone down the swanny! I'll settle today's bill for both of us, okay?"

"Fair enough. I'll go for the sirloin steak!"

Momentarily a wave of alarm crossed his face.

"Don't worry. I'm only joking. It's only a little cafe, not a Michelin restaurant."

He was embarrassed that his alarm had registered in his face, and he re-grouped by offering her anything she wanted there on the menu. They sat and perused it together. Here he was again, with this perfect stranger, the only person in the world who knew that he had been suicidal. It was such a surreal situation. As he mused, the gerberas caught his attention again.

"Aren't these just so beautiful? When you look closely at the petals, you can't help noticing that each one is perfect, like each one of the thousands of feathers on a bird is. Isn't creation amazing?"

She picked one of the flowers out of the vase and examined it closely.

"Now that you say so, I suppose you're right."

At that moment, the waitress arrived. "We charge extra for the flowers, you know," she stated, with a twinkle in her eye. Charlotte laughed a little.

"I was just admiring it. That's all. Isn't nature wonderful?"

The waitress looked a bit puzzled at this admiration for flowers.

"Are you ready to order yet?" She asked.

Today, they both ordered something more substantial. They opted for paninis with salad and coffee. Charlotte looked at Peter with concern.

"How are you doing?"

"Ok, I suppose."

"Have you spoken to your wife about the other night?"

He looked horrified. "Of course not."

"I don't want to pry into your relationship or anything like that, but don't you think she'd want to know that you got so close to, well, you know."

He cowered for a few seconds and then responded quietly. "It's embarrassing and difficult to talk about, and I don't want to worry her. I really don't want her to know."

Her pained expression clearly indicated that she was struggling with his logic. "How do you think she's going to feel if she gets a sudden unexpected message that you've hurt yourself? Don't you think she might have wanted the opportunity to talk things over with you first?"

He just looked at her blankly. He didn't know what to say. She was right, of course. She just looked at him unsure of what to say next. She was no counsellor, far from it, and she didn't feel at all qualified to stray into that sort of territory, so she changed the subject.

"I'm sorry, Peter. I'm not supposed to be challenging you. Sorry. I went off-piste there. I was being nosey. We'll just stick to the agenda."

He looked at her kindly, appreciating her concern for his wife but also pleased that she was not going to pry any further about his marital relationship. It would have been nice if their food arrived now. They could do with the distraction, but it didn't, and there was no distraction, and they both felt awkward. Charlotte spoke first.

"Do you remember where you left off last time?"

"Yes, I do. Do you?"

"Yes, I think so. You were about to tell me about the visions this bloke John was about to get regarding the tribulations."

Peter nodded, his mind beginning to focus on the terrors. "Okay. Then I'll pick up where I left off."

"Great! I'm all ears! *He that hath ears let him hear!*" she proclaimed rather loudly, mimicking him from last time.

He smiled. She had been paying attention! She looked at him rather gleefully.

"Yes, I think I got up to the point where the lamb of God was the only one worthy enough to open the first of the seven seals, and all the angels and beasts and elders worshipped him. Seven is a common number in the Bible. It represents perfection, like when God made the earth in seven days."

She said nothing but just looked at him rather wide-eyed. Their food and drinks arrived, but he barely broke his stride.

"After the first seal was broken to the sound of thunder, John saw a rider on a white horse let loose upon the earth. The rider had a crown and a bow. Remember. This was a vision, and the things seen are representative. The white horse and the bow and crown represent a conqueror going into battle. At this time, there was much warfare on the face of the earth. Then the second seal was broken and he saw a red horse and rider with a great sword going abroad on the earth to kill. Red represents blood and death. I suppose that's logical in the face of extensive warfare. After the third seal was broken, he saw a rider on a black horse going forth and he was carrying weighing scales. Black and the scales represent famine. The fourth seal was broken and a rider on a pale horse went forth. The name of the rider was Death and Hell, and power was given to him to kill a quarter of the world's population by the sword, hunger and wild beasts."

He stopped for a moment to gauge her expression. She felt that she ought to make comment.

"Why was all this happening? Does it say?"

"I suppose it was God's wrath being poured out on the people of the earth for disobeying him and his commandments for so long."

She looked a little subdued. "That's not very nice, is it?"

"No, it's not. But the people had been given plenty of chances to repent, but they chose to defy God and make up their own stupid rules, and eventually it was time for a big reckoning."

"Hmmm," she said, clearly not impressed with God's behaviour. "Was that it?"

"No. Those were only the first four seals. There are lots more to come."

"Can't wait," she said dryly. "Go on."

"The fifth seal was broken and John saw the souls of those slain for their faith under the altar in heaven. They were crying out for vengeance on those who had killed them, but they were told to wait a little longer until their fellow brethren on earth had also been killed."

At this point, Peter looked positively terrified. His skin had gone pale and his palms were sweating and he had gone quiet. She could see the genuine fear in his eyes. He took a few desperate gulps of coffee.

"You really believe all this stuff, don't you?"

He looked at her sincerely, and answered quietly. "Yes."

"Is there any good news?"

"Not till a long time later."

The dialogue paused as they started to eat in silence, as if they were putting as much effort into digesting his words as the food and drink. A few minutes passed quietly until he was ready to carry on.

"The sixth seal was broken and there was a great earthquake. The sun turned dark, the moon became as blood, and the heavens rolled up like a scroll. Stars fell to earth and every mountain and island moved. All men hid. They were terrified of the wrath of God, and called for the mountains to fall on them because they didn't want to face the future. Four angels held back the four winds of the earth but they were instructed not to harm the earth until one hundred and forty-four thousand servants had been set aside to preach the gospel in the coming troubles. There were twelve thousand from each of the twelve tribes of Israel. Did you know that this is where Jehovah witnesses get their notion from that only one hundred and forty thousand people will eventually get into heaven?"

"No, I didn't know that." She tried to sound interested. "That's not very many people when you look at the bigger picture is it?"

He took the last bite of his panini and washed it down before answering.

"True. Especially when you consider all the generations that have been on the earth. They've misinterpreted this whilst completely ignoring the messages in the entirety of the rest of the Bible. That's what all religious sects do. Anyway, that was just a little extra nugget of knowledge for you."

"Yeah, thanks," she answered dryly.

"Meanwhile, a great multitude of men stood before the throne of the lamb in heaven. They were wearing robes of white which meant that they had been cleansed and redeemed by the blood of the lamb. They praised God. One of the elders asked where they had all come from and he was told that they had all come out of the tribulation."

She interrupted him. "Through death?"

"Yes, they were martyrs who came through the great tribulation. They had been persecuted and slain because of their faith. Then the seventh seal was opened and there was silence in heaven for half an hour."

"Is that unusual?"

"Yes, I think so, normally lots of music, singing and praising. The seven angels that stood before God were given seven trumpets. Another angel was given much incense and he offered it at the golden altar before God with the prayers of the saints, and the smoke and the prayers rose up before God. And this angel took fire from the altar and cast it down to earth, and there were loud voices and thunder and lightning…"

"And earthquakes per chance?"

"Yes. How did you know?"

"I think I'm beginning to get the picture. Does it say why there was silence though?"

"Not really. I think it must have been like stunned awe because they could see what was coming next."

She looked surprised. "There's worse?"

"Loads more worse, I'm afraid."

She looked subdued and he carried on.

"Now there follow the seven trumpets. After the first one sounded, hail and fire mingled with blood rained down on earth and destroyed a third of all plants."

"There always seems to be a lot of blood."

"Yes, and fire; they signify sacrifice and cleansing. Got to have plenty of blood and fire."

"With a little brimstone too?"

"Why not? For good measure! Then the second trumpet sounded, and a great burning mountain was cast into the sea and a third of the sea became as blood and a third of all life in the sea died."

She finished her coffee. "More blood. Would you like another drink by the way? I'm going to get another one."

"Yes, okay."

"Red wine perchance?"

"No, just another coffee please."

She meandered her way around the tables and occasional buggies to the counter and ordered two more coffees before sauntering back.

"Would you like something else to eat too?" She enquired kindly. "Something not too hot or brimstoney?"

"No, I'll be fine, thank you."

"Okay. I've ordered a chocolate éclair as well, and jam doughnuts, as you're paying." She smiled cheekily. "Please, do continue."

"Trumpet number three sounds and a great burning star fell to earth and polluted a third of the earth's rivers and lakes. Then trumpet number four, and a third part of the sun and moon were smitten and daylight on the earth was reduced by a third."

Their extra coffees arrived. The waitress gave Peter a slightly concerned look. He appeared quite frightened and a little trance-like. Charlotte smiled at her sweetly as if to say that everything was alright; well, for the time being anyway. She looked out of the window. She couldn't see any horsemen or angels of death in the street. Not yet anyway. And the sun was still shining. Bonus! Peter continued.

"Then an angel announced 'Woe unto the earth' for the next three trumpets. A woe is a very bad thing, you know."

"You could have fooled me. More woe-ish than all the other woe-ish things that have happened so far?"

"Definitely!"

"Oh, dear," she looked positively downbeat.

"Trumpet number five sounded and a star fell from heaven to earth with the key to the bottomless pit…"

She interrupted him. "Bottomless pit?"

"Yes, it's a reference to hell or hades, the place of eternal fire. I think it's the same place as the lake of fire which gets mentioned in the Bible quite a lot too."

She hesitated thoughtfully. "I'm not sure I can help you on the point of information."

He continued purposefully.

"The door to the pit was opened and a huge plume of smoke escaped which darkened the sun and moon, and out of the smoke came a swarm of locusts, but these weren't your normal locusts."

"M and S locusts?" She interjected playfully.

"You could say that," he replied, but without the hint of a smile. "These were like winged horses prepared for battle. They had breastplates of iron on them with gold crowns on their heads. They had the faces of men, with long hair, but the teeth of lions with tails like giant scorpion tails, with terrible stings in them. They were told not to damage the plants of the earth or the one hundred and forty thousand saints, but only to torment all other men for five months, during which time men would beg for death to escape them, but death would evade them."

"Do you think that John might just have been having a terrible nightmare? It does sound like a nightmare don't you think?"

"Yes it does, but he believes that God was showing him a real vision of the end times. He didn't think it was just a nightmare and neither do I."

She frowned a little. "Drugs maybe?"

"I don't think so. He was in a jail, don't forget."

"Did they have LSD in those days? Apparently, that can repeat on you without notice."

"LSD was first synthesised in the thirties, the nineteen thirties."

He looked at her as if to ask if he could proceed.

"Okay. Please, carry on."

"Okay. Then trumpet six, the second woe! The four angels which were bound in the great river Euphrates were released for one year, one month, one day and one hour to slay a third of the men on earth with an army of two hundred million horsemen. Their horses had the heads of lions and tails like serpents with heads that bit. Out of the lions' heads came fire and brimstone."

"More fire and brimstone!" She exclaimed, almost joyously.

"Yes, but John was told that despite all this, men refused to repent of their idolatry, devil-worship, sorcery, theft, fornication and murder."

"Sounds like people get worse in the end times," she mused in curious fashion.

"Just a little,certainly very obstinate, that's for sure."

"Are we out of our woes now?"

"Not yet. One more woe to come. Trumpet number seven. Another mighty angel came down from heaven in a cloud with a rainbow around his head and a face like the sun. His feet were like pillars of fire. He stood astride the sea and the earth and roared like a lion and seven thunders roared. He declared that there should be time no longer. He had a book in his hand and John was instructed to take the book and to eat it. It was sweet in his mouth but bitter in his stomach."

Charlotte screwed up her face. "Fire, warfare, pestilence, strange creatures with a mixture of animal and human features and stings in their tails are all palatable, but making someone eat a book? Too much! How could anyone eat a book?"

"It tasted sweet. It must have tasted good."

She didn't look convinced and he continued.

"This seventh angel banished time and ordered John to prophecy to men that in these times, two witnesses would appear who would prophecy in God's name for three and a half years."

"Wait a minute, you just said that the angel banished time and then you went straight on to mention three and a half years. Which one is it?"

"Yes, it's a bit confusing, isn't it? But I can't explain everything in one brief summary. Let me come back to your point a little later."

He looked at her with a kind of enquiring expression.

"Okay," she agreed. "But don't forget!"

"Okay. So, these two prophets were very special anointed people. They had God's divine protection. If anyone tried to harm them, fire would come out of their mouths and kill their attackers. They were also given power to stop it raining, to turn water into blood, and to smite the earth with more plagues."

"More plagues?" She enquired. She was surprised. She thought that the earth had had enough plagues by now.

"Yes, and if you want to know what sort of plagues we're talking about. You could read about them in the Old Testament. God used them then to torment the Egyptians many thousands of years ago."

"Ooh yes. That would make great bedtime reading. Thank you."

"In the book of Exodus."

"Okay, Exodus, got it. Please, go on."

"So, at the end of their allotted time of three and a half years of ministry, the beast of the bottomless pit was allowed to attack and kill them. Their dead bodies were left to rot in the street for three and a half days, and the people celebrated because these prophets had tormented them. But then the spirit of life from God entered into their dead bodies and they stood upon their feet. The people who saw this were terrified, and there was a great voice from heaven calling the two men up to heaven, and they ascended, and there was a great earthquake, and a tenth of the city they were in was destroyed, killing seven thousand men. And now, it's judgement time."

She stared at him mesmerised and said nothing. She had many questions inside her head, but she didn't want to interfere with his flow, and judgment time sounded rather engrossing, like the climax to the story. Peter brought a hand up to his face and covered it. He was clearly beginning to quietly weep.

Charlotte spoke quietly. "Peter, I'm so sorry this has upset you. I obviously don't want to put you through any kind of trauma."

He said nothing as he took a few moments to compose himself.

"I'm sorry. It's been playing on my mind a lot lately, what with the state of society today as well, and it just gets too much."

"There's no point talking about it if it just upsets you. I'm sorry. I thought it might be good to share your concerns. You know, a problem shared is a problem halved and all that."

"No, please don't apologise. I am very grateful for you taking an interest."

Nevertheless, as he sat there, rather slumped, he looked drained and weak. Charlotte was sensitive enough to realise that he'd had enough for one day.

"Well, clearly we've covered enough misery for now. Let's call it a day, and maybe we can meet again and talk about something nice next time, like holidays or kids."

"I haven't been on holiday for years and I haven't got any kids."

She gulped at thin air. "Well, something, maybe hobbies or house prices."

He looked at her sullenly. "The manse comes with the job. When the job goes, the manse goes too."

He seemed to be sinking into more and more of a hole.

"Okay. Can we agree to meet again and we'll talk about anything that you think might help?"

She was wondering how counsellors managed with this kind of thing, day in, day out. She gave him her most sincere expression, but she could see that he was in two minds.

"Please, Peter. I don't want to leave it like this, with you getting upset. If we're going to finish this exercise, I want to do it on a positive note."

He got a hanky out of a pocket and wiped his face whilst he thought.

"Okay. When did you have in mind?"

"A couple of days again? Give you time to build up your emotional strength."

"Saturday?"

He pondered for a few moments. "Okay, but it will have to be in the afternoon. I'm doing something with the wife in the morning."

"Fabulous. Saturday it is then. Three o'clock here, okay?"

"Yes."

Chapter 8

Samuel sat with Sky on her bed. They moved her pillows against the wall so that they could sit comfortably propped up by the wall with their legs straight out across the bed. Sky's feet reached just below Samuel's knees. His feet hung over the side of the bed. She loved to be read to, unlike Bronson who considered stories to be childish and much preferred screen time. Samuel had left the main light off, but they could see adequately by the fainter light of her bedside lamp. He opened the book, and announced its title in grand fashion.

Watership Down By Richard Adams.

The book was pictures only. Years ago it had come with an audio tape of the story, but that had long since worn out, so now it was up to Samuel to remember the story, prompted by the pictures. If he forgot a small detail, she would readily remind him. He leafed through the first pages. Sky settled down, expectantly sucking her thumb.

"You've done the bit about Fiver having his terrible vision?" Sky nodded gently without removing her thumb.

"And the bit about Hazel taking him to see the chief rabbit to warn him of imminent danger?" Again, Sky nodded.

"And the bit about the Owsla Captain Holly trying to arrest Bigwig for spreading dissent, and Bigwig beating him up so they could get away?"

She nodded again, and her face looked more intent as her mind was beginning to delve into the story.

"Which rabbits left the warren?"

Without hesitation, she answered faultlessly. "Hazel, Fiver, Bigwig, Blackberry, Silver, Hawkbit, Dandelion, Speedwell, Acorn, Buckthorn and Pipkin." She then decided to add a bit of information for her dad's benefit.

"Silver was almost as strong as Bigwig, but Pipkin was a really weedy rabbit just like Fiver."

"Yes, dear. I think you're right. Did Mum do the bit about Dandelion telling them the story about Frith, their animal God giving all the different animals' special qualities?"

"Yes. He gave foxes sharp teeth and cunning. He gave cats silent paws and eyes that see in the dark."

"And what did he give rabbits?"

"Big strong back legs that made them the fastest runners in the woods."

"Did she do the bit where they had to cross a river to escape a dog?"

She nodded. "That's the bit we got up to."

"Okay." He checked the pictures. There was a picture of an enormous fluffy rabbit on the other side of the brook to the weary bedraggled travellers.

"Well, some of the rabbits were beginning to think that they'd made a big mistake leaving their home warren at Fiver's insistence. The woods and fields that they had been traversing were strange and had hidden dangers. Badgers. Foxes. Crows. Men. They were all tired, scared, fraught and exhausted, and they could see no end to their troubles. Then Hazel spotted a strange rabbit on the other side of the brook. He took Blackberry with him to check out this stranger. He was immediately struck by the obvious health of this massive rabbit, whose condition spoke of good eating and fine health. He seemed remarkably relaxed and completely unperturbed by the arrival of these strange rabbits.

"His name was Cowslip, and he readily invited them to join his warren, which was apparently large and had plenty of empty burrows. He then lolloped off towards his warren, leaving Hazel to mull over this offer. Hazel had found him strangely welcoming, yet he couldn't make sense of it. Normally, a warren would be wary of strangers, for fear of them stealing their does. He returned to his own rabbits to discuss the situation.

"They all formed the opinion that there was nothing to lose in giving the hospitality a try. Only Fiver was opposed. He had a very bad feeling about it and warned the others that they should have nothing to do with them. Just then, it started to pour with rain, and the thought of being underground in proper burrows was just too appealing, and they went across the brook towards the warren.

"The warren was strangely open, with obvious runs towards it. They were welcomed by two rabbits expressing weird patterns of welcoming behaviour, which were very un-rabbit-like, and were then led down into the huge underground chamber. The strange rabbits all had the same opulent smell as Cowslip. Hazel spent some time talking to one of the new rabbits called Strawberry, but he found him bizarrely uncurious, and inclined not to answer questions directly, as if he didn't like questions that began with 'where' or 'why'. After some time, Hazel invited his troop to go above ground to graze. Cowslip was most surprised as they had plenty of food underground, here in the dry, and outside, it was raining, but Hazel and his rabbits went above ground anyway.

"Eating underground seemed unnatural. He asked them what they thought of this new place. They had all noticed that with these new rabbits, despite their apparent good health and physical vitality, they seemed to be sad and melancholy. After sharing their thoughts and grazing for a while, they all returned to the burrows, and found an empty one which they shared together for the night.

"The following morning, Hazel woke to a strange and dangerous smell, that of cigarettes which men smoked. Shortly after this, Strawberry was making a commotion and stamping his feet. Hazel asked him what was wrong. Nothing was *wrong*; he was just alerting the rest of the warren that fresh food had been dumped nearby. Hazel exited the burrow with caution, but Cowslip came up behind him and boldly exited himself, telling Hazel that there was nothing to be worried about. He led him down the field to a fresh pile of carrots dumped in the hedgerow. There was usually something fresh put out every day, and it varied from day to day. Apples, corn, cabbages, etc. After nibbling on the carrots for a while, Hazel mused to Cowslip.

'With all this abundant food, your warren should be full of...'

"He didn't get to finish his question as Cowslip asked him to carry some carrots back to the warren. This was not a trick his rabbits had ever learned, but they gave it a go. Only Fiver refused to act *like a dog*. He remonstrated with Hazel that this arrangement of men putting out food for rabbits was wrong, and carrying it underground was wrong. Hazel replied that it clearly wasn't poisoned and there were no men nearby shooting them, so what could be wrong?

"They all returned to the warren and in the big chamber, where Dandelion was invited to regale them all with one of his stories. It would be the one where the fabled chief rabbit of folklore, Elharairah, stole all the king's prize lettuces, and that, my dear, is where we shall leave this story for today."

Sky must have been tired, because she didn't argue. He got off her bed and helped her into it and pulled the quilt up to her neck.

"Sweet dreams, precious one."

He kissed her on the forehead, turned off her lamp and exited the room, shutting the door gently behind him. He briefly went into Bronson's room and found him glued to his computer game.

"Bronson, you've got ten more minutes." There was no response. Bronson couldn't hear him because of his headphones. Samuel manoeuvred himself as best he could between Bronson and the screen and mouthed his request very slowly as he emphasised the ten minutes with his fingers. Bronson gave him a darting dirty look and carried on. Samuel then went down to the kitchen where Abi was laying the table. He sat at the table.

"Abi, do you think Richard Adams wrote Watership Down as a veiled message to mankind?"

She looked at him curiously. "What veiled messages?"

"How people can allow themselves to live in a trap and pretend that's ok?"

"I've read that he never meant his work to be allegorical."

"Maybe he never meant it to be, but is it nevertheless?"

"I think it's a story mainly about change, only he uses rabbits instead of people because kids love animals. We all have to learn to adapt to change."

She dished up steaming spaghetti Bolognese and red wine. "Bon appetit!"

They both started to eat, but between mouthfuls, he continued to pontificate.

"We got up to the bit where Hazel and his troop had entered the well-fed warren, and they'd all gone down into the big chamber to exchange stories. Dandelion would go first and tell an inspiring story of Elharairah the legendary chief rabbit that was full of trickery and cunning and he used his resourcefulness to trick the king out of his prize lettuces. It was a story the celebrated cleverness and bravery."

"Samuel. It's me, Abi. You're supposed to be saving this story for Sky, not me. I know it as well as you do."

"Yes, I know that, darling, but I just want to expand on it with you in a way that I can't with Sky, because I tend to think of you as a little bit more grown up."

He looked at her and smiled nicely.

"Go on then."

"Ok, so then one of the resident rabbits Silverweed recited a poem. Cowslip explained that they no longer harped back to the times of Elharairah and of valour and bravery. They were more into dignity and resignation. It was like these rabbits were new age, rejecting the lessons of their ancient culture and just reinventing their way of life however it suited them, but then we go on to learn that they are effectively being farmed for their pelts and their meat, and they have come to accept this treaty with the devil because until they get caught in a trap, life is safe and easy."

"Your point being?"

"Well, are we like this too?"

Abi looked genuinely perplexed. "Do you think someone is after your pelt, darling?"

Samuel chuckled. "Do we ignore danger just for an easy life?"

She still looked perplexed. "Give me an example."

"Okay. So, as mobile phones started to take the world by storm, there were people warning of the dangers of the radiation. Then came Wi-Fi, and again, there were warnings of the dangers of EMFs and microwaves on the brain. But as far as I know, none of this was taken seriously."

"Isn't that because none of these fears were proven?"

"But how would we ever know? Cancers are increasing as is Alzheimer's, etcetera. How could we possibly ever know what part these new EMFs may have played in it? Aren't we just like those rabbits? Just pretending that the danger doesn't exist because we all love our phones and wireless internet so much?"

Abi thought for a moment. "I don't think it's us being apathetic about danger though. I think we trust the experts to find out about these things, and then to let us know if there are any real dangers."

"Yes, but it seems that not much new tech gets properly tested for safety. Did you know that there are 80,000 chemicals produced for commercial purposes in the world each year? How many of those have been tested for effect on humans?"

"No idea."

"Just fourteen per cent. Fourteen! Who cares what they do to us?"

He looked at her. She made no reply. He carried on.

"And what if, on the rare occasion tests actually are carried out, these so-called experts are bought off? And they only provide the evidence the companies want to see?"

"Now you're getting all conspiratorial."

"Come on, Abi, we know full well how corrupt everything to do with commerce is. I see a lot of correlation between Adams's stories and modern life, which is weird because he wrote these fifty years ago, way before mobile phones and Wi-Fi, and don't get me started on 5G!"

"Don't worry. I won't get you started on 5G! Please eat up. You're going to need your energy. For afters, I'm coming after your pelt!"

With that, she gave him a saucy look and smiled mischievously.

**

Alexander was sitting in the lounge with his mum. He had come down to watch the news. He generally couldn't bear TV. For him, only wildlife programmes and some documentaries with a sprinkling of news. The rest of it in his opinion was just a complete waste of time. The older he got, the more he wanted to use his time usefully and not fritter it away on needless so-called entertainment.

"Mum, did you know that a twenty-week-old female foetus has all the eggs that she will carry for the rest of her life in her womb already?"

"No, I didn't know that, dear."

"In fact, she has six million at that stage which will be reduced to one million at birth."

"That's incredible, dear. What happened to the other five million?"

"Must have got reabsorbed I suppose."

She looked at him and smiled.

"I can vividly remember you sitting on that settee when we first got it. Your feet didn't even reach the edge of the seat."

She chuckled.

"Mum, you mustn't live your life in the past."

She put her knitting down and looked at him rather sternly.

"Son, you will find that there comes a point in your life when you can't look forward to the future any more. You will have done all the things you wanted to do if you could have afforded it. There is no longer any ambition. Simply getting up each morning becomes its own achievement. Ignoring aches and pains and staying mobile is in and of itself an accomplishment. Your children will be grown up and often distant. Your best friends and relatives will be going senile or be popping off one by one. Apart from simply having a roof over your head and enough food in your belly, material things will no longer matter. When you reach that point, you get your enjoyment from looking back, not from looking forward. Memories become treasured valuables, not money or jewellery. You think about past episodes of your life and smile at what you did right and wrong. I think often about how I met your dad and relive our best times together inside my head. He's gone now, but the cherished memories and feelings live on in my heart. They make me smile. It's those that I look forward to. What would be the paucity of my life if I distracted myself from those memories and feelings because of some vain pointless ambitions?"

Alexander felt rather humbled. He understood what she was saying. Perhaps he was not that far away from that same pivotal point in his own life.

"I'm sorry, Mum. I didn't mean to be insensitive. I was just talking like a parrot without thinking. It's what everyone keeps saying to me when I start talking about Prescilla."

Dawn gave him a cold mean stare. She didn't like that name mentioned in her house. How dare that woman abandon her son in middle age? She didn't understand modern women at all. "You can talk to your friends about her if you must, but please, not to me."

**

Munther lay on the bed next to Samuel and Abi. They had just made love, and both felt sated, lying in each other's arms in post coital comfort. Munther spoke gently into his ear.

"This is it. This is the best you're going to get out of life. Young children who still think you're someone special, but they will grow up to feel like they've been had. You know, some parents lose all contact with their kids once they've grown up, so what was the point of all those years of hard work? And Abi. Do you think she'll always be there for you? By your side? Faithful and devoted? It doesn't happen like that anymore. When the kids grow up, she'll be gone. If not before. New horizons. Trendy feminist ambitions that require freedom from oppressive relationships. That's today's culture."

Samuel looked at Abi, her head resting on his chest, her arms entwining his torso.

"Darling, are you happy?"

She was close to sleep and only mumbled very quietly. "Tomorrow."

"Tomorrow what?"

"Talk."

"I want to know what your ambitions are?"

"Tomorrow," she mumbled again, sounding slightly as if she was in pain.

She didn't have much experience of different sexual partners, but all the others had gone quickly unconscious after ejaculating. Only Samuel seemed to be somehow weirdly mentally stimulated, but she wanted to relax. She'd had a long day, and this had been a lovely way to end it. He was afraid of the future. He knew things through the bank, about how drastic changes were being planned by the self-appointed elite that would make life much harder for everyone apart from the very richest, and he wondered how they would cope when things got tougher.

"Darling, do you think that we are on the cusp of a neo feudal system? A new age of lords and serfs? That's how it's always been for time immemorial. This new-fangled development of a middle class is just a blip on the millennial graph, a recent phenomena and social experiment that won't be tolerated for much longer."

She didn't answer. She was pleasantly falling asleep. This was no time for conspiratorial discussions. She ignored him.

"See?" Munther said quietly. "She doesn't care. Women pretend to be just like men, but they're not. They feel differently. They think differently, and you'll never really know what's going on in her mind. She'll stay with you for as long as it suits her, and then she'll really surprise you one day, and shit on you big-time."

Samuel looked down at Abi's thick hair splayed over her pretty face and his chest. He held her a little more tightly. He loved her. He admired her. He knew that he always had trouble really understanding her, but he didn't want to lose her, ever.

Chapter 9

Saturday afternoon found Peter and Charlotte sitting in Billie's Bistro for the third time that week. Who would have thought that they were more or less perfect strangers? He had already had lunch with his wife Elsie, so he was happy just to have just a coffee. She by contrast hadn't eaten much at all that day, and so she ordered another panini with a doughnut and coffee. After the last session where Peter had become quite upset, she was thinking that maybe they should just have a little chit-chat this time but her curiosity was too overwhelming.

"Peter, the last time we spoke, you ended up getting quite distraught. Is there anything you can talk about in Revelation which is not upsetting?"

"Well, I think we've covered most of the worst stuff. Would you like me to continue the story?"

"Yes. Strangely, I would. Maybe at heart I'm just a boring little masochist. But can you do it without upsetting yourself?"

"I'll try."

He chortled a bit, and got straight on with it.

"Well, John saw a heavenly temple open up and there was of course much thunder, lightning and great hail, and he saw a woman clothed with the sun and the moon was under her feet. She had twelve stars on her head and she was delivering a child."

Charlotte looked very surprised. "You mean a real baby. She was having a baby?"

"Yes, but there was danger. A red dragon with seven heads and seven horns and ten crowns was waiting to devour her new-born baby. He swept his tail and drew a third of the stars from the heavens and cast them to earth to demonstrate his power. He stood before the woman so he could devour the child as soon as it was born. The woman brought forth a man child who was to rule all nations with a rod of iron. The child was immediately taken up to the throne of God and the woman fled into the wilderness where God had prepared a place for her to be fed and sheltered for three and a half years…"

"So, the baby didn't get eaten by the dragon after all?"

"Correct. God protected the baby and the woman. Then a war was fought in heaven. The archangel Michael and his angels fought the devil and his angels. Michael won and the devil was banished to the earth, but was full of wrath because he knew his time was short. He tried to persecute the woman in the wilderness, but she was given the great wings of an eagle to fly to a place of safety. The devil caused a great flood to swallow her up, but the earth helped the women by swallowing up the waters and in his frustration and anger, he made war against the remnant of her seed."

Charlotte interrupted him. She was getting quite confused. "I get that this is all about good versus evil, but who is this strange woman, and who are her seed?"

"The woman represents God's church on earth—the bride of the lamb, and her seed are the believers—the saints—spiritually, the children of God."

"Oh, okay, and just remind me again. Who is the lamb?"

"That's the son of God, Jesus Christ, who in the end times is going to return to the earth to be with his bride."

"Oh, that's nice. Every great story has a bit of romance in it."

She smiled coyly at him. He wasn't quite sure what to make of her, as usual, so he just carried on.

"Now this is where it gets really bad."

"Now?" She queried. "Didn't it get bad enough already?"

"No. Now a beast rises up from the sea. It's like a leopard with seven heads, ten horns and ten crowns. It has the feet of a bear and the mouth of a lion and blasphemy is written on its head. This is the antichrist. This dragon blasphemed God and was given power on the earth for three and a half years to persecute and overcome the children of God. One of its heads had a deadly wound on it but it was healed, and the entire world worshipped this beast."

"The beast?"

"The devil, serpent, and Satan. All interchangeable in Revelation."

"I see. But the dragon can give the beast its powers?"

"Yes. The devil is the prince of this world."

"What, even now, today?"

"Yes. Look around you. It's a fallen, evil, sinful world."

She briefly pursued the various happy diners around her, supping their beverages and discussing such trivia as soap operas, football and the weather, and she looked rather perplexed.

"Maybe not in here," he added, reading her thoughts, "although you don't know what these people get up to behind closed doors, but there are terrible things happening all the time all over the world."

"Oh, okay. You mean like child labour, slavery, sex trafficking, illegally harvesting peoples' organs and politicians fiddling their expenses?"

"Precisely, and worse. So, this beast makes war on all the saints, to overcome them. A second beast appears with two horns which spoke like a dragon. It had all the powers of the first beast and more. It could perform miracles and call down fire from the heavens but its job was to get all the earth to worship the first beast, the antichrist. A great idol was made of the antichrist and the second beast gave life to it, and the idol called for all that do not worship it to be put to death. That's a tricky one for Christians who are instructed to have no other God apart from the one true one."

"So, if they stick to their guns, they'll be put to death?"

"Undoubtedly, and to make matters worse, this is where the mark of the beast comes along. Everyone is ordered to have the mark of the beast on his hand or forehead, and without it, he will not be able to buy or sell."

She looked at him curiously. "666?"

"Yes."

She looked very pleased with herself. "How did I know that?"

He was not impressed, and he answered very evenly. "I think it entered into common folklore a long time ago. Now things start to come to a head."

"About time," she agreed.

"Remember the one hundred and forty-four thousand messengers of God we spoke about earlier?"

"Vaguely. An awful lot of death and destruction has happened since then."

"Yes, quite, but not to them. They had a mission to preach the gospel to all the earth during these times, and they had God's protection. Nothing of the tribulation touched them. Well, now their mission is over, and it's time for judgment. Seven angels in heaven made proclamations. The first one announced that the Day of Judgement had come. The second one announced that Babylon had fallen—I'll explain that in more detail shortly. The third one announced that every man who had the mark of the beast and who had worshipped the antichrist would now suffer the wrath of God. The fourth one ordered the earth's people to be reaped. The fifth angel went forth into the earth with a sickle."

"What, like the grim reaper?"

"Yes, I'm afraid so. And the sixth angel ordered the fifth angel to begin harvesting, and the seventh angel announced more plagues!"

"Surely not more plagues again?"

"Yes, I'm afraid so. The first one was that men who had the mark of the beast were covered in sores. The second one turned the sea into blood, killing all the creatures in it."

Charlotte was shocked. "All of them?"

"Yes, all of them. We're getting close to the destruction of the earth. The third one was that the rivers turned into blood."

He anticipated her question. "I suppose that killed all the creatures in them too. The fourth one was that the sun turned hotter and scorched mankind. The fifth one poured out his vial on the seat of the beast, and his kingdom was full of darkness and pain. The sixth one poured out his vial on the great river Euphrates which dried up so that the way for the kings of the east might be prepared. Three unclean spirits like frogs come out of the mouth of the dragon and were able to perform miracles, and they gathered together an army of men to rebel against God at Armageddon."

"Armageddon! I've heard of that, but I can't think why."

"It's something else that has seeped into common folklore along with the mark of the beast. I suppose it represents the final battle between good and evil. Number seven is thunder, lightning and the biggest earthquake the world has ever seen. So big, that it destroyed whole islands and flattened whole mountains. Oh, and this was accompanied by massive hail, each one weighing up to sixty pounds."

"Sixty pounds? That's the size of a child!"

She was astonished. Pete was nonchalant.

"Apparently, but now John was going to be shown the judgement of the great whore with whom the kings and peoples of the earth had committed fornication. An angel carried him away in the spirit into the wilderness where he saw a woman sitting upon a scarlet beast with seven heads and ten horns. She was arrayed in scarlet and purple and was bedecked in gold and precious stones and pearls and held in her hands a golden cup full of the abomination and filthiness of her fornication. On her forehead were the names 'Mystery', 'Babylon',

'Mother of Harlots', and 'Abomination of the Earth'. She was drunk with the blood of the saints."

"Someone didn't like her, did they? I mean, she doesn't sound very nice."

"Quite. Well, I mentioned the fall of Babylon earlier, and here we get more detail. Babylon represents all the sinful ways of the world. Modern culture if you like, a culture that has turned its back on God and has embraced all kinds of false religions and perverse practices. She's like a city, and her ways were responsible for the persecution and death of the saints. The beast she sits upon is the devil himself. The seven heads are seven mountains with seven kings. Five are fallen, one is, and one is yet to come. The ten horns on the beast upon which she sits are ten kings on the earth with no kingdoms, but are given the powers of a king for but one hour to make war on the lamb with the beast, but the lamb will overcome them all. These ten kings will turn on her, and burn her and eat her and her kingdoms will be given to the beast."

Charlotte sat quietly. There was just too much fantasy for her to understand but she didn't want to complicate things further by asking more questions. Peter continued.

"John then saw an angel with great power come down from heaven and all the earth was lightened with his glory, and he announced with a mighty voice that Babylon had fallen. He cried out that Babylon had become the habitation of devils and every foul spirit, and that all nations had drunk of the wine of the wrath of her fornication, and that the merchants of the earth had waxed rich through her abundances, but she had incurred God's wrath. Another voice from heaven boomed out calling for God's people to come out of her and to not be partakers of her sins. He announced that she would be destroyed in but a day with plagues, famine and fire, and she was."

"All merchants mourned her passing as all trading ceased. All riches become as nought and there are no more musicians or craftsmen. The city will be cast down with such force that there will be nothing left of her. This was God's judgement upon her because of all the blood of the saints and prophets that was shed by her. There was much celebration in heaven at her passing and praising of God, and now the marriage of the lamb was announced as the wife had made herself ready. She was arrayed in fine white linen which is the righteousness of the saints."

Charlotte looked perplexed and wanted to affirm this point. "The wife being the church, the saints, on earth?"

"Exactly. Then heaven was opened, and the faithful and true one was seen sitting on a white horse. He was ready to judge and make war in righteousness. He had eyes of fire and wore many crowns. His raiment was dipped in blood. He was 'The word of God', 'the king of kings', the 'lord of lords'. He charged out of heaven, followed by an army on white horses, and a sharp sword came out of his mouth to smite all nations. The beast and the kings of the earth were ready to make war with the lamb, but the followers of the beast were slain by the sword and the beasts of the air were invited to feast upon their flesh. The beast and his false prophet and all those who had been deceived and had the mark of the beast upon them, were cast into the lake of fire and brimstone. Then John saw an angel come down from heaven, and he held the key to the bottomless pit and had a great chain in his hand and he bound the beast and sealed him in the bottomless pit for one thousand years that he could deceive no more. But after the thousand years he would be loosed once more for a little season."

"Is he eternal, like God?"

"Yes, he is, just like we all are."

She looked at him quizzically, and added, "God likes horses, doesn't he?"

Peter was taken aback by her rather random observation. "Yes, I suppose he does, and eagles, and lions." Then he got back to his account.

"John saw the souls of the saints who had been beheaded for not worshipping the beast or for not getting his mark, and they ruled over the earth with Christ for a thousand years. This was the first resurrection. All the other dead saints would rest until the end of the 1000-year reign."

Charlotte looked quite befuddled. "Who are all the other dead saints?"

"All the saints who have died over the course of time prior to the tribulation."

"That must be a lot of people."

"Yes, I suppose so. I mean, I hope so."

"And the ones who are resurrected now, who are they ruling over?"

"Whatever people managed to live through the tribulations, pestilence and wars."

"Oh," she said, musing on all the multitude of deaths which must have occurred and wondering just how many people might have actually survived.

"That can't be very many people, can it?"

"I suppose not."

"Surely it can't be hardly anyone, because you said that during the reign of the antichrist anyone who *didn't* have the mark of the beast wouldn't be allowed to buy or sell, or do anything, so presumably they all starve to death, and then you said than during God's judgcmcnt, he destroyed everyone who *did* have the mark of the beast."

Peter looked unsure. "I don't know all the answers, Charlotte. Maybe the ones who refused the mark of the beast weren't all put to death. Maybe some of them were just used as slaves, or were simply imprisoned for their faith, like John was. I don't know."

She looked thoughtful if not confused, and he just carried on.

"After the one thousand year reign, the beast is released from the bottomless pit, and yet again, he goes abroad on the earth to deceive people, and he raises an army the size of which is like the sands of the sea. He gathers up a vast army to take back the earth…"

Charlotte looked quite confused. "But where did all these vast numbers of people come from? I thought that after all the plagues and wars etcetera, there was hardly anyone left."

Pete looked at her with a little twinkle in his eye.

"I think you're forgetting that one thousand years have now passed, and that's a lot of sex and babies!"

She mused on that thought for a moment and then queried.

"Would God allow sex?"

"My dear, God invented sex!"

He proclaimed this rather too loudly and was aware of many heads turning towards them. He carried on a little more quietly.

"Satan and his army surrounded the beloved city where the saints were, but God rained down fire upon them and rather undramatically, the devil's army was suddenly and completely devoured by fire and all his human followers perished. Once again, the beast is cast into the bottomless pit, but this time, he will be tormented there for all eternity, along with the antichrist and his prophet, and he won't be released again."

"Why did the beast get released though?"

"I don't know. Maybe a final cleansing of the earth of those willing to rebel against God?"

"Peter, you began all this by explaining that for believers to gain their salvation, they had to be overcomers, yes?"

"Yes."

"That they had to overcome the trials and horrors of the tribulation, yes?"

"Yes."

"Well, don't you think that you could be one of them? Your faith seems very strong."

Peter's head dropped and his voice lost its energy. "Oh Charlotte, I wish you were right, but I know my weaknesses. I can't even bear the thought of a cold shower let alone any real pain ands certainly not torture. I know I would give in. That would make me a traitor, and God wouldn't forgive me. I would get the mark of the beast just to avoid pain and discomfort, and to be able to eat, and so eventually, on judgement day, I would be cast into the lake of fire with Satan."

She looked at him sadly. Somehow she sort of understood his dilemma. She tried to console him. "But maybe you're wrong. Not many people would take all of this stuff literally, and even if they did, what is to say that any of it might happen during your lifetime? I mean, haven't people been waiting for the return of Christ ever since he was crucified? When was that? Two thousand years ago?"

He looked forlorn. "I take your point, Charlotte, but there seem to be so many signs that the end times are upon us. I really can't help feeling that this is going to happen in my lifetime. I just know it."

She looked at him compassionately seeing the need to divert him from his dejection.

"Did anything else happen?"

He looked pensive. "Yes, of course. John saw a great white throne in heaven with God sitting on it, and earth and heaven fled away from him. Books were opened and the dead, great and small, stood before God, and they were judged according to their works. The sea gave up the dead in it, and death and hell gave up the dead which were in them. Death and hell were cast into the lake of fire and whoever was not found written in the book of life was also cast into the lake of fire. Every man and woman who has ever lived was judged."

"What about babies?"

"What about babies?"

"Well, did they get judged too?"

"Yes, according to their works."

She pulled a face.

"What about aborted babies? Do they count too?"

"Of course, they count. Their spirits are eternal just like yours and mine."

"But how could they be judged?"

"I suspect that they will be found to be blameless, and their names will be in the book of life."

"But they didn't have names."

"God will have named every single one of them. He knows how many hairs are on your head."

He smiled, thinking about the loving side of God's nature, and she felt her hair, wondering how anyone could know how many individual hairs were in there. John smiled some more.

"Finally, we get to the good bit. The old heaven and earth pass away, and John saw a new heaven and earth, and he saw a new holy city, New Jerusalem coming down out of the new heaven as a bride adorned for her husband. A great voice announced that God was coming to dwell with men. He would wipe away all tears from their eyes and there would be no more death nor sorrow nor pain nor crying. He sat on the throne and declared that old things had passed away and he made all things new. He that overcometh shall inherit all things. An angel took John to see New Jerusalem, and he saw that it was made of pure gold like glass, and was adorned with all manner of precious stones. There was no need for the sun and the moon as the glory of God himself illuminated everything. There will be no night any longer."

He suddenly stopped speaking. That was it. He had worked his way succinctly through the entire book of Revelation. Charlotte looked at him with an almost disappointed look on her face.

"Is that it?"

He giggled. "What do you mean, is that it? The whole earth has gone through tribulation after tribulation. The entire heavens and earth have been destroyed. The sun and moon are no more. Every man, woman and child who has ever lived have been resurrected, judged and either cast into the lake of fire with the devil himself or have been allowed to dwell upon the new earth with God himself in blissful eternity. What more do you want? Little umbrellas and a slice of lemon?"

She laughed. "I don't know. That just seemed like such a sudden end."

"It's not an end. It's a wonderful new beginning."

"Yes, I suppose so."

But this was the end for them, and she wanted to see him again. He had done everything she had asked him to do and she had no right to encroach on his life any further. She felt awkward.

"That's it then. I mean for us."

He looked at her quizzically. "Yes I suppose so."

He looked a little sad himself. Perhaps it had been cathartic for him to run all this Revelation stuff by someone else.

"But I'm still worried about you."

He laughed. "Please, don't be. God has taught me a valuable lesson through you."

"Just because you've told me all about Revelation doesn't mean that you will be any less scared of it."

She looked very concerned. He did his best to reassure her.

"Yes, that makes sense, but let me assure you. God used you to intervene and frustrate my purpose the other night, and I have to attach the relevance to that which it deserves. Maybe I should trust him to give me the courage that I lack, or even to graciously spare me from the tribulation somehow because I'm such a wuss."

He smiled at her quite broadly and for the first time, she saw hope in his eyes. That made her feel so much better.

"That's fantastic, but I feel that somehow we need to maintain our connection."

She wasn't brave enough to explain to him that in a weird way he had given her a sense of purpose that felt rather wonderful. He looked awkward, but thoughtful. It had been right to meet her and to explain why she had found him in such a state the other night, but now it would feel wrong to meet her again. He could only offer her one opportunity.

"You could maybe come along to my church?"

"Oh, oh yes. I'd forgotten about your church. Which one is it?"

"It's the Baptist church in Jeremiah Street, in between the massage parlour and the betting shop."

With that, they wrapped up their meeting with a polite and rather formal handshake, and before departing, he told her that he hoped to see her in church soon.

Chapter 10

Elsie picked up the mail on the doormat. This was a routine, almost unconscious act. There were several dull-looking brown envelopes addressed to the right reverend, and just one for her. It was not brown. She was curious! She rarely got mail just for herself. And it was actually handwritten. She opened it immediately:

Dear Elsie, I am so sorry to be the bearer of bad tidings to you, but obviously I feel that you would want to know this. On several occasions recently, I have witnessed your husband, the right reverend, canoodling with a young woman at Billie's Bistro during the day. I don't wish to stick my nose into other people's private affairs of course, but I am pretty sure that she is not one of your church members and I suspect that he has succumbed to an illicit relationship, and that you would want to know about this. I wish to remain anonymous because I don't want to get drawn into a potentially unpleasant domestic situation, but I can vouch that I am telling the truth.

Yours sincerely, a well-wisher.

A cold shiver went down her spine and her legs felt noticeably weaker. She felt that her brain had just received a jolt from something indescribable. Suspicion takes root and festers as easily as a snake squirming down a hole in the ground. This letter wasn't even signed. She had no idea who had written it, so of what substance was it really?

Munther whispered in her ear, "How could he do this to you? You've given him the best twelve years of your life. You've been totally faithful to him and you were stupid enough to trust him back. He's taken advantage of you. He's lied to you and deceived you. He's been unfaithful to you with a much prettier and younger woman. He doesn't deserve you. It's time for you to stand up for yourself and show him you're not just a doormat."

She went into the lounge and sat down and read the letter over and over again, wondering if the writer was simply malicious or had misinterpreted something. Peter was out. She immediately racked her brain. Where was he? She didn't always pay much attention to his appointments. She considered his days quite dull. He had a diary in his office, on his desk. She got up and went there to peruse it. Appointments most days. Just names. All names of people she knew from their church. This morning he was visiting the Fitzroyals. She knew that they were having issues with their fifteen year old son wanting to transition into a woman, and they wanted advice from a man of the cloth. She looked back over the past four weeks. No entries about Billie's Bistro, and no names which she didn't recognise. She was feeling more than a little panicky, but she was also wondering if this letter was a crank letter from some vile person just trying to stir up trouble within their marriage. She would just have to wait until he returned. Then she would show him the letter and see what he would say.

Later that day, after being confronted by Elsie, Peter left home feeling bereft but determined. Munther was talking sternly in his ear.

"How could she suspect you without any real evidence? Why should you have to explain your meetings with a woman who had come to your aid in your hour of need? Why can't she just trust you when that's all you need from her—just a little trust? If she truly loved you she *would* trust you, instead of immediately and unfairly making false accusations against you. You'll never get her trust back. Your marriage is sunk. Your career is over. No one will be willing to listen to a preacher who has been caught out shagging. You know how these things get exaggerated. The next thing they'll be saying is that you're a kiddy-fiddler. You are so totally fucked."

He needed her to trust him. There could be no future without it, but obliquely, trust is hardest to give just when it's most needed. He got in his car and drove straight to the bridge. He stopped the car in the middle of the road and got out. He put the handbrake on but he didn't bother turning the engine off nor closing the door. He'd always wanted to abandon a car like that in the middle of traffic, just like they do in films. He went to the fence and looked down. Yes, a great drop to the rocks below. Last time he had made the mistake of hesitating and thinking. This time he wouldn't prevaricate for a moment. He surprised himself as to how effectively he scaled the fence. It must have been the adrenaline. The driver in the car behind his got out and shouted, "Oi, mate!" as he watched Peter take a flying leap into the abyss. Seconds later his body was pulped and lifeless, shattered bones held together loosely by skin and cloth. No more fear. No more uncertainty. No more mistrust from anyone.

Munther and Quithel high-fived happily!

"Success! Finally! Now let's go to work on that Charlotte bitch!"

**

Police constable Amelia Smithers arrived at the manse later that evening. Her male colleague Robert drove her there, but he wouldn't be going in. It was probably much better just woman to woman he said. He would sit outside in the car and wait. He was only there for moral support. She lamented, "Oh God, I hate doing these. I can't stop myself getting emotional."

"I know. They're evil. It's probably one of the hardest parts of the job. You've just got to detach yourself."

"Yes, I'll do that. I'll just sit here in the car, detach myself, and let you go and tell her."

He smiled. "Woman on woman. I'm here if you need me."

He looked at her and said, "She's probably seen our car. She'll already be fretting, especially if she's already missing him. You'd better get on with it, or in a minute she'll be out here banging on our windows."

Amelia knew he was right. She reluctantly opened the door and walked slowly towards the house. What had once been a garden was now an open-plan, paved parking area for two cars like most former formal front gardens. It was dark but a street lamp was very close by, and it was quite sufficient to illuminate the house for her to find the house name. There it was on a wooden plaque just to the side of the oak front door, 'The Manse'. The doorbell was illuminated by the side of one of the jambs. She liked it when they had lights. It meant that they were actually working. Just as she was about to press it the door opened and Elsie stood there looking terrified. She spoke immediately.

"Officer, what's wrong?"

"Mrs Magnusson?"

"Yes, please, what's happened?"

"Mrs Magnusson, please may I come in?"

Elsie moved backwards without taking her eyes off the officer's face. She was terrified that something terrible had happened, and she was intensely searching for visual clues. After all, she and Peter never normally rowed. That was most unlike them, and now they were both out of sorts and he had rushed out in a state. Amelia closed the front door. Elsie was just standing there in the hallway with a look of consternation all over her face. Amelia was trying to put off the moment of truth for a few more precious seconds.

"Please, can we sit down?"

Elsie quickly moved into the lounge and sat on the sofa. She was desperate for the news. Amelia stood. No matter how many times she had delivered this kind of message, it never got any easier.

"Mrs Magnusson, I'm afraid I've got some terrible news for you."

"Has something happened to Peter?" She immediately asked in a tense, nervous voice.

Amelia tried to stay calm and level-headed. "Yes, I'm afraid so."

She looked directly into Elsie's eyes and wondered if this was the best time to just blurt out the cold, blunt truth. It was as good as any.

"I'm afraid that he jumped off the Brunel Bridge."

Elsie gulped breath for a few seconds like a beached fish and then remonstrated strenuously. She would clutch at straws. They usually did. "No, that couldn't have been him. He wouldn't do such a thing. I thought you were going to tell me that he'd had a car crash or something. Jumping off a bridge? Not him. Not in a million years."

"I'm afraid that we have identified the person concerned. It was Peter Magnusson."

"How can you say that? Do you know him?"

"Mrs Magnusson, he left his car at the scene. People saw him leave it and jump. There was identification on his body."

"His body? What do you mean, his body?"

"Mrs Magnusson, I'm afraid that he didn't survive the fall."

Amelia chose her words carefully, avoiding cold, stabbing words like 'dead' and 'head smashed to smithereens'.

Elsie retorted automatically. "There must be some mistake. He would never do a thing like that. He cherished life. He believed in living life to the full. He had no reason to want to hurt himself."

Despite her protestations, she was now sobbing heavily. She didn't mention the fierce argument they'd had only an hour or so earlier. Amelia sat next to her and risked putting an arm across her shoulder. "I'm so sorry, Mrs Magnusson."

Amelia felt useless. There was so little that she could do to ameliorate the situation.

"Is there someone I can call for you so you've got some company?"

"No, I'm sure Peter will be back soon. I'll wait for him."

She continued to cry. Realisation was often slower to arrive than a snow storm in summer. Then, much later, acceptance.

Amelia wanted time to fly. Instead, it was standing still.

"Please, Mrs Magnusson, let me call someone for you. A tragedy has happened and people often struggle to come to terms with these things and they need friends or family with them to support them. Who can I call?"

Elise didn't answer. She just carried on crying, cuddling her wet face in her hands.

"Do you have any children?"

"Fuck you!"

Amelia removed her arm. People sometimes acted quite out of character in these circumstances, anger and aggression not being an uncommon response. As a messenger, she knew she might take the brunt of someone's initial frustration and anger.

"Fuck you! Fuck you!"

Amelia had the maturity and common sense to remain silent. The least she could do was allow Elsie to vent her anger on her, so long as she didn't actually start hitting her. She put on her very best soothing, sympathetic voice.

"I'm so sorry, Mrs Magnusson, to have brought you this terrible news, but I'm not going to leave until I know someone else is going to be here to support you."

Elsie stopped crying. She looked like she was thinking.

"I'll need my mobile phone. I want to phone Peter."

She looked at Amelia imploringly.

"You can try, but I can assure you that he won't answer it. In fact, I think we've got his mobile for safe keeping along with a few other personal possessions."

Elsie stared at her blankly as if she hadn't understood what she had just said.

"I'm sorry, Mrs Magnusson, but you've got to try to accept that he has gone. Who else can you call?"

Elsie was quiet for a long minute.

"Can I fetch your phone for you? Where is it?"

Elsie still looked blank and trance-like. Amelia looked around the lounge but she didn't spot a mobile anywhere.

"Do you get on well with your neighbours?"

"Yes," she answered very quietly.

"Which side do you get on best with?"

Elsie looked from side to side as if she could actually see her neighbours and then she pointed to her left. Amelia got her own phone out and called Bob.

"Bob, can you call on the house next door, the one to your right, and see if there's anyone there who can come in and be with Mrs Magnusson please?"

"Sure. Do you know their names?"

"No."

"Is it going okay?"

"Of course not."

"Ok. Be around shortly, hopefully."

**

The next day Alexander returned from work exhausted. He didn't personally subscribe to a fit bit, but other posties spoke of walking thirty to forty thousand steps during their rounds. He let himself in as usual and the first thing he did was slump onto the sofa. His mum would make him a nice cuppa. The TV was on and blurting out its usual daytime rubbish. He wondered why daytime TV had got such a bad reputation, because, in his opinion, prime-time TV was no better. Mum must be in the kitchen. As he waited for her to emerge and offer him a cuppa, he started to nod off. Usually, after drinking a cup of tea, he would happily fall asleep there on the sofa for an hour and a half. He was torn between relaxing into sleep and fighting it until his mum showed up. He nodded off briefly, but his anxiety about not seeing Mum yet shook him out of his stupor, and he got up and went into the kitchen, calling her name.

To his horror, he saw a large, lumpy floral dress on the floor. He only recognised this as his mother when he realised that those were two legs sticking out at the bottom. One pink slipper had been kicked off. He went to the further end of this mess where his mother's head was. He shouted, but there was no response. He looked at her face turned to one side and saw that she had been sick and that her face was laying on this gloopy sticky mess. He quickly pulled the shoulder end of her body a foot or two to the side to get her face out of the vomit.

She was clearly at least unconscious if not dead, so he knew not to turn her over at this stage for fear of her choking, but he needed to know if she was still breathing, and if she had a pulse. He dug his fingers firmly into her neck where her carotid artery would be. He felt nothing, but her body was still warm. He rummaged around the carotid area until he felt a weak pulse but it was very irregular. She was best left in that position whilst he raced to the house phone and dialled 999.

After what seemed ages, he returned to his mother.

"Hang on, Mum. An ambulance is on its way."

He struggled to turn her onto her back. The operative on the emergency line had suggested that if her pulse was very weak and erratic that he should give her CPR. She was still unconscious, but he was concerned that if he turned her onto her back, she might choke. Before turning her over, he stuck two fingers inside her mouth to scoop out the sticky sick that was still in there. When he was happy that her airway was as clear as it could be, he rolled her onto her back. He held his cheek close to her mouth and nose and after a while felt the faint passage of air. He was at least relieved that she showed no signs of choking, so he got on with pumping her sternum. By the time the ambulance arrived, he had almost passed out with exhaustion.

**

Samuel was snuggled up with Sky again, on her bed, leaning against the wall and flicking through the pages of Watership Down.

"Did Mum do the bit where Bigwig got caught in a snare and nearly died?"

Sky nodded quietly, sucking on her thumb as usual.

"And how Cowslip and his rabbits refused to try to help them free Bigwig?"

She nodded again as she scoured the pictures intensely.

"And how they ran away from this warren of death to build their own new warren somewhere far away?"

More silent nodding. Samuel was checking the pictures to make sure he didn't miss out anything in his quick summary.

"And how Holly and a few others from their old warren joined them after the builders gassed and destroyed their old warren?"

Sky nodded and then added enthusiastically. "Fiver was right, wasn't he? Something terrible did happen, didn't it?"

"Yes darling. His premonition was correct. Just goes to show that sometimes, when there's a little voice inside your head warning you about something, you should listen to it. Always remember that. Pay attention to that still, small voice."

He looked at her with gravitas and she nodded again.

"Did you do the bit where they found an ideal place to build a new warren?"

Again, she nodded.

"Well, maybe you'd better show me the part you got up to with Mummy, or I'm going to spend all evening finding the right place."

She enthusiastically leaned across and turned a few pages and pointed silently at a picture, thumb back in mouth.

"Okay. So, they've made a very strange friendship with Kehaar the seagull after they found him injured and kept him alive by feeding him?"

More nods.

"And now he wants to return the favour by helping them find some mummy rabbits because they're all boys, and they're worried that their new warren will die out without any baby rabbits?"

"Kittens," she corrected him, "and the grown-ups are called bucks and does. Didn't you remember that Daddy?"

"Yes, sorry. I was simplifying too much. I forget how clever you are."

She carried on staring at the page, her own mind telling her the story.

"Well, those lazy bucks had to do their own digging to make a nice new safe warren, even though that was not something they were used to because digging was always the work of the does."

"But they had none," she explained quietly.

"Exactly, quite a problem. Dig or die! Well, having found their way to this lovely hill called Watership Down, which Fiver thought would make the ideal place to build a warren, they committed to digging out their own new warren themselves, whilst Kehaar was recovering enough to start flying again. Then, when he was well enough, he flew off looking for other rabbits, and returned with the news that there was another warren just two or three rabbit days away. Hazel decided to send a few envoys on their behalf, to ask the other chief rabbit if he would be kind enough to let them have a few of their does to start populating their own new warren."

She looked at him with an air of authority. "Kehaar also found some rabbits in cages at a farm that was guarded by cats and a fierce dog."

"Yes, darling, that's true, but that's a story for another night."

She sat back quietly. "So, who do you think Hazel chose to visit the other warren?"

"Holly, Silver, Buckthorn and Strawberry," she answered certainly. "Especially Holly, because he had been the Owsla chief at the old warren. He knew how to be important."

"Very good, dear. Yes, quite right. So, these four made their way, with occasional visits enroute from Kehaar to point them in the right direction, and when they were near the warren they bumped into a lone hare. They asked him where this other warren was and the hare named it Efrafa, and advised them to run off in the opposite direction as quickly as possible, but just then three big authoritative rabbits appeared and demanded to see their marks."

"Marks? What marks?" Holly answered.

"Apparently, all the rabbits at this warren had identification marks torn into their flesh when they were young, and then they always belonged to the group that carried the same mark, and they weren't allowed to mix with other marks. Holly and the others were marched off unceremoniously into Efrafa."

She leaned across and turned the page, eager to see the next picture, even though she knew exactly what was coming.

"They discovered that this warren not only has an Owsla but also a council, and each member of the council was responsible for one area of rabbit life, such as feeding, breeding, concealment etcetera. This was a highly organised warren where the residents sacrificed freedom in exchange for safety. The council ensured that the burrow entrances were well hidden, that all rabbits did their poos somewhere hidden, and that only a small portion of rabbits were allowed above ground at any one time. Each mark had a specific and limited time each day, and everything was monitored by captains, guards and patrols. Sometimes, a mark wouldn't see the light of day for a few days if their allocated feeding time was during the night. Members of the Owsla would go out on wide patrol for days at a time. This was to make them tough and cunning in order to survive. If they found any straggler rabbits from anywhere else, they would take them prisoner or kill them. All the orders emanated from the chief rabbit Woundwort, who was huge and very strong and terrifyingly scary, and was a complete control-freak. What do you think of them so far, Sky?"

"I think they sound mean."

"Yes, I agree. Anyway, Holly and the others spent some time underground talking to some of these new rabbits, and they formed the opinion that none of them thought for themselves. They were all too scared. They just did whatever they were ordered to do. He also discovered that the warren was under great strain because the does far outnumbered the bucks, and they had outgrown their burrows. Holly thought that this was very positive for their mission, and he was very hopeful that when they were taken before the council, headed up by the fearsome Woundwort, their mission would be met favourably. But they had to wait their turn. The council had other business to attend to first. Another rabbit was waiting with them; Blackavar. He had been apprehended trying to escape the warren. He was clearly terrified.

"Inside the council, they ripped his ears to shreds. They were duly told that he was lucky to escape with his life. Then it was their turn. When they went in, Woundwort simply started explaining the rules for new residents. Holly interrupted him and tried to explain what their mission was, and that they were only there to deliver a request from a neighbouring warren, and they certainly didn't intend to stay, but Woundwort turned him down flatly and told him that they would not be leaving at all. They were allocated to a mark and were dismissed.

"Well, they were all rather stunned, and kept a low profile in their new burrow with the rest of their new mark. That night they were led outside with the others to graze, but there was no opportunity to make a run for it because there were too many sentries. Holly realised that the only way of escape was to use cunning and deceit, so the next night when they all went above ground to graze, he immediately approached the captain and confidently told him that the council wished to see him immediately. The captain queried him, but Holly made him scared of the consequences if he didn't go down to the council straight away. He went, and Holly ordered the two sentries with him to stay there and wait for the captain's return. Then he and the other three bolted for it.

"On their way out, they were intervened by two other sentries, but because there were four of them they were able to fight them off and keep running. However, it wasn't long before they heard a rabbit posse catching up with them in the rain and the dark. Those Efrafan sentries were tough and capable, and they were faster than Holly and the others. And that, my dear, is where we will leave the story tonight."

"Dad! No. Please do some more."

"No, my girl, it's getting late. You must wait for tomorrow like a good little Efrafan rabbit."

"I don't want to be a good little Efrafan rabbit. I want to be tough and strong like Holly and Bigwig."

"Okay. Well, be a good little girl as well and get your beauty sleep, or you will never grow up to be a big and strong rabbit like Bigwig."

He tucked her in kissed her as usual and turned off the lights.

"Sleep well, gorgeous."

Chapter 11

It was just over a week since last seeing Peter when Charlotte turned up at his church for the Sunday morning family service. She had checked the start time on the internet and had allowed herself twenty minutes to walk there to arrive five minutes early. She was feeling nervous, mostly because she didn't really understand why she felt the desire to go in the first place and also because she didn't know anyone. It took all her courage to boldly attend as a stranger.

She was kindly greeted in the foyer by an ancient man in an ancient off-green suit with obvious curvature of the spine and a pronounced stoop. He offered her a weak floppy handshake as he tried to lift his head as much as his arthritis or osteoporosis allowed him to in order to look at her properly.

He beamed a genuine smile at her. Even his pale yellow eyes seemed to brighten a little. He announced in a soft strained voice, "Welcome, miss. Lovely to see you."

He had a booklet in his hand which he offered her and asked if she would like a Bible. She thought that might be a good idea and politely accepted. He turned around and carefully plucked one from a shelf behind him, handed it to her and ushered her towards the main hall with a stiff awkward arm. She cautiously walked through an open double door into the capacious hall. There were no old-fashioned pews, just single plastic seats arranged in blocks and in a gentle semi-circular fashion. About half of the seats were already taken. Almost as many other people were standing around greeting each other rather noisily. Children seemed to be running around everywhere. She was surprised at the age range. She had expected to see mostly old people here, but this crowd were in fact largely families. The building was well lit. It was modern, and it seemed like nothing she had come to know about traditional churches. She was immediately captivated by the music. No organ! Despite almost total disregard from most of the chattering congregation, a group of musicians were seriously engaged in making music at the front on a raised platform: Two guitarists, a keyboard player, a violinist, three vocalists, and a drummer in a Perspex cage. A few people near the front were singing along and waving their arms in the air rhythmically. For the time being, the group were functioning as background music whilst people increasingly began to settle down as the half-hour approached.

She took a seat near the back in a row which was still almost empty, but within the next few minutes, she found herself completely surrounded. She watched a suited man walk across the front of the hall from a side room and he stood in front of a stand which she supposed stood in as a pulpit. The musicians stopped playing and the man at the front adjusted a microphone clipped to his suit collar. He began by welcoming the entire congregation and was soon lamenting a tragic event of the past week, and spent some time offering the congregation his condolences.

Charlotte was not really focussing very well on what he was saying because she was still quite preoccupied with all the visuals. All these people, the bright lights, the ethnic mix of people with the attendant kaleidoscope of vibrant colours. Some children were still unsettled between rows or tugging at their mothers. Others seemed happy and playful being on their best behaviour near their parents, mostly playing with toys and doing their best to respond to the regular shoosh signals they were being fed. She was concerned that she hadn't seen Peter yet. She turned to the large black lady sitting to her left and whispered quite closely to her ear, "Excuse me, this is the Baptist church, isn't it?"

The lady tapped a hand on Charlotte's knee and spoke quietly back.

"Yes, dear. Did you think you've got lost?"

Charlotte smiled at her politely. "No, it's just that I was expecting to see someone I know here."

"You mean someone in particular?"

"Yes."

"Do you have a name?"

At this point, Charlotte realised for the first time that she didn't actually know Peter's surname. She looked and felt embarrassed.

"It's okay. I expect that I'll find them later."

The black lady smiled. This was no time to have a conversation. The preacher was engaging them in a rather serious introduction. Then there was a prayer, then the first song. Words came up on large screens at the front, but Charlotte realised that she could also use the booklet she had been given on entry instead. They all stood to sing and then, when that song was over, they sat again for the notices.

The main announcement was the funeral arrangements scheduled for three weeks' time, for the late pastor Magnusson. The words rang unharmoniously in Charlotte's ears. The late pastor? Her heart started beating rapidly. She felt a panic attack coming on. She turned to the black lady and asked in an urgent tone.

"Is Pastor Magnusson Peter?"

The black lady looked rather puzzled. "His first name is Peter."

With that, Charlotte stood up immediately and started pushing past all the legs in her row, unceremoniously and as quickly as she could. She trod on a few toes but carried on without apology. Tears were already running down her face. She was struggling not to vomit. She rushed out into the street and walked as fast as she could. The black lady decided to follow her out to see if she was okay, but by the time she got outside onto the street, there was no sign of Charlotte.

**

Come Tuesday morning, Elsie got another letter. It was addressed in the same handwriting as the original one that appraised her of her husband's infidelity. She was terrified of opening it and put it to one side immediately, but of course, no other thoughts could now enter her mind apart from wondering what this stranger's letter would have to say. Before long, she phoned her best friend from the church for advice.

"Mary," she exclaimed without any kind of salutation, "I've got another of those letters."

Mary took a few moments to collect her thoughts. She was busy at the church's food bank dishing out packages to the needy that were also stopping for coffee, biscuits and chat, so she had to adjust her thoughts. After focussing, she asked purposefully, "What does it say, Elsie?"

"I don't know. I haven't opened it."

"Don't you want to?"

"I don't know."

Mary discerned that Elsie was in a bit of a state.

"Honey, there are plenty of helpers here. I'll come straight over."

Elsie didn't even get a chance to respond. Mary switched her phone off straight away and made her excuses at the food bank and left. Ten minutes later she was seated with Elsie in her front room.

"I want to open it, but also, I don't. It was because of her last letter that Peter is gone."

She started crying and Mary embraced her. "Oh dear, this is a tough one. Shall I open it and see what I think first?"

"What do you think it might say?"

"Honey, I wouldn't like to guess. It might just be them offering their condolences."

"Or it might be information about another affair."

"Sweetheart. You are overthinking this. Maybe you should just throw it away."

"No. I'd always be wondering."

They both realised that she had to read it, but this was going to be hard, possibly dreadful. They opened it together with bated breath.

"Dear Elsie, please excuse me writing again. I really didn't intend to, but I thought that you should know that your late husband's lover, the one I saw him with several times at Billie's Bistro, turned up at church last Sunday. I thought that was a bit rich considering what has happened, and I thought that you should be aware of this. A well-wisher."

Elsie stared at Mary, her mouth agape. She was crying, but that was nothing unusual. She had been crying so much since Peter had gone. Triggers could be minute. She didn't know how to formulate the struggle in her head into words, but finally a single poignant, "Who?" seeped out, like air escaping from a punctured tyre. She looked shocked and puzzled. Who was this person sending the letters? And more to the point, who on earth might this adulterous woman be? She didn't recall seeing anyone unusual at church last Sunday. She looked inquisitively at Mary and asked her.

"Did you see any strange women at church last Sunday?"

Without waiting for an answer, she suddenly jumped up and rushed into Peter's office and returned with his day-diary. She sat back next to Mary and started working her way backwards. Everyone in here was suspect. She had examined this diary several times already with a fine tooth-pick, and had found nothing suspicious, but now she needed to look again. She looked at Mary intensely.

"Mary, I don't want that woman coming to my church!"

"But you don't even know who she is, and thanks to your husband's sterling efforts, the congregation is now quite a size. I don't think I know everyone any more. What can you do?"

Elsie repeated herself with a cold determined expression and in a cold steely voice.

"I don't want that fucking woman coming to my church, ever!"

**

Munther and Quithel were resting on a church roof looking down on a broad river flowing majestically by it.

"I've drowned a few in there!" Munther announced proudly. Quithel could tell that he was in one of his rare, slightly pleasant, conversational moods.

"Please, tell me more about the councils."

Munther looked at him scornfully. "Why do you want to know more about them? They're not your job."

"Yes I know, but from what you've already told me, I think that the more I know about them, the better disposed I will be to do my actual job."

Munther was not convinced and a sceptical expression twisted his pale black face. However, he decided that if he was to educate Quithel some more, then, maybe he would shut up and stop asking questions.

"Okay. Well, you know I've mentioned that some of our colleagues sort of work behind the scenes. Well, they still work on people, but with a view to impact the bigger picture for the benefit of the rest of us, so they don't work like we do. They are attached to councils. They kind of pave the way for our work, to make it easier."

He looked at Quithel to see if there was a spark of understanding, but Quithel just looked back at him with a puzzled look on his face. "Go on."

"What I'm saying is that their objectives are always to do with the bigger picture whereas we work on harm to individuals."

"You mean like what you told me about Traxodyl and Malin and what they achieved?"

Munther shook his head and looked cross. "No, not like them. They stumbled individually on a couple of great ideas which they then managed to push globally. No, the councils don't come up with great new projects. That is not their job. They plod away constantly building on the kinds of things that we have worn humans away with since the beginning of time. Common predictable things."

Quithel looked at him quizzically. "Such as?"

Munther closed his eyes and started opening up his closed fists, one finger at a time as he counted out the basic areas of work. Poverty, sickness, war, false religion and child abuse, slavery, fear, anxiety, frustration, injustice, to name the first ones that come to mind. He had run out of fingers, so he thought that was enough.

"So, each council is responsible for growing those areas of development, which warms people up for us?"

"Yes, exactly, I mean, take frustration, for instance. If people are constantly frustrated, they are much more likely to give up, to become depressed and harm themselves, yes?"

"Yes, I suppose so. But how does the council do that?"

Munther sighed as if he thought that Quithel was being particularly dense today. "So, in that area, as an example, the council works to encourage governments to be greedy, so that people never seem to be able to earn enough money, or to encourage societies to become tediously bureaucratic, so people feel that it is too hard to achieve things because of the trivial rules and regulations that seem to hinder them. Stuff like that wears people down and makes it easier for us to work on them."

"I see. So, they work on influencers who can make people's lives less worthwhile?"

"Yes. You're getting it. In some countries, they convince the rulers that the country's wealth belongs to only them, and then those rulers will happily make the rest of the people in that country destitute. In other countries, it might not be acceptable for the rulers to own everything, so then the council will encourage the leaders to waste vast sums of money which helps keep the workers impoverished. Those leaders will happily do this as long as their palms get crossed with some incentives. Don't ever forget—money is what makes the human world go round. Everything is about money and greed. The basic areas which the councils cover don't change. Humans are humans no matter what epoch you look at, but we need to use different tools in different eras. They have to be constantly adapting."

Munther noticed that Quithel still looked rather quizzical, so he elucidated.

"Take fear, for example. In the dark ages, people were afraid of their lords and of hunger, so the councils then worked on encouraging lords to be cruel and evil towards their serfs, and to deprive them of almost all of life's necessities. In the modern age, fear has to come from more subtle sources because the structure of society has changed. People in different parts of the world fear different things. Here, people are worried about not being popular or keeping up with the Joneses, whereas in third world countries they are still afraid of poverty and diseases. As technology has developed, the councils also have new tools."

"Such as?"

"Take television, for example. Suddenly people all over the world can be communicated to instantly, and all day long, so the fear council works on the programmers to push them towards delivering bad news constantly, and also to influence general entertainment in a way which undermines people's standards and ethics. When TV was young, it presented us with quite a challenge. Programmes were being made about wildlife and nature which were bringing fantastic new insights to people all over the world about the wonders and diversity of the planet. The Dark One was worried that such information was making people consider a creator and question evolution, so the fear council had to step in urgently to encourage the programme makers to steer away from what was so amazing about nature, and towards what was going wrong with it instead. Now wildlife programmes are more about species extinction, shrinking habitats, chemical poisoning, pollution, poaching, climate change, etcetera, and of course, it's all man's fault. So, we manage to turn wonderful things into causes for despair, depression and anxiety. We harp on about how they all contribute to carbon poisoning and pollution, and what woman of a certain age has never bought a fur coat? They're all guilty. The council also ensures that all wildlife programmes are heavily interwoven with evolutionary themes, obviously."

Quithel was impressed. He hadn't realised just how organised the dark side was. "Is there any benefit to being on a council?"

"I don't personally think so, but that's because I like to be a free spirit, and to be free to pick and choose my victims. I can only see it appealing if you prefer team work. Perhaps if you lack initiative, like you do, you would perform better in that environment. Maybe it would suit you, but I honestly don't know if you're going to be good at anything in particular."

Quithel was fascinated. In due course, he would like to experience working on a council. He thought that might make better use of his intelligence and resourcefulness. He kind of despised Munther for having been stuck in the same job for so many thousands of years. He lacked ambition and that was pathetic.

Chapter 12

Dawn was lying in a hospital bed in a small ward of just eight patients. Some had curtains pulled around them, and quite a few beds had quietly talking, reassuring relatives around them. All the patients in this ward had serious heart issues. Dawn mostly slept, interspersed with occasional arousals where she would start to speak, and Alexander, who sat dutifully by her side, would insist on her not talking, but resting further. He looked very tired and anxious. Seeing the drip feed going into her arm and the oxygen pipe going into her nose, and the electronic monitors she was wired up to, made him feel weak. He hadn't slept well. Occasionally, a nurse would swan by, check the dials and make a little cheerful small talk. In time, an Indian doctor arrived and pulled the curtain around the bed to give them some privacy.

"Hello, how are we today?" He asked brightly, smiling.

Alexander presumed he was referring to him rather than his mother as she could barely talk. "Yeah, I'm okay, doctor. Bit tired of course. More to the point is how is my mum?"

The doctor adjusted the white plastic chair on the opposite of the bed so that he could sit down. Of course, he was carrying a clipboard and had a stethoscope around his neck—still an essential badge of office. He briefly scoured the page on his clipboard before placing it down on the bed.

"I am Doctor Patel. I operated on your mother yesterday. I must say she is really lucky to still be alive."

Alexander didn't know whether to take that as a good or a bad thing. It would depend on what she was or was not capable of now, but he thanked him very sincerely anyway. The doctor continued.

"I can't believe that you performed CPR on her for over two hours."

He looked at Alexander with genuine awe and admiration in his eyes.

"She is my mother," Alexander responded simply, with a sense of gravitas that explained why he had applied himself so fully. The doctor nodded to convey his understanding and empathy.

"Well, congratulations. There is no doubt that you kept her alive."

"Thank you, but where do we go from here?"

The good doctor leaned back and took a deep breath.

"Your mother is eighty-three, and as is often the case with people in their eighties, she has quite bad atherosclerosis. Plaque has been building up inside her arteries for years, decades probably, and I'm afraid that she has reached that point where some of her arteries are so clogged up that not enough oxygen can get to her heart muscles and that has caused a myocardial infarction."

Alexander interrupted him, "A heart attack?"

"Yes, exactly. We overcame the immediate obstruction by performing a balloon angiography, that is, we inserted a small balloon to open up the artery sufficiently, but really, this is just a temporary measure."

Alexander looked at him appealing. He wanted to know what the permanent solution would be. The doctor understood the look.

"Ideally she should get a coronary artery bypass or two, or maybe three."

Alexander interrupted him enthusiastically. "How soon can you do that?"

The doctor sighed. "I'm afraid that it's not that simple. Your mother's heart muscle will have suffered some damage in the left ventricle, and that means that she will suffer some degree of contractile dysfunction."

"And that means?"

"Her heart will be weaker anyway, even if we were to perform heart bypass surgery."

"But the bypass would keep her alive, yes?"

"Well, yes, hopefully for a period of time, but there are no guarantees."

"Okay. So, what are the timescales?"

The doctor sucked in a deep breath. He was trying to delay his response.

"Mr Maitland, are you familiar with the term ESG?"

"Yes. That's an electrocardiogram."

The doctor gave a small smile. "That's an ECG, no; ESG stands for environment, social and government guidelines."

Alexander looked puzzled. He was only vaguely aware of ESGs but couldn't see the relevance here, at his mother's hospital bedside whilst discussing intricate and urgent heart matters. The doctor leaned back and folded his arms, as if trying to distance himself from the subject he was about to try to explain.

"As you know, when covid struck some years ago, the government saw fit to suddenly take charge of everyone's health directly, and we, the medical profession were side-lined in favour of political dogma." A weary expression crossed his face, and he added apologetically.

"I'm afraid that we doctors have always been accustomed to just following orders from the top-down, and this was no different. As you know, the overreach soon mushroomed. They decided that they could tell people not to go out, not to see their own families, what chemicals to stick in their bodies, and what chemicals not to stick in. I'm sure you well remember."

"Of course."

"Well, at that time, it was a bit like a war-time commandeering of the medical profession in the face of a terrible enemy, for the good of the people, of course. Trouble is they never relinquished control. Now I'm sorry to say that we are even more of a tool for government political policies than we ever were before."

"Sounds about right," Alexander agreed, trying to sound agreeable. "What's your point though?"

"Well, as they have continued down that road of dictating what we doctors should or shouldn't do, it's no longer a matter of us using our discretion or our medical expertise in any given situation. *They* have introduced rather a lot of blanket diktats and tick-box assessments to govern us directly."

Alexander was beginning to get impatient. "I'm sorry, but what has this got to do with my mother?"

The doctor looked at him sympathetically. He appreciated that a man of any age wants the best for his own dear mother.

"Under the guise of ESGs, they manage what we are allowed to do or not do, you know, to ensure that valuable resources are used in the best possible way, to save the planet, and all that."

Alexander was beginning to feel a little cross with himself because he was feeling somewhat thick. He still didn't know what the doctor was so carefully driving at.

"I'm sorry. I get the impression that you are beating around the bush. Please be honest with me. I am a grown man. I'm sure I can take it."

"What I am driving at, Mr Maitland, is that we have specific guidelines for what we are allowed to do. Specifically, in this case, the government has dictated age limits on certain operations we perform. After all, there is already a waiting list for eight million operations, and we have ever-dimishing resources."

The penny was starting to drop, and now confusion was giving way to incredulity.

"You mean my mother is too old to operate on?"

The doctor pulled a twisted, troubled face. It was not easy telling a man who so obviously loved his mother that there was little hope for her. The good doctor however was able to offer a small ray of hope.

"Mr Maitland, it's not a completely lost cause. These ESGs are theoretically only guidelines, but unfortunately, as an NHS hospital, we have no choice but to follow them to the letter because we are government funded. Our funding depends upon our compliance with the ESGs, and as you can imagine, the management are completely fixated with them and getting the right ticks in the right boxes."

Alexander looked dejected. The doctor tried to be positive.

"You do have options though. You might be able to get help privately. A privately funded company would not be absolutely obliged to follow the guidelines as we are."

Alexander sat forward with a slightly more optimistic expression on his face.

"My mother has paid into the system all her life. My father worked until he dropped. He never even got to draw any of his pensions. Are you sure she can't be helped by the NHS?"

The doctor's expression went blank, and he gently shook his head. He had heard all these points before. He leaned back. He really didn't want to get into the politics or unfairness of it all. That was not his job. He had done his best to save Dawn's life, and now was delivering the message which he was obliged to deliver on behalf of an all-knowing, all-powerful government, who incidentally paid his wages, and he had done this as gently and as kindly as he knew how. After a little more thought, Alexander asked a pertinent question.

"So, you're saying that there is an age limit on bypasses?"

The doctor looked at him drily. "Seventy-three or four I think."

"Seventy-three? That's no age at all these days."

"I suppose the government wants people to take much more responsibility for their own health."

"I bet there's no limit for politicians. I bet that's in the ESGs."

The doctor shrugged his shoulders. "Like I said, there's always private."

Munther was by Alexander's side. "Alex, you did your best, mate, but the system is letting you down now. There's nothing else you can do. Just let her go peacefully, without any more traumas. That would be the kindest thing to do."

**

Amelia attended the manse at Elsie's request. On the night of the death message, she had left Elsie her card with an exhortation to call her if there was anything she could do to help. Now that exhortation had now come to fruition. Elsie politely invited her in, sat her in the lounge, and fetched her a nice cup of coffee. Then she showed her the letters. Amelia read through them respectfully. She thought that the chain of events was rather sad, and she fully understood why they had caused Elsie such consternation, but no offences had been committed.

"Elsie, I'm sorry that these have upset you, what do you want me to do?"

"I don't want this woman coming to my church, ever!"

Amelia looked down at the letters on her lap as she wondered how she could bat this one off without causing offence. She spoke softly and slowly, as if to appeal to the understanding part of Elsie' nature.

"Elsie, your church is a public place when its doors are open, with an implied invitation to one and all. Jesus stands at the door with open arms to everyone, especially sinners and adulterers, does he not?"

She looked firmly at Elsie to gauge her reaction, but Elsie just gave her a quiet, determined stare back.

"No, Jesus does not stand at my church door with open arms because I don't want that woman coming to my church again!"

Amelia prodded further.

"Have you found out who this woman is?"

"No."

"If you knew who she was, you could kind of ban her I suppose, and hope she stays away of her own accord."

"That's the problem. I don't know who she is. That's where I need your help."

Amelia gave a little chuckle. "And how do you think I am going to be able to identify her? You said you don't know her. Nobody knows who she is. She may not even be real. She exists in these letters, but you don't even know who is writing them. It's anonymous information."

"I don't know how. You're the police officer, aren't you? That's your job."

Amelia wasn't going to be backed up into an impossible corner. "Elsie, we're not clairvoyant, and I would need something to go on, a reason to investigate, and I don't think we have that."

Elsie looked at her sternly. "What *can* you do to help?"

"I don't know. What can *you* give me?"

"Nothing more than these letters."

Amelia tried not to let her exasperation show.

"So, all we know is that a woman whom we don't know *allegedly* attended Billie's Bistro a few times with Peter, according to an anonymous letter-writer, during the week before he passed away, and you don't want her casually popping into your church when it has its arms wide open to all and sundry and especially sinners."

"Yes," Elsie answered very sternly, as if that made perfect sense.

"And that's it?"

"Yes."

"Elsie, I can only get involved if there's a crime of some sort."

"She's harassing me."

"By going to your church?"

"Yes!"

"Elsie, I can tell you now, that this is going nowhere, but if you're determined to make an official complaint anyway, I just might be able to find this woman's identity. The most I can do is ask her on your behalf to stay away from your church, but I can assure you that under these circumstances there could be no prosecution of any kind. I'd be doing this just as a kind of favour for you, and it really is a long shot. Do you understand that?"

"That's fine. I just don't want this woman coming to my church. Jesus or no Jesus."

Amelia finished her coffee, and then got up to leave. At the door, she summarised. "Okay. I'll give it a shot. I'll record a complaint of harassment against person unknown, with you as the aggrieved party, and make a few enquiries at the cafe. I really can't do anything more than that. Do you have a recent photo of Peter that I can use please?"

Elsie quickly fetched her a photo of her and Peter together, and Amelia left, feeling caught between a rock and a hard place. She really didn't want to waste her time, yet at the same time, she couldn't bring herself to just flatly turn this poor, grieving widow down.

**

Munther and Quithel were in the bedroom of a ten-year-old boy called Thomas. He had his computer on and was about to do a dare on a social media challenge. His room was not well lit with just a bedside lamp alight next to his bed, together with the flickering glare of his computer screen. He had two incense sticks burning on his desk, with some heavy metal music blaring quite loudly from the speakers, but not too loudly. He didn't want to attract the attention of his mum downstairs. The video camera was switched on and he was connected to a crowd of about a dozen viewers on a zoom call. They were all egging him on. Quithel was not conversant with what was going on. He asked Munther cautiously.

"What's he supposed to be doing?"

"He's going to asphyxiate himself."

Quithel looked very puzzled. "Why?"

"It's a social media challenge. They've become quite popular, thanks to our death council. They come up with ideas that challenge people to do stupid or dangerous things just for media attention. They call it kudos. Quite often things go wrong and then they die. Kids this age are particularly impressionable and vulnerable. I've told you before haven't I? Humans are quite unpredictable."

Quithel was astonished. He had thought that people only hurt themselves because of depression or mental illness, not for fun.

"Is it a big thing?"

"No, not really. Mostly impressionable young people trying to make a name for themselves. Quite productive though. They don't mean to actually kill themselves of course, but the whole point is that these things are dangerous, and naturally, they go wrong sometimes."

Quithel was most curious. "What kind of dares are there?"

"Oh, they change over time. They're just passing fads really, but the internet popularises them really quickly. Things like setting yourself on fire, doing dangerous things whilst blindfolded, and pouring boiling water on someone for a laugh. Swallowing dangerous objects. Can you believe it?"

Quithel looked quite aghast. "Anything else?"

"Skull breaker challenge. That's where they get someone to see how high they can jump, but then when they're in the air, they kick their legs from under them and try to make them land on their head."

"Nice! What else?"

"Car surfing."

"What the heck is that?"

"What do you think it is? It's where someone sits on the roof of the car whilst it is driving along."

Quithel was speechless, so Munther carried on.

"That's harmless enough." He paused, and then added, with a laugh, "Until they fall off."

Quithel had a question. "Which ones are the most fatal?"

Munther thought for a moment, and then answered quite certainly. "Performing stunts on tall buildings. They might get away with it a hundred times, but when it does eventually go wrong, that's bye, bye baby every time. It's almost as if they have to keep doing more and more risky things until they reach the limit, and then it's adios, senior!"

He smiled his creepy indulgent smile.

"What about this asphyxiation though?"

"Not often fatal. Usually they just pass out. It used to be just an auto-erotic thing for grown men. Apparently, they have a bigger orgasm if they are at the point of passing out at the same time, or so they think, anyway. So they would half strangle themselves with a tie or scarf tied to a door knob or something like that, whilst they played with themselves. Again, if they did it often enough, the time would come where they would actually accidentally asphyxiate themselves. These kids don't seem interested in the auto-erotic side of it. They just do it for an online dare. Thank goodness for the internet, eh?"

He turned his attention to Thomas. "Come on, Thomas, you've got quite an audience now. Show them how incredibly daring you are. See how many likes you can get."

Thomas got up from his chair, ensured that the computer screen was angled towards his bedroom door, and he went over to the door with a necktie. He made a loop and tied it to the door handle. He squatted against the door as he awkwardly inserted his head into the loop. Then he slowly sagged into the sitting position. He'd seen other people do this online.

"That's it boy," Munther encouraged. "Let it take your weight. Your viewers really admire you. You're so brave!"

Thomas's face went red and bloated as the noose tightened and took most of his body weight. Only his lower legs were on the floor. He tried to hold his breath, but it was impossible to overcome the automatic instinct to breathe. However, the blood flow to his brain was rapidly diminishing and he got quickly drowsy. Moments later, he passed out. In a few more minutes, he would be dead. His viewers were cheering, but he couldn't hear them.

Suddenly, there was a strange presence in the room and both Munther and Quithel began retching violently, overcome with an intense noxious feeling, for which their only instinctive reaction was to fly out of that room as fast as they possibly could, and keep going.

An angel stood magnificently in the room looking angrily at Thomas as he walked over to him, and violently ripped the handle off the door. Thomas's body slumped to the floor, unconscious. The angel was full of righteous anger and he threw the defunct handle at the adjacent wall, smashing the handle to pieces. Downstairs Thomas's parents were watching the TV, but they both felt the whole house suddenly shake.

"What the fuck was that?" Thomas's mum shouted, as she instantly jumped up and made for the stairs. She instinctively went for Thomas's room. She tried to open his door, but it would only open slightly.

"Gerald! Quickly. Help!"

Gerald made his way up the stairs in much more sedate fashion, but when he saw the alarm on his wife's face he immediately became energised and thrust his considerable weight at the door. After three hefty shoves, Thomas's body had been swept along enough for them to gain entry. Thomas's life had been saved.

Munther and Quithel re-grouped on a distant church roof.

"What the fuck was that?" Quithel asked, quite alarmed.

Munther looked at him with a rather dejected expression. "That, my friend, is what it feels like when a light-rep shows up."

He was breathing heavily and spitting a nasty taste out of his mouth. Quithel had nothing to say as he mulled over the sensation that this had been the worst feeling he had ever felt, and by a very long chalk. Finally, he commented.

"Well, I hope that doesn't happen too often. It was horrible."

Munther reassured him. "Light-reps very rarely intervene, thank goodness, but when they do, it does feel awful. You've just got to get out of there as fast as you can."

"Is it always that bad?"

"Yes. The only time I've ever felt worse was quite a few thousand years ago when I was harassing the Israelites in the desert. Inadvertently, I got too close to the Ark of the Covenant. It must have been a few hundred metres, but even so, that was too close. That time I felt like my insides were about to erupt and I was going to explode. I honestly think I was lucky to survive. It took every speck of effort I could muster to pull myself away. I just know I was very nearly a goner."

Quithel looked at him with alarm. "Remind me to never go near the Ark of the Covenant."

Munther smiled. "That would be unlikely. No one knows where it is. It's been hidden for the past two and a half thousand years at least."

"Why?"

"Who knows? I just hope it doesn't suddenly show up somewhere near me."

Chapter 13

The next day Amelia made time to pop into Billie's Bistro. Being in police uniform, her presence caused quite a stir. She could feel all eyes boring into her immediately and she didn't feel that she would ever become truly insouciant about being stared at, much as she tried. She walked to the counter and asked if she could speak with the manager. A waitress quickly disappeared into the kitchen and just as quickly returned with an aproned Billie.

"Hello. How can I help you?" Billie asked brightly.

"I wonder if I might have a word in private."

"Yes, of course."

Billie tried to maintain her equanimity but she looked a little flustered. People almost always wondered if they had done something wrong when a police officer turned up out of the blue. She led Amelia through the kitchen to a small office to the rear of that, and then as quickly as possible she asked what this was about.

"There's nothing for you to worry about. No one is in trouble. I'm making enquiries in a missing person inquiry and I wondered if you had CCTV here?"

"Yes we do, but we only keep the records for two weeks. They are automatically erased after that."

Billie was suddenly wondering if her use of CCTV was fully legally compliant.

"That's fine. I only want to go back two weeks. I have just two or three days I want to look at if I may?"

"May I ask what this has got to do with my cafe?"

"Of course. I believe that someone came here to meet someone. I have a picture of the first someone, but I want to try to identify the second someone." She smiled at Billie.

"Clear as mud," Billie responded.

The office was rather small and cluttered with paperwork and files, but it did have a proper computer and desk, and Billie sat Amelia in front of the screen and showed her how to interrogate the CCTV records. Amelia had been pleased to learn that they had CCTV records, but at the same time, she was not pleased, because this would now tediously drain her precious time, and looking through hours of tapes, albeit speeded up as fast as she wanted, was no fun at all. She wasn't sure if she would get it all done today. If a call came in, she would have to leave.

"Well, if you'll excuse me, I must leave you to it and get on with my work. I'll be in the kitchen if you need me. Would you like a coffee?"

Amelia accepted the offer of a coffee and got in with the task at hand. It was fully two hours and three coffees before she found an image she could use. She rather triumphantly announced to Billie that she had found a useful image and asked if it could be sent to her by email. Of course, Billie wasn't sure. She had never actually taken anything off the system before.

Explaining her uncertainty, she said, "It's really just a deterrent, you know. Signs up in the cafe telling the clientele that they're being spied on. Cameras swivelling around from the ceiling, making them aware that they really are being spied on. Since installing it, I think we've recovered the cost of the system through saved teaspoons."

Between the two of them and after playing with various drop-down menus for five minutes, they managed to send Amelia the image to her work email. Things had gone better than she had expected and she was really quite pleased.

"Thank you so much for your help. This is going to be so useful in my inquiry."

"No problem. Happy to do my bit for my Queen and country. I hope you catch your missing person."

**

That afternoon Amelia texted her old school friend Stacey who worked at GCHQ.

"Hi, Stacey. Hope you are well. I'm after another favour if I may. Just want to ID a face. No offences involved. Sort of official, but only a little bit if you know what I mean. Let me know."

It wasn't long before she got a response.

"In the interests of national safety or security?"

"Of course."

"What have you got?"

"A CCTV image."

"Depends on the quality."

"Willing to try."

"Okay. I'll check this out for you. You remember that this can't be used in a court of law and you can't reveal your source? Purely intelligence, just a favour, okay?"

"Of course."

Stacey had to send her a current email address as she changed them regularly, and used a different one for every single inquiry she was working on. Amelia sent her the image of two people, explaining that it was the female that she was interested in. The police service still didn't have facial recognition software. Too many do-gooders out there protecting ordinary peoples' rights and privacy, but it was a completely different kettle of fish for GCHQ. They had access to anything and everything, no questions asked. The legislation which restricted police electronic surveillance didn't apply to them at all, because they were saving the country from being blown up. Nobody scrutinised proportionality or considered potential collateral consequences. The RIPA act was something they didn't have to worry about. They probably didn't even know what the initials stood for let alone what limitations it imposed on law enforcement in the real world. It was all okay because they operated in a world of total secrecy.

Later that afternoon, Amelia got an email which she knew would be untraceable.

"Charlotte Blaithwaite. Uses facial recognition on her iPhone and bank account."

Stacey even supplied a current address, although Amelia liked to think that could have worked that bit out for herself. Now she would be able to do Elsie a favour.

**

Several days had lapsed, and Amelia had not found the time to visit Charlotte. It was tricky because she had so many other more important inquiries to busy herself with. Real crimes. Burglaries, thefts, assaults, etc. So, she kept putting off this tricky visit. What was she supposed to say anyway? "I'm here to ask you not to go to church because it might upset someone you don't know for reasons which might be purely spurious? But in law, you're perfectly entitled to go there whenever it is open." She hated these kinds of scenarios where she was treading on very thin ice. There were so many shades of grey. She was struggling to get motivated and kept avoiding the issue.

Friday evening arrived and she had just started her evening shift with Robert when a call came over the radio. "Brunel bridge—possible jumper. Female. Late twenties. Dark red coat."

Robert pressed the transmit button on his radio. "Ten four. Bravo 34 enroute. Eta five minutes."

He immediately flicked on the blues and twos and sped into action, driving chillingly fast down the centre of the road, traffic on both sides slowly melting into and over the kerbs. Red lights became green lights but proceed with caution. Just as they approached the road with the bridge, they killed the blues and twos, and pulled up quietly about thirty metres before the place where they saw the woman standing alone near the centre of the bridge. Amelia was the first one out of the car and she started slowly walking towards her with her arms appealingly out in front of her. Very slowly.

"Please don't do anything hasty. We just want to talk to you."

"Stay away. I *am* going to jump."

Amelia stopped walking. She really didn't want to provoke the lady. On the night, she had delivered the death message with Robert, she had said that delivering death messages was just about the hardest part of the job. In fact, she had been told by other officers that the worst thing any officer could experience would be trying to talk a person down from jumping to their death or from shooting their brains out, but they jump or shoot anyway, right there in front of you and then questions will plague your mind forever more. "Did I say the right things? Could I have handled the situation differently? Was I too pushy?" and so on. The questions continue, day and night, never-ending.

She pushed these thoughts out of her mind and focussed. She could see the woman clearly in the street light, but not really her face. Momentarily, Robert illuminated her with a bright light. He just wanted to satisfy himself that she wasn't carrying a weapon. Yes, he was concerned about this strange woman, but he was also concerned about his colleague and himself. He decided that she was not a serious threat to them and extinguished the light. Amelia's mouth dropped and she realised that she had seen that face before. The woman, who was still twenty metres in front of her, suddenly started to scale the fence. Amelia would not be able to reach her in time so she screamed instead. "Charlotte!"

The woman froze, straddling the barrier with a look of shock on her face. She stared at Amelia.

"How do you know my name?"

"Peter sent me."

Charlotte looked as though she was melting. The energy and vitality of her limbs seeped out of them and she collapsed in slow motion onto the barrier. Moments later, both Robert and Amelia were holding her safely, then gently lowered her onto the pavement.

Amelia and Robert drove a sobbing Charlotte home. Robert gave Amelia curious looks, wondering how she knew this woman, but he didn't want to ask in front of Charlotte, who seemed inconsolable in the back seat of the car. Although she was terribly upset, she was not in need of any medical attention, so it was just their duty to take her somewhere safe. They had asked about friends and family enroute, but got nothing back other than harsh, sad, negative responses. They had barely got inside her flat when a call came over the radio for assistance needed from a fellow officer.

"We've got to go!" Robert stated quietly but firmly to Amelia. Amelia was just in the process of sitting Charlotte down on the sofa. She turned to him with a strained look on her face.

"We can't just walk out on her now."

"It's a ten zero!"

"It must be Wally. He calls in a ten zero if his shoelace has come undone."

"Amelia, we have to go."

She looked at him with pain in her eyes. "You go. I'll call you when I am finished here."

He gave her a hard stare which she interpreted as a silent but loud sigh, and left immediately. He didn't have time to argue with her. It was a ten zero after all. Moments later Amelia heard the siren blaring and fading into the distance. She looked kindly at Charlotte.

"They won't need my help, I can assure you."

"Shouldn't you have gone?" Charlotte queried, beginning to pull herself together.

"What and then find that I've got to go to the Brunel Bridge again to pick up your pieces? I don't think so."

Charlotte made no comment. Her face still carried a strained expression of desperation and sadness.

"I think I need to stay here for a bit and find out why you're so desperate."

"That's not your job."

"It is my job as a human being."

Charlotte cried and Amelia did her best to comfort her. Eventually, Charlotte's mind started to clear.

"How did you know my name, and how do you know Peter?"

She was very confused. How could anyone know that she even knew Peter? Over the next half an hour a slow gentle conversation revealed to Charlotte that it had been Amelia who had delivered the death message to Peter's wife, and that Elsie had made a complaint about the mysterious woman who had been seen with Peter in the bistro. Charlotte was mulling it all over.

"She doesn't know that Peter went to the bridge before, planning to jump, does she?"

"No, it seems not. I don't think anyone knew this apart from you."

"And she thinks that Peter was having some kind of affair with me?"

Her voice carried her incredulity, and the shocked look on her face portrayed it.

"It looks like it."

Charlotte was puzzled. "But Peter was adamant that he hadn't told her about that night, or meeting me at the cafe because he didn't want her to know what it was about. That's all. Why would she think we were involved?"

"I think someone spotted you and added two and two and came up with twenty-two."

Charlotte went quiet for a while, lost in thought.

"I was so upset when I found out he'd killed himself. I really thought I'd helped him to see that it wasn't right for him, but I was wrong, as usual. My life is so shit."

Amelia didn't know what to say other than simply, "I'm so sorry."

She waited for Charlotte to say something else, but now she seemed lost in thought. Tears occasionally trickled down her cheeks.

"Well, Charlotte, we need to get you some help. I'm sure that your future is not as bleak as you make out."

Charlotte looked anything but convinced. Amelia carried on.

"Have you ever tried counselling?"

"Do you know what they charge for that? And where am I going to find the money for that? I'm on benefits, you know."

The harshness in her voice indicated that she considered it horrendously expensive. That it wasn't a service that a poor lowly person like her could avail themselves of.

"Surely your life is worth whatever it costs to get you back on track."

"I've never been on track in the first place."

Amelia spent a few moments collecting her thoughts. She looked around the living room. It was fairly barren. No pictures. No photographs, hardly a souvenir in sight. The furniture was minimalist. She could imagine all the bits and pieces having been supplied by free-cycle. She knew that she couldn't stay long but she didn't want to leave until she had somehow inspired a little hope into Charlotte's life.

"Look, I won't be happy unless you agree to get some help. We have a list of approved counsellors which we dish out where necessary."

"I can't afford that."

"You won't need to worry about the cost. I'll take care of that."

Even as she said this she wondered what on earth she was saying. As a police officer she knew that she shouldn't get personally involved in any of the situations she came across, but somehow this one was different. Something was tugging at her heartstrings, as if a higher authority was directing her. She simply felt compelled to reach out for Charlotte, who responded only by looking gobsmacked.

"I take it you have a mobile phone?"

"Yes."

"Okay. Give me the number so I can follow this up."

Charlotte nodded and provided her phone number.

"Great. Thank you. Look, in the car I should have details of recommended counsellors. When my partner comes back, I'll get you them, okay?"

Charlotte looked back at her still wearing a look of hopelessness, but Amelia was doing her professional bit and taking charge of the situation.

"I want you to promise me to see one of them, okay? I'll foot the bill. I want to do that for you."

Charlotte didn't know what to say, and only managed a weak, "Are you sure?"

"Yes, I am. Lots of people give charitable donations each month, and this is my way of making a small contribution to help someone else for a change. You! I don't have to waste all of my spare money on clothes and make-up that I don't need. I'll phone you in a day or two to see how you're getting on and to find out who you're going to see. Okay?"

Charlotte just nodded, staring into her lap. Amelia then phoned Robert.

"Hi, Rob. You can come back and get me now please, and can you bring up a list of counsellors from my information folder?"

A droll reply, "I'm waiting outside."

"Oh! The big fracas didn't come to anything then?"

"It was more a case of Wally tripping over his shoelaces as usual."

She smiled and looked at Charlotte kindly.

"I'll leave the front door open so I can get you those details, okay?"

Again, Charlotte only nodded weakly, and Amelia really didn't know if she was just wasting her time. She returned moments later with the list.

"Look, there are ten approved practitioners here. We have to give you lots to choose from so that we can't be accused of being partial, you know, taking bribes to favour one of them, that kind of thing, but I don't want to blind you with science. I've heard that this one is really good."

She drew a ring around one of the names-Cynthia.

"Please promise me you'll call her."

Charlotte nodded weakly again, and then spoke feebly, choking back sobs. "Thanks for your concern. I do appreciate it."

Amelia waited a moment before adding, "Don't forget. I'll foot the bill."

Charlotte fought back tears and Amelia went to leave, close to tears herself.

"Wait!" Charlotte barked out as she stood up. She walked over to Amelia and gave her a big hug. "Thank you. Thank you so much."

As Amelia made her way back to the car, she was fighting tears herself. Munther was at her side.

"You stupid cow! You won't last in this job for five minutes if you want to put the world to rights. You'll just end up losing your job for being unprofessional, or becoming emotionally burnt out. Why on earth would you use your own hard-earned cash to try to help a loser like that? You need those clothes and that make-up. Charlotte would be just wasting your time and money. You've got to show strength, not weakness, clear-headedness, not this kind of emotional frailty that leads to such poor decisions. You're going to have to go back on your word to her when you come to your senses."

Chapter 14

Alexander attended the nearest branch of his bank. It was hardly local. Local banks had gradually all but disappeared from the high streets over the past ten years, as services had gone online. He had to go into the city because he had demanded a face-to-face meeting with someone in authority. Apparently, there were issues concerning the money he had raised for his mother's private operation, and wanted a face-to-face discussion with someone to sort it out.

He wore a nice smart suit for the occasion. If he wanted to garner respect, he would have to show respect. He entered the reception and approached a very smart middle-aged lady in bright blue two-piece sitting behind an open desk. It felt nice when there were no Perspex barriers. He announced his purpose confidently.

"Good morning, miss. I am here to see Mr Shepherd."

He tried not to look embarrassed as he instantly realised that he might have started off on the wrong foot by presuming to call this lady 'Miss'. Old habits die hard. Fortunately she appeared completely unperturbed by his minor faux pas. And she smiled at him nicely.

"May I have your name please sir?"

"Yes of course. Alexander Maitland."

"Ah yes, Mr Maitland. I'll buzz Mr Shepherd for you. He is waiting to see you."

As she made a quick phone call, Alexander checked his watch. Was he late? Had he got the time wrong? He had expected to be kept waiting.

"He will be with you shortly, Mr Maitland. Can I get you a hot drink?"

Wow, he thought. They certainly were polite and efficient here.

"No, I'm fine, thank you." Just then a very smart youngish gentleman pushed his way through the double doors and held out his hand. They shook hands as he introduced himself.

"Good morning, Mr Maitland. I'm Mr Shepherd, head of the compliance department. Thanks for coming in to see us. Please follow me."

Mr Shepherd showed him down the corridor to a medium sized office. He politely ushered him inside and invited him to sit on a comfy chair. The room was weird. It had no windows and to that extent felt rather claustrophobic. To one side there was a very large desk with a huge computer screen on it with big plush office chairs on either side of it. He was shown not to one of those but to a comfy chair to one side of the desk. He sat and then Mr Shepperd sat in an identical chair at a strategic forty-five degrees to his. Only a low circular coffee table separated them.

"Would you like some cool spring water, Mr Maitland?"

He indicated the fresh water dispenser by the wall.

"No, I'm fine thank you."

"Okay. That's fine. Well, I've looked through your correspondence and I've invited you here to explain this very delicate and unfortunate situation in person."

Alexander looked at him quietly and expectantly.

"You may or may not know that over the years, financial institutions have been given more and more responsibility to protect their clients. Here in the compliance department everything that we do is purely to oversee matters that protect our clients' interests, and to ensure that this bank operates entirely within the law."

Alexander just nodded. He wasn't here to be impressed or listen to rules and regulations. He just wanted to get his mum a life-saving operation.

"You have deposited a large amount of money into your mother's account."

He started to flick through the papers in front of him. "Seventy-five thousand pounds to be exact."

"We got it through an equity release scheme. It only took a few days because her house is worth a lot of money."

"Yes of course, we are not at all concerned about the source of these funds, Mr Maitland. I have read through your documentation and I can see that the source is all legitimate. The problem is what you want the money for."

He looked directly at Alexander to gauge any signs of understanding. There appeared to be none, so he carried on.

"You have pointed out that these funds are ear-marked for an operation for your mother in a private hospital."

"Yes," Alexander answered eagerly. "A triple heart bypass. She needs it to survive."

"Mr Maitland, have you ever heard of ESG?"

Alexander looked puzzled. "No," then he suddenly remembered the term from his discussion at the hospital.

"Wait. Yes, I think that's what the cardiologist told me about when he was talking about my mum's condition. He said that they prevented the NHS from operating on my mum but that it should be okay if we went private, so that's obviously what we are going to do."

Mr Shepherd looked at him sympathetically. "I take it that you have found a private hospital that is willing to operate?"

"It took a few goes, but yes, we found one that was agreeable."

Mr Shepherd sucked in his breath. "I'm afraid they've been a bit naughty. The guidelines also apply to them."

"But they said that so long as we pay privately it would be fine."

"Yes, but it's not just them is it? They might be willing to bend the rules to make a few quid, but we have your money, and we have our obligations to the guidelines too, and they dictate what reasons we can release it for."

Alexander was beginning to feel cross, and the tone of his voice was becoming sharper and louder.

"What do you mean release it? It's our money. My parents both worked hard all their lives for what they managed to accrue. Surely my mum can spend it on a life-saving operation for herself, otherwise, what's the point of it all?"

Mr Shepherd shook his head slightly. "I know it's very difficult for you to accept, and I am really sorry for your plight, but we are governed by those ESGs. We have no choice but to comply."

"So, are you saying that you can't release our own funds for a life-saving operation for my mother?"

"I'm afraid so."

"Yet you say that this department operates in order to safeguard its clients' interests?"

"Yes, exactly."

"Do you not think that a life-saving operation is in my mother's interests?"

"This is not about protecting a client from fraud. Your mother is simply too old. The government decides where valuable resources can or cannot be expended now."

Alexander was thoughtful. "How old is too old?"

"For that kind of surgery, the cut-off point is seventy-four for a woman, and seventy-one for a man."

"And who checks her age? Does she have to take her birth certificate to the operating room?"

Mr Shepherd just looked at him. He didn't think it was necessary to answer that question. Alexander asked another question. "What if I want the money for a flash car?"

"That depends on what kind of car it is. Would it be electric?"

"Of course," he answered, clearly sarcastically.

"Then that would be fine."

"Great. I need seventy thousand pounds, please, to buy a nice new ESG-compliant electric car."

Mr Shepherd shook his head more firmly this time. "You can't withdraw large sums of money as cash."

Alexander was surprised. "Since when?"

"Mr Maitland, that has been the case for many, many years."

"But it is our own money."

"Yes, but it comes back to our duty to protect our clients. It used to be the case that when large sums of cash were withdrawn, they were often used for criminal purposes, or the client was the subject of a scam or was being blackmailed. We must stand by our duty of care towards our clients at all times."

"So, your duty of care doesn't extend to allowing your clients to use their own funds for life-saving surgery, but they can buy a big flashy car, so long as it's electric, and you call that duty of care?"

Again, Mr Shepherd considered that to stay silent was the best response. Alexander looked defeated.

"I'll have that cup of water now please?"

Mr Shepherd happily got up and approached the water dispenser. "Cold or room temperature?"

"Cold please. Definitely cold."

He filled a paper cup and handed it to Alexander who stood up and promptly threw the contents directly into Mr Shepherd's face before marching out of the office and then the building, a very unhappy man.

**

135

Later that day, when home and after showering and changing, Samuel stated to Abi in an even tone.

"Something unusual happened at the office today."

She was stirring a large pot of chilli con carne mince on the aga. She didn't look up.

"Don't tell me you finally shoved the vice-chair out of the window?"

"No."

He knew she'd have another stab.

"Did you punch that arse Mr Womble in the face?"

"No, nothing nearly so dramatic."

She looked disappointed. "Tell me then."

"I got assaulted."

She turned from her cooking to take a good look at him, much more interested now, and asked brightly, "Oh, that sounds exciting. Did you get hurt, darling?"

"You're supposed to be sympathetic."

"I am being sympathetic. Show me the bruises."

She put her hands on his shoulders and examined his face. "You don't look injured."

"I had a cup of water thrown at me."

"Oh. Could have been worse. I take it that it wasn't boiling water? Your skin still looks intact, I think. It looks a bit saggy, but I think that's just your age."

She smiled coyly.

"No. It was cold. Very cold," he said in a low, slow, and dramatic voice.

"Oh dear," she replied slowly and rather sarcastically.

"Is this what you call being sympathetic?"

She put on her world-weary expression. "One of the kids cuts or bruises themselves every day. I've become a tough cookie when it comes to blood and guts. Who threw it at you? Were you staring at someone's tits at the time?"

"This is serious."

"I'm sure that the only thing that got slightly hurt was your pride. What did you do?"

"You mean to deserve it? Like I was guilty of something?"

"Well, people don't normally take water pistols to work at a bank do they? So, what happened?"

He sighed. "I was having a private meeting with a customer to explain ESG limitations, and he wasn't very happy with the outcome, and he took it out on me."

She looked genuinely curious. "Really? Why wasn't he happy?"

"He was only hoping to be allowed to use his own money to pay for a life-saving private operation for his dear old mother, but she's too old."

"I would have thrown more than a cup of water at you."

"Thanks. Thanks for the moral support."

"Well, that doesn't sound very fair to me."

"Look, I don't make the rules but I do have to enforce them."

"And is that okay if you don't agree with them?"

"Who said I agree with them or not? It's my job to be dispassionate."

"Hmm. That doesn't sound like the man I married."

"Excuse me? I think this conversation is getting a bit out of hand!"

Samuel was getting more annoyed with her than he had been with Mr Maitland. She explained.

"Look, I'm not being mean, dear, but one of the many traits I admired in you when I first got to know you was your integrity."

Samuel felt offended. "And?"

"Well, don't you think that the bank is trimming your wings a bit in that area?"

"What do you mean?"

"Well, it does sound like 'I was just doing my job'. Bit weak, don't you think? Did you explore other alternatives?"

"Such as?"

"I don't know. You say yourself that there are always loopholes in all the rules. Politicians deliberately incorporate them so they can exploit them. That's what you always say. Did you look for one?"

Samuel almost looked confused. "Are you judging me?"

"No, darling. I just wonder if sometimes you just act like a robot, that's all. I'm not saying it's your fault. It's what the bank expects of you, but funnily enough, it's not that endearing. It doesn't take much character to be a robot."

"And what kind of loopholes should I have looked at?"

"I don't know. That's your job. All I know is that for me as a teacher, they want us to just be robots delivering whatever the latest fad is from the government, but I never forget that I'm there to help these beautiful children develop in all sorts of ways, far beyond what the government want, and sometimes I say 'fuck the rules'."

She smiled at him, innocently. He was rather dumbfounded. He hadn't expected her to put him on the spot like this. She continued pensively. "Does this old lady have any special qualities? Does she work? Does she contribute anything to society? What's her blood group?"

"Now, you're being really random. What's her blood group got to do with anything?"

"Well, suppose she has a really rare blood group. Wouldn't that justify keeping her alive if she was a donor?"

Now Samuel was feeling rather useless. Indeed he hadn't explored any possibilities. He wanted to be cross with her for being unsympathetic, but really, he knew she was right. He had been lazy, and she expected more of him, and he was not annoyed about that. She had actually made him annoyed with himself.

"What time will dinner be ready, beautiful?"

**

Alexander got home no less angry than he had been at the bank about an hour earlier. He found his mother sitting in her usual chair watching her usual programmes. Since her heart scare, she got up from her armchair far less often, and Alexander insisted on cooking for her and fetching her teas when he was at home. There had been a role reversal. An oxygen bottle with plastic tubing was now positioned right beside her should she have breathing difficulties, but she refused to use it. He had suggested that she set up bedroom in the lounge so as to avoid using the stairs, but she was resolute about sleeping in her proper bed, the one she had shared with her husband for forty years. She wasn't going to be treated like an invalid even if it did take her three times as long to get up the stairs. He sat on the sofa, grabbed the remote, and muted the TV. She looked at him expectantly. He looked so sad.

"Mum, it's bad news I'm afraid. Apparently, they're not allowed to perform heart bypass operations on somebody as old as you."

She looked disappointed, but she was determined to be generous.

"That's alright, dear. I can understand that, saving their resources for younger people with a life ahead of them."

"It's not fair, Mum."

He actually started to cry. He felt a failure as well as being upset about the hopelessness for his mum. She hadn't seen him cry since he was a child, not even when his wife left him. Tears welled up in her eyes too.

"We've just got to make the best of it, son, and trust God."

**

Munther was having another go at Amelia. She was out on patrol with Robert, patrolling the quiet dark streets until a call might come in. Quithel was a bit worried that he was overdoing it.

"You said that we have to drip feed or they will tune us out."

"Don't be so dense, Quithel. There are times when they are particularly vulnerable, and at those times, we have to put in more effort. In time, you might learn to discern the difference. People are easily unsettled when it comes to job security. I can use that with Amelia to get her to let Charlotte down. Charlotte has to be let down. That is what she is used to, and the danger right now is that Amelia is giving her hope." He turned to Amelia.

"That counselling is going to cost you fifty quid a pop. You can't afford that, and what if your colleagues find out? They're going to think you're a complete nutter. And it's against the rules. You're not supposed to get emotionally involved in any of your cases. You're risking getting the sack for being emotionally insecure. Why? It's just not worth it. You could end up losing your job. Show some insight and pull right out of the situation before it's too late."

She was scouring the streets, looking for anything to distract herself from the voice inside her head. Munther turned to Robert.

"How did she know what Charlotte looked like? Why was she so keen to help her? That's not normal. Ask her. Ask her!"

Robert gave her a quick sideways glance as he held the car steady. "Amelia, how did you recognise that suicidal woman the other day?"

She shot him a look of surprise. Was he a mind reader?

"Excuse me?"

"You never told me how you knew her name. And who the fuck was Peter?"

"I don't do everything with you, you know!"

"I know. That's why I'm asking."

She thought carefully before answering. "Peter was that vicar chap who jumped a few weeks ago. You know the one where you made me deliver the death message."

Robert smiled. "One of the few things female officers are better at than us men."

"Are you allowed to say that?"

He smiled some more. Amongst themselves, with colleagues they trusted, officers were anything but politically correct. "But how did you know Charlotte?"

"His wife, Elsie, asked me to pay her a visit. Someone sent her an anonymous letter implying that Peter had been having an affair."

"I thought vicars were only interested in children."

She punched him in the arm. "Don't be so mean."

"And was he?"

"I don't know. I don't think so. Anyway, I made a few inquiries and established that there was a connection with Charlotte."

"You're doing PI work now? Does that pay well?"

"Shut up. It's all above board."

He looked at her curiously, but didn't ask any more questions. Munther spoke to her again.

"You see. They'll catch you out. You've got to drop that Charlotte girl. She's going to be nothing but trouble for you."

Chapter 15

Amelia phoned Charlotte. She would have preferred to actually drop in to see her, but she had been simply too busy over the past few days to find the time. A phone call would have to suffice. She felt relieved when the phone was answered.

"Hi, Charlotte. It's Amelia, the police officer."

Charlotte chuckled a bit. "You don't have to remind me that you're a police officer."

"Sorry, it's just that some people struggle with names."

"Not me."

"Great, listen, just a quick call. I'm just ringing to see if you called that counsellor I gave you the details for?"

"Yes."

Amelia felt delighted. She really hadn't known what to expect but now she felt pleasantly surprised.

"Oh, that's great. I'm so pleased."

She then sounded more business-like. "Get her to send you a bill for the first session or two, and then forward it to me at the police station, okay? Have you still got my card with my details on?"

"Yes."

Charlotte sounded unsure. "Are you sure you still want to pay for this?"

"Of course, I wouldn't have offered if I didn't mean it."

Charlotte was greatly moved. It had been a very long time since anyone had shown concern for her. She barely managed a soft, squeaky 'thank you' before ending the call.

**

It was late afternoon. Alexander was at home making a hot drink for his mum when his phone rang.

"Mr Maitland?"

He kind of recognised the voice but couldn't place where from.

"Yes?" He replied quizzically.

"Mr Maitland, it's Mr Shepherd from Everyday Bank."

Alexander grimaced a little. He was not given to using expletives often but this was definitely one of those times. "What the fuck do you want?"

Samuel refused to be offended by the rudeness.

"Mr Maitland, I want to apologise for the other day. On reflection, I feel that I allowed myself to be governed too absolutely by the rules and regulations to the extent that maybe I didn't cover all the bases."

Alexander's mind was racing. His initial thoughts had been that Mr Shepherd was calling for the personal satisfaction of informing him that he had made a complaint of assault to the police about the water. After all, virtually every public place these days prominently posted notices informing the public that bad behaviour towards their staff would not be overlooked or accepted, and that there would be a zero-tolerance approach.

"I don't understand."

"I'm sorry but there were a few questions that maybe I should have asked you but I didn't, such as 'what does your mother do with her time?'"

"Is that really relevant?"

"It might be."

Alexander presumed that he had nothing to lose so he might as well cooperate, even though he had been brooding an increasing distaste for this particular individual over the past few days.

"Ok. So, not a lot. She just sits around at home watching TV soaps, and knits. She can't run marathons anymore."

"I'm sure. In your opinion, does she do anything that benefits society?"

Alexander stared at the phone with some disgust. This kind of questioning seemed so distasteful, but he answered civilly anyway.

"Who decides? I mean, that's a bit of a subjective question, isn't it? She helps look after me I suppose, and that benefits the part of society that I make up. Is that good enough?"

Samuel appreciated the insensitivity of his questioning.

"I'm sorry if I'm coming across a bit blunt, Mr Maitland. I am trying to help if I can. Really I am. Does she do anything outside of her home?"

"Not any more. She used to be a seamstress, but she's been retired for a very long time now."

It sounded like Samuel was reading through a pre-prepared list of questions so that he didn't miss one out this time, but it made him sound so impersonal.

"Does she have any outstanding skills or knowledge?"

"None that I can think of. What are you looking for?"

"I don't know."

He could hardly actually say that he was looking for any reason that might justify keeping her alive. He persevered.

"What blood group is she?"

"Excuse me? What is that relevant to?"

Samuel just repeated the question. "Do you know her blood group?"

"No," Alexander was feeling increasingly annoyed, but he reminded himself that he needed to cooperate because this was about his mum, not him.

"I am at home. I can ask her."

"Please do."

Alexander was perplexed by this question, but nevertheless, he wandered into the lounge and asked his mother who unflinchingly answered, "O negative."

"O negative," Alexander repeated into the phone.

"Hang on. Let me check."

There was a half a minute's pause before Mr Shepherd resumed.

"Ok, it's not the rarest type, but it is rare, and it is highly sought-after as it is the only type that can be given safely to all of the eight blood groups. I think that's very special. Is your mother willing to donate blood?"

Alexander thought that this conversation had become quite weird, but he asked his mother anyway.

"I'm too old to play rugby," she joked in response.

"Mum, this is serious."

She stared at him curiously. "Okay then. I suppose so. There's a first time for everything."

"Yes, she says yes."

"Great. Has she been vaccinated?"

"What? Yes, I suppose so."

"I mean specifically the new mRNA ones."

"Oh, yes. I think she had them all. Is that relevant?"

"Blood group O negative is really good, but if she was also unvaccinated, that would be like the Holy Grail. There is huge demand for unvaccinated blood."

"Really? Why on earth would that be?"

"God only knows. Listen, I need you to register her with a blood donation service and then confirm to me her blood type and that she's enrolled in a donation scheme, and when I get that, I think we can release those funds for you."

"Really? You mean for her operation and not a new car?"

"Yes. I don't want to sound trite but it seems that your mother can still be very useful to society and for that, we can definitely bend the rules."

Alexander turned the phone off as he sat quietly on the sofa and cried for the second time in a few days.

**

Charlotte got the bus to Cynthia's home. It was a twenty minute bus ride, but she had to walk another ten minutes, as Cynthia was not close to a regular bus route. It was however a pleasant walk in the warmth of the early summer afternoon. There were beautiful trees to look at on the way, and on passing some gardens which were abundant with plants and flowers, she picked up the delightful sweet smell of nectar, which pleased her enormously.

Of course she was feeling very nervous, even though she had had a long conversation with Cynthia a week earlier covering all her basic queries and terms and trying to put her at ease. When she arrived, she noted that it was a lovely big detached house, and she felt somewhat out-of-place approaching the front door. It helped that the front garden was small with just a short walk to the sturdy oak front door. She steeled herself and tentatively crept up the path. She faced the brown oak door and paused. She hoped that she wasn't being filmed. She wasn't comfortable with her appearance and didn't like the idea of people watching her on camera, anywhere and at any time. Everywhere you went these days, you were being filmed. However, she couldn't see any obvious cameras and summoned the courage to press the bell.

Cynthia came to the door beaming. She was very welcoming and had a relaxing way about her that helped to put Charlotte in a slightly more comfortable frame of mind. They shook hands, which felt rather formal, and she was gently led into the large counselling room down the hallway and was offered a seat on the two-man sofa. As she sat she took in the ambience. The room looked freshly decorated with rather trendy pale green walls, contrasted occasionally with rich dark green in the lit alcoves and on what might have once been chimney breasts. There was bright daylight streaming in through the large patio doors, and there were nice ornaments around and fascinating paintings on the walls. She liked the smell of the candles. *Vanilla*, she thought. It all made her realise how little effort she had put out over the years personalising her own flat.

"I'm so glad you could make it, Charlotte. I realise that for you to take the trouble to come here to see me was possibly a big step for you. It's great to meet you in person."

Cynthia readily and naturally displayed her big warm smile before continuing.

"We talked on the phone briefly about the basics of your needs, but before we go any further, I want to make it clear to you that from my point of view, this needs to be a kind of team effort."

Charlotte looked quite confused, sincerely hoping that other counsellors weren't about to burst out hiding places, like a surprise party.

"I want to help you to build a support network around yourself, and I will be a part of that network."

Charlotte looked worried. She was a loner. "Who do you mean?"

"That's something we will begin to look at today. Do you have any close family?"

"No." Her answer was quick and curt.

"Friends?"

"No."

Cynthia gave her an encouraging look and added. "I'm sure we can find some people in your circle who can help. Do you have access to a computer and the internet?"

"Yeah, I've got an iPad."

"Oh, that's good, and are you okay at using the internet?"

Charlotte looked at her a little disappointedly. Did she think she was really that thick that she didn't know how to use the internet?

"Of course."

Cynthia read her tone. "I'm not trying to undermine you, Charlotte, in any way at all; I just need to get my facts straight so that I don't make any incorrect assumptions, okay?"

"Okay."

"We're going to start off by making a list of people who can be of help to you right from the off, okay?"

"If you say so." She didn't sound very convinced.

"So, the first person is your GP. Do you see them regularly?"

"Not really."

"Does he or she know that you tried to take your own life?"

"No."

"Well then, I want you to make an appointment to see them and let them know what's going on with you emotionally."

"Why?"

"Because your main care-provider is your GP and they need to know what is going on with you."

"Do you think I should be on more medication?"

"I'm not asking you to see them to get more medication. They might choose to change your medication, and they might not. What they will probably do is refer you to the mental health team, and they will probably make a home visit to you to talk to you in confidence about your issues, and about the support they can provide you with. I'm thinking more about emotional support, lifestyle and practical advice."

Cynthia smiled at her warmly, trying to ease her obvious discomfort, but Charlotte looked at her quizzically. The only thing she knew about GPs was that they dished out prescriptions. That was all.

"Who else?" She queried.

"The council provides a service called 'I-Talk'. They have a great website and they offer a variety of courses to support people to deal with loss, depression, financial hardship, etc. There are online courses and you can book into real courses like cognitive behaviour therapy too."

Charlotte looked a bit nonplussed.

"Don't worry; I'll give you a print-out before you leave with all these details on. You can also phone them for advice and support. They also have a helpline phone number."

Charlotte wasn't particularly responsive. She was still very nervous about what was going to happen with Cynthia right now. She was sitting there like she was in church. Bolt upright. Knees together. Hands folded, on her very best behaviour. Cynthia continued, going on to explain further help that was available from organisations like Mind, the Samaritans, Suicide Watch, Survivors of Suicide, and others. She reiterated that these people were there for her, to help provide support generally and particularly in times of stress and that they could all be easily researched online.

"Have you ever been in contact with any of these groups?"

"No."

"Okay, well, I am insisting that you see your GP, and I am earnestly encouraging you to research these other organisations to make use of their resources. You can do it online, but there might come a point where you would like to engage with their face-to-face courses. That would be a great way to make new contacts. A lot of their courses are conducted for a group of people, and that will give you the opportunity to make new friends with people like you."

Charlotte nodded, unsure of how much she would push herself into new and strange endeavours, and she wondered what Cynthia meant by 'people like you'. Did she mean other complete losers? Cynthia then started to delve into what was motivating her to consider hurting herself. She coaxed information from her about her upbringing, education, family, friends and work experience. She began to build up a picture of her lifestyle and her ideas about her own self-worth and purpose in life. They appeared to be very low. Then she began to explore her strengths and potential, so that further down the line, they could look at ways she could help improve her belief in herself and explore what goals might be realistic for her to attain more from life. The session seemed to fly by, and at the end of it, Cynthia had gleaned a picture of where Charlotte was emotionally, a little of her life's journey, but much less about the recent events involving the tragic vicar. She reiterated the safeguarding information before handing Charlotte written information. She wouldn't make another appointment with her until after she had confirmed to her that she had arranged an appointment to see her GP.

Sitting on the bus on the way home, Charlotte felt surprisingly pleased with herself. Going out to see a counsellor was quite an achievement for her. The dissatisfaction with her life still weighed heavily inside her, as did the trauma of Peter's death, but now this was slightly lightened by knowing that someone was willing to help her try to improve her life and her mental wellbeing.

Munther was sitting next to her. He whispered in her ear.

"Well, that was a waste of time, wasn't it? How can a well-paid woman like that, who lives in a big luxurious house in a highly-affluent area, know or understand anything about your miserable life? She's only in it for the money, preying on the multitude of poor, broken, low-lifes like you. Easy money. All those services she mentioned? They're in place just to ease the social conscience. Organisations set up just to ease the guilt and responsibility of the rich and successful, so they don't have to face or deal with the issues of unfairness and discrimination, which they have themselves imposed on innocent people like you. Don't listen to her. She's just being selfish. You've already got the right idea. Escaping this awful life and putting an end to the misery. The end is inevitable. Don't let her make you drag it out necessarily."

Charlotte winced. Her mind was muddled, and she really didn't want to go and see her doctor.

Chapter 16

Samuel was standing in front of his huge office window, taking in the inspiring rooftop view outside, as he often did. It made him feel important. Even on a dull cloudy day like this, the magnificence of the view impressed him. The river below looked particularly dark and brooding today, swelled and muddied by a recent storm that had left the air so fresh, cool and clear. He was speaking to a client on the phone. As he did so, there was a brief knock on his door, which opened simultaneously, as Mr Mainwaring lunged his bulk through the doorway. He strode purposefully towards Samuel's desk, indicating with his arm and an annoyed look on his face, for Samuel to finish his call. Samuel thought that this was very rude, and he instantly felt his blood pressure rising.

"Look, I've got to go. I'll call you back later," he explained tersely to his caller, restraining from putting his thoughts into words—"Sorry! I've just had a rude ignorant bastard barge into my office demanding my instant attention."— He turned and walked towards his desk. They both sat on opposite sides, and as usual, Mr Mainwaring leaned across the desk in that manner which Samuel found rather disgusting.

"Samuel, we've got a problem, a big problem."

He looked around the large office as if spying for hidden personnel.

"Go on, sir."

"There's this smart Alec in the accounts department. I don't know what got him on the trail, but he found something that didn't seem right to him, and like a Terrier trying to dig up a bone, he did enough digging to come up with something."

"Are we talking insider trading?" Samuel asked nonchalantly.

Mr Mainwaring leaned back into his chair. The folds of his fat belly had become uncomfortable pressed against the edge of the desk. There was a light sheen of sweat on his fat face. He must have used the stairs.

"No. It appears worse than that. Some kind of embezzlement. Something to do with some very clever software creaming off lots of tiny sums of money. Lots of it. Clever bugger! Didn't think tiny quantities would get noticed."

Samuel froze. Inside he felt the fight or flight response innervating his nerves, but he had to force himself to appear insouciant.

"Do we know how this has happened, sir, or where from?"

"No idea at the moment. It is early days. I felt that as head of compliance, you ought to be made aware of the situation, but this information is to go no further than this room, you understand?"

"Of course, sir."

"As yet we've got no idea if it's an inside job, or whether our firewall has been breached. It's probably a firewall breach by some spotty, autistic progedy who lives on the other side of the planet who never leaves his bedroom, who probably doesn't even understand the concept of money. Most importantly, Samuel, we have our professional reputation to protect. We have to cover this up at all costs."

"Of course, sir. Who's working on the investigation?"

"We're bringing in specialists."

Samuel didn't know what else to say. He didn't want to seem unduly interested, but at the same time he was terrified that his involvement in the fraud would be discovered.

"Can we trace where the money has gone?"

"Not yet. Whoever is behind this has covered their tracks very well. Smart Alec downstairs has closed down the programme, but he said that where the money had gone was untraceable. Far too heavily encrypted. Must have been a clever bastard. That's the problem these days. We all have to have the cleverest programmers, or we'll be outsmarted by cleverer ones."

Samuel hoped that the terror surging through his head was nor revealing itself in his eyes or in the strain of his mouth, or his pulsing veins, or his sweaty palms. At least he wasn't in the habit of shaking hands with Mainwaring. He wouldn't want to touch the man at the best of times let alone when his palms were sweating. Palms only ever sweated through anxiety, not heat.

"Okay. Well, thanks for letting me know, boss. It sounds like the matter is in good hands."

Mr Mainwaring took stock of him silently for a moment, as was his style, and then he got up and left quite abruptly, duty done. Samuel immediately checked his watch. He needed to know the time because he needed to do something, urgently, but he didn't know what. His scam programme had apparently already been shut down. All he could actually do was hope and pray that he had sufficiently scrambled the payment pathways to make them untraceable. He daren't make any connection to his Cayman Island bank account in case this was a setup. Maybe Mainwaring's visit was just to provoke him to make a move. No, he would have to sit tight and hope he'd already done enough to protect himself.

The last couple of hours of the working day dragged by insufferably, but eventually, 5.30 p.m. arrived and he was free to leave. He needed to leave, and think. His head was a swirl of messy thoughts all the way home.

Munther was in the car with him.

"Look, fellah, don't worry about it. You've covered your tracks brilliantly. You'll be fine. All you've got to do is keep your nerve and keep up the pretence of ignorance. That's all. Whatever you do though, don't tell Abi. You've got to keep her in the dark. You've got to keep it a secret from her."

When he got home, Abi was already there. She had to be home for when the kids got back from school. She was in the lounge with them, watching something loud, very colourful and very childish on TV.

"Hi, hun!" she shouted out as she heard him enter the hall. There was no reply. She waited. No response. "Hi, hun!" she shouted again, slightly more quizzically this time. She heard him grunt a response from the kitchen. They had been married for twelve years and after that amount of time together, little signals were instantly recognisable, especially for her as a woman, and she sensed that something was wrong. She excused herself from the children and the sofa. They didn't seem to notice as they were mesmerised by the overly-colourful and overly-loud programme, and she joined him in the kitchen. She looked at him with an intensity that was clearly looking for clues. It wasn't difficult for her to see that his face was tense and frightened. Correspondingly, a worried look came over her face too.

"What's wrong?"

He just looked at her. Part of the trauma inside his head was wondering what to say to her, if anything. She repeated her question, and he knew that he couldn't hide it from her. He hesitated. He was feeling vulnerable enough and he no longer wanted to shoulder the burden of keeping a secret from his wife.

"Honey, there's something that I've got to tell you."

"I can see that. What is it?"

She was thinking that someone close to them had died. There had been a lot of unexplained sudden deaths in recent years. In fact, they had become something of an on-going pandemic that one was supposed to pretend wasn't happening. Or worse! Maybe he was about to confess an affair! He was leaning back against the work surface, as if any kind of support was much appreciated at this awkward moment. She stood rather magnificently with her arms folded as if preparing herself to fend off tragic or life-destroying news.

"I've got a problem at work."

He was going to drip feed this stuff. Let her down gently.

"Go on. Don't keep me in suspense, please!"

"Look, I don't expect you to understand this, but I've had a little sort of petty scam going on at work, to help us with our retirement."

Her mouth dropped and her folded arms relaxed a little. The realisation that someone hadn't actually died, and he hadn't been shagging the office junior in the broom cupboard, gave her a little, fleeting relief, but now there was a mystery to unfold, and she didn't like the feeling of this one little bit.

"Stop talking in riddles and tell me what you've done."

This was hard. He didn't want to be judged. He had done what he had done for all the right reasons, but he didn't know how to explain himself without sounding like he had done something wrong.

"Well, it's not a scam exactly. No one gets hurt, or misses any money as such."

She knew that he was squirming.

"Samuel. Please cut to the chase and tell me what has been going on for goodness sake! Or do I have to resort to the rolling pin?"

She looked at him with her most demanding expression. He softened.

"Some time ago, I put a little programme in place that creams me off a tiny bit of commission, only pennies, from clients' charitable donations."

He paused to look at her to see how he was doing.

"You're stealing from charities now?"

Her face was a picture of disbelief. He spoke more loudly now.

"No, of course not stealing from charities, just rounding down the pennies. Hardly anything really."

"So, stealing from charities then."

She stared at him as if to say so many things like 'how could you be so stupid?' And 'how could you stoop so low?' But she didn't want to verbalise her thoughts immediately. She didn't want to shut him down whilst he was spilling the beans. She gave him an awkward silence in which to continue.

"Look, you know how difficult it is to make ends meet these days. It was just to slowly build up a bit of spare money for a rainy day, which nobody would miss but would come in very handy for us later."

"What? Handy in the sense that you have to look for another job, with a criminal record behind you?"

He said nothing and just looked at the floor.

"What? Handy in the sense that you get fired from your well-paid job and totally jeopardise everything we've worked towards for the past twelve years?"

He said nothing. She was growing increasingly cross. The arms were no longer crossed. They were pushing him in the chest, as if trying to force his lungs to express some sense out of his mouth.

"Explain to me the bit about just how that is worth it?"

He looked dejected. "Nobody should have found out about it."

She looked at him with a look of disbelief. "Except that they did, didn't they?"

He was quiet for a moment as he desperately tried to think of something positive to say. Sky wandered into the kitchen.

Abi looked at her fiercely. "Sky, go back into the lounge, now!"

"But Mummy…"

"Now!" Abi shouted, and Sky turned and ran away, crying.

Samuel moved off the counter. "There's no need to take it out on her."

"Don't you try hiding behind our daughter! Now that they've found out about your thieving, what happens?"

"Look, the programme has been discovered, but they won't be able to find out who's behind it."

"What? Like they weren't going to find out that you were creaming off their money?"

He looked sheepish. What could he say? He hadn't expected them to discover his programme, but some smart Alec had.

"Well? How long before they put two and two together?"

"Sweetheart, you're over-reacting!"

This time, quite a hard shove to the chest. "Don't you sweetheart me. You deceive your work. You deceive me, and you expect me to be okay about it? What other secrets have you been keeping from me? Have you been shagging the office junior in the broom cupboard?"

He looked at her very quizzically.

"What? Darling, you really are over-reacting."

She'd had enough, and turned away. She stopped in the doorway.

"I want you out. Go and stay with one of your darling golf buddies. I need time and space to think."

He looked horrified. "Darling, you cannot be serious."

"If you're not out that front door in ten minutes, I will personally phone your beloved Mainwaring and tell him exactly what you've just told me."

**

Munther and Quithel were taking a break on a church roof. This one was situated towards the outskirts of the city, and was surrounded by shabby high-rise buildings full of flats. It was late evening, and most windows in the adjacent buildings still gave out that yellowy fluorescent glow mingled with slowly flickering colours from innumerable television sets. From this small distance, all the noise merged into a low dull humming sound. Munther spoke with undisguised disgust.

"Look at them all. Crammed in like rabbits in their concrete jungle, living life more or less vicariously. What a fucking life. They spend most of their time watching how the rich and famous live their lives of succulent luxury whilst they themselves scrape along on supermarket value-brands, wearing tacky clothes made in foreign sweatshops."

Quithel looked on the bright side. "If they live like that, virtually and in relative poverty, that's good for us, isn't it?"

"How?"

"Well, you know, like you've said before. If they're unhappy and unfulfilled, they're going to be much more vulnerable to us pushing them into desperation and despair."

"Not necessarily, my dear fellow, not necessarily. Yes, as I survey the surrounding buildings, I can happily recall several instances where I succeeded

154

in encouraging tenants to launch themselves victoriously onto the streets below, but it's not often so straight forward."

Munther's red eyes narrowed as he pulled his thoughts together and spoke slowly. "There are three things you must remember about human beings, Quithel."

Quithel racked his brain, trying to remember the previous times when *three things* had been mentioned, wondering if these would be the same three things again, or different ones. He waited silently, as he wanted to get Munther in the mood to talk as he had an important question for him. Munther carried on.

"One-They envy rather than celebrate the success of others. They readily allow jealousy to eat them up, even to the point where they don't acknowledge their own success. Two-Almost all of them lack self-belief, again, no matter what they sometimes manage to achieve. Three-They are insatiable. No matter what they get, they always want more."

Quithel looked puzzled. "So, are you saying that impoverished people are no more vulnerable than wealthy and successful people?"

"It seems that way. The highest suicide rates are for doctors, vets and pharmacists, people with high social and economic standing. See, nothing is predictable with people."

Quithel was quiet for a moment as he wondered if this was a good moment to risk asking a question.

"Munther, can I ask you a question?"

Munther's face dropped a little. "Must you?"

"I know that some people get demon-possessed. How does that happen?"

Munther laughed. "You do ask some weird questions. Why do you ask?"

"I don't know. I suppose I still feel new at all this, and I'm just trying to understand the bigger picture."

Munther scoffed a little. He didn't really understand Quithel's curiosity, and he answered tersely.

"Why can't you just focus on what you're supposed to be doing instead of being a prat?"

"I do focus on what I am supposed to be doing. I was just wondering, that's all, but if you don't know about that subject, that's fine."

"Look, I've been doing this for millennia. Of course I know about it. I know all about it."

"So, go on then, explain it to me."

Munther sat quietly for a moment, racking up some stories in his mind before he spoke.

"I've known a few devils that've done it. They say it's a weird experience because for the first time in their existence, they acquire a body, and moreover, they're usually stuck in it until that person dies. Weird! Doesn't appeal to me, being confined like that, but it takes all sorts I suppose."

"Yes, but how does it happen to some people and not others?"

Munther looked at him disparagingly.

"Generally, we're not allowed to do it. As you know, our influence is limited to cajoling, beguiling; deceiving etc. We're not allowed to force things to happen. However, some people engage in what they call devil-worship. They devise all kinds of rituals to demonstrate their serious intent to make contact with the dark side, and to become a part of it. The devils who are assigned to them have to test them for quite a while to ensure that they are wholly sincere and not just playing around, but if these people persist, there comes a point when a devil feels able to enter them. I don't know how they know, but they just do."

"Do they then take control of them?"

"Pretty much. The person still has their own mind and personality, but apparently, it's far easier to influence someone from the inside than the outside. They say it's difficult to explain, but the results are astonishing."

"In what way?"

"All the world's most evil men have been demon-possessed. Mass murderers, war-mongers and terrorists. Most of the famous tyrants of history. It's like they no longer have a conscience or the ability to empathise with people any more. Why? Do you fancy it?"

"I don't know. Is there any reward for doing it?"

"Not specifically, but when you're free again, you do have a lot of kudos with other devils because so few have experienced it, not to mention the notoriety of their subjects. But no rewards as such. Why? Is this also going onto your bucket list?"

Quithel smiled in a deprecating way. "Not necessarily. I just like to know how things happen."

"Well, I'll show you how things get done. It's time for us to get up off our butts and go visit someone!"

**

156

Alexander was waiting in the relative's lounge which was closest to the operating theatre. He had been with his mother the evening before. They had wanted her in for certain tests the day before the operation, and he had been allowed to spend the night in a guest room. He was tired now. He hadn't slept well, for no particular reason. It had been surprisingly quiet and it was warm and comfortable, but that slightly uncomfortable feeling of being somewhere strange had irked him. Also it hadn't been dark enough for him, and obviously, he had been worrying about his dear mother, about to undergo a major operation. Now it was midday and the first operation should be nearing completion soon. There were two other visitors in the lounge. Gill and Elizabeth. They were both wives, quite a bit older than him, waiting to find the outcome of heart operations on their dear husbands. Alexander wondered if they had experienced similar problems gaining permission for the surgery. They probably weren't *too old*. He didn't ask.

They had all briefly conversed at first, to discover what their relatives were in for, but after exchanging pleasantries and establishing some basic details, they had all gone quiet. This was no place for small talk. They were all too nervous just to chat aimlessly.

A surgeon walked into the room. He was clearly more or less straight out of the operating theatre. His green overalls were bloodied. His face looked sticky and sweaty, a plastic cap still covering his thin hair. Alexander just about recognised him as Mr Cartwright, the main surgeon, even though he looked quite different in his surgical togs. Alexander had spoken to him earlier that morning when he had been wearing a rather dapper suit. His face carried disappointment and sadness. He stood a few feet from Alexander and looked at him intently. His mouth was straight and stern.

"I'm sorry, Mr Maitland. We did everything that we could, but I'm afraid she didn't make it."

Elizabeth stood and went and sat next to Alexander and caressed his back. She carried a look of shock and horror.

"I'm so sorry, Alexander. I'm so sorry."

Mr Cartright left the room. Alexander was stunned. Yes, of course he had been worried about his mum, but he genuinely hadn't expected her to pass away during the actual operation. At first, he was motionless, as if he was unable to process this development. Then he leaned forward and cried. Gill came and sat on the other side of him and also put an arm around him. The two ladies stared

157

at each other across his huddled shoulders, terrified of what might become of their husbands. This situation lasted for about ten minutes before a very kind nurse joined them.

"Mr Maitland, is there anything I can do to help? Call someone for you maybe?"

Alexander just carried on crying. He had barely heard her voice. The nurse just stood there patiently until Elizabeth gave her permission to leave, stating that they would fetch someone when he was ready. Half an hour later, he stood up. The two ladies looked at him as if he had just come back from the dead.

Gill pleaded quietly, "Is there anything we can do to help you?"

He was holding a hanky tightly to his face. He just shook his head and stumbled out of the waiting room into the corridor. He remembered that he needed to find the lifts. He looked for signs as he wandered slowly down the corridor. A man in a white coat stopped him, and asked him what he was looking for.

"Lift." Alexander answered quietly, as if too many words might drain the very life-force out of him. The man gave him directions and pointed. He seemed to instinctively know what had happened. He got into the lift with a few other people, but he didn't look at them. Someone asked him which floor he wanted. "Ground."

On the ground floor, he exited the lift hurriedly and made his way to the exit. There were cabs nearby and he got in one and barked out his address hoarsely. His own car was somewhere in the hospital car park, but he couldn't be bothered to try to find it. He didn't feel like actually doing anything, like manoeuvring a car. He had also left his overnight case in the guest room. These things really didn't matter. Outside his house, the cab driver asked for sixteen pounds and forty pence. He silently gave him twenty pounds and walked off up the drive without waiting for change. What did change matter? At the front door, he frisked himself for keys. He found none. He must have left them at the hospital in his bag. He picked up a large stone on the adjacent flower bed and smashed the window in the front door, and reached in to open the door from the inside. He just wanted to be at home, his mum's home.

Chapter 17

Charlotte had struggled with the idea of continuing to engage with Cynthia. The initial session had gone well, but her anxiety and lack of self-confidence were now undermining her hugely. Munther had been busy all week trying to put her off going again. "How could this strange woman possibly help you? You have nothing in common at all. How could she possibly understand your situation?"

However, in response to Cynthia's encouragement and advice, she had researched all the organisations online which she had told her about, and she was amazed at the amount of support that seemed to be available. She decided that before engaging with even more strangers, she should try seeing Cynthia again first. She hoped that Cynthia could help build her confidence up. She needed to do that. So, she made that appointment with the GP and then a second appointment with Cynthia.

Cynthia gave her a warm welcome as always and settled her down in the counselling room. After some small talk to help her feel comfortable, she got started.

"Charlotte, it's great to see you again and I am pleased that you will be seeing your GP soon. That's great. How are you feeling today?"

"Yeah, okay."

"Have you had any suicidal tendencies since we last met?"

Charlotte paused and looked at her clasped hands thoughtfully. "No, I suppose not."

"That's good. I am pleased to hear that. What would you say is bothering you the most at the moment?"

Charlotte inspected her hands some more as if they were going to suddenly open up and reveal some object of enlightenment. After baring her empty palms, she answered quietly, "Elsie."

Cynthia looked puzzled. "Who is Elsie?"

"The vicar's wife. Peter's wife."

159

"Oh, I see." Only a few details about the vicar had been mentioned last time. "And why is she troubling you?"

"The police officer, Amelia, told me that Elsie had got a letter from someone telling her that Peter was having an affair with me."

She shot Cynthia a stern look. "I wasn't, and I'm not happy for Elsie to be thinking that. It's not fair on Peter. He was a really good man."

Cynthia waited. Nothing more was forthcoming, so she commented.

"And it's not fair on you either. Is there anything you can do to rectify this?"

Charlotte looked at her somewhat shocked. "Do you think I should?"

"I think that if it's bothering you, and I totally understand your concerns, then you should definitely consider what you can do to clear that situation up. I think you need to get some restitution, both for Peter and yourself. What do you think you could do?"

Charlotte stared into the middle distance. "I don't know. I don't know the woman. I don't know who sent her the letter. I don't know what I could possibly do."

Cynthia thought out loud for her, "Well, could you visit her, or send her a letter explaining things?"

Charlotte reacted in animated fashion. "I couldn't possibly visit her. Amelia told me that she doesn't even want me visiting her church, and I've been warned that for me to do so could constitute harassment, and certainly a breach of the peace, because she'd go ape if she knew it was me."

"Okay, so could you write to her?"

Charlotte sat quietly mulling this over, and then, "Remind me, why I would want to do this?"

"To clear Peter's name. Elsie has been led to believe that he was unfaithful, and you can vouch that this isn't true. That would help her a lot too."

"Only if she believed me."

"Why wouldn't she? You have nothing to hide, right?"

"Of course."

"And you said last time that Peter hadn't mentioned you to her because he didn't want her to know that he had considered suicide, yes?"

"Yes."

"And now that he sadly has, don't you think she deserves to learn the truth? Is there any reason not to be honest with her?"

"No, none."

"Well, there we are then. I think you should write that letter, but I'd like to see it before you send or deliver it. Elsie will be in a state of grieving, and I wouldn't want you saying anything that might inadvertently hurt her more."

Charlotte nodded, thinking deeply. Cynthia then asked the next question.

"How would you get the letter to her?"

"I don't know. I suppose I could leave it at the church, or maybe Amelia would deliver it for me. It was Elsie who got her involved after all."

Cynthia looked quizzically at her. "Remind me why Elsie got her involved again please?"

Charlotte answered sadly. "Initially, it was Amelia who delivered the death message to her, and then after she got the second letter telling her that I—the woman in the affair—had been to her church following Peter's death, she called Amelia and insisted that I be banned from her church."

"Even though nobody knew who you were."

"Yes. Sounds silly, doesn't it?"

"Elsie was grieving and in shock. She was just trying to do anything that might somehow improve the situation for her."

They spent the rest of the session discussing what might go into the letter and how this would be good for both Charlotte and Elsie. Again, the session seemed to fly by, and Charlotte left with the mission to write that letter and to think about engaging with Mind or 'Survivors of Suicide'. They fixed a date for another session a week later.

On the bus home, Munther tried to dissuade her about the letter.

"You owe that vicar's wife nothing. She has made assumptions about you undermining your integrity. She would scratch your eyes out if she could. You owe her nothing. Leave her to wallow in her own misery. It's of her own making. You really don't need to make her feel any better at all. She has been really unfair to you. She has judged and condemned you without reason. She has let her own husband down with her lack of trust. She deserves what she's got now. You owe her nothing. Writing that letter will just upset you. Forget her! She's just a miserable, bitter old cow! Let her go."

**

Abi had put the kids to bed. She had been short and out of sorts with the kids, and she didn't even feel in the mood to do some more of the Watership Down

161

story with Sky, and now she was sitting down to a lonely dish of tuna and pasta. Without Samuel, her evenings actually felt lonely. The small TV in the kitchen was on, but she couldn't focus. She was so angry with him, but at the same time, she missed him terribly. The house seemed so quiet and empty without him. There was a knock on the door. She opened it fiercely. She had told him to stay away, but to her surprise there were two reasonably smart gentlemen on her doorstep, neither of whom was Samuel. One held out his identification and announced himself.

"Good evening, madam. I hope I am not disturbing you. I am officer Evans from the Community Cohesion Agency, and this is my colleague, officer Shakenhurst. I am seeking a Samuel Shepherd if I may."

Her heart sank. That didn't take long for them to get onto him. So much for his cleverness at evading capture. She really wanted him to be there with her, right now, by her side so that she could slap his face, hard. She hadn't taken in what department the officers were from because her mind was swimming with thoughts of an incarcerated husband and no home with two young children to look after single-handedly.

"He's not here."

"And who might you be please?"

"I am his wife, Abi Shepherd."

The officer looked at her cynically. He clearly didn't believe that Samuel was not there.

"Mrs Shepherd, it is better for us to get this done now rather than later."

She stepped away from the door, leaving it wide open. "You can come in and check if you like. I can assure you that he is not here. Just the kids."

The two officers did indeed step inside, but they gave no indication that they intended to search the premises. They just stood in the hallway.

"May I inquire as to where he might be please?"

She was embarrassed to explain, but she decided that honesty was the best policy.

"We had a bit of a falling out a couple of days ago and he is staying with friends for the time being. I don't actually know for sure where he ended up. I pretended like I didn't care."

Her countenance dropped. The words made her feel guilty and a little traitorous. She did care. The officers looked at each other. They both looked convinced.

"Mrs Shepherd, we need to speak with him. Where can we find him?"

"To be perfectly honest with you officer, I really don't know, but I can call him if you want? I'm sure he will answer his phone to me."

They both nodded, curious to see where this would lead. She got her mobile out of her back pocket and phoned him. He answered quickly, "Darling, how are you?"

"Not brilliant. I've got two strange police officers on the doorstep looking for you."

There was a pause. She wondered what on earth he felt like. It was bad enough for her, but they weren't trying to cart *her* off.

"How strange?"

Trust him to make a joke of it.

"Very strange."

"I'll come back."

She looked at the officers. "He's coming back."

"How long?"

"How long?" She repeated into her phone.

"Fifteen minutes."

With that, he was gone. She looked at the officers. They'd heard that.

"We'll wait outside in the car. Thank you for your help."

She watched them through the lounge window. Their car was directly in line with the house. She went into the kitchen to make a hot drink. She'd lost her appetite for the half-eaten pasta, and returned to the window in plenty of time to see Samuel pull up behind the officers' car. They all got out. There was a brief chat on the pavement before Samuel had his hands cuffed behind his back and was placed into the rear of the police car. Then they drove off. That was so sad to watch, and she sat on the sofa and cried.

At the police station, Samuel was taken into the custody suite, still cuffed. It was quiet and echoey. The lone custody sergeant sat unassailable inside a pentagon of wood and Perspex that fully enclosed five booking-in cubicles. A very scruffy older man, who looked like he was a street dweller, was just being led away by custody support staff. Samuel gagged slightly at the stench of body odour and urine that clung to the air. Now it was his turn to be 'processed'. The officers briefly explained why they had arrested him and then left, leaving Samuel in the charge of two uniformed custody assistants. They removed his cuffs, removed his personal possessions, took his details, recorded his fingerprints, photo and DNA and then he was given a form telling him of his rights.

"Can I see a solicitor please?" He asked the custody sergeant who was busy examining his computer screen.

"Not at the moment, Mr Shepherd. The officers need to interview you first."

"I thought that it was my right to be represented if I want it."

The sergeant barely looked up. This was all so repetitive and routine for him.

"Not anymore, I'm afraid. The human rights act was replaced some time ago with different legislation. Stuff that does more to protect society. That changed most of the details. It's not about individuals anymore."

Samuel looked at him with some alarm in his eyes. "Are you saying that I don't have any human rights?"

"Mr Shepherd, I am not here to give you a lesson on the law. I am here to ensure that the law is adhered to. I have given you a form with the relevant information on. You need to read that."

He looked at the assistants and nodded, and Samuel was duly led away and shoved into a cell. The huge dense metal door crashed shut behind him like a car crash. The surprisingly alarming sound literally made him jump. He took in his surroundings. He had never actually been in a cell before, but he'd seen them on TV, so he knew roughly what to expect. The atmosphere was what hit him. It was cold, sterile, inhuman, and disheartening. The pale yellow walls glowed in the reflection of the bright fluorescent lights built into the high ceiling. The concrete bed extending out of the wall was barely inviting. The stainless steel toilet stared directly up to the CCTV built into the ceiling. There was no sound. It was bland and echoey. He sat on the then mattress on the bed and read his notice.

Apparently, his need to have someone informed of his arrest, and his right to speak with a solicitor was subservient to the needs of the community, and it was the job of a 'social conscience officer' to assess those needs in the light of the best outcome for the community, whose interests always superseded those of any particular individual. He was shocked, and wondered to himself how a new, thinly-disguised communist regime had so subtly replaced the fragments of a decaying democracy. Where had the public outcry been? He decided that this was bullshit. He stood up and went over to the door. There was a button next to what appeared to be a speaker built into the wall. He pressed it. He immediately recoiled due to a piercing screeching sound, which continued until someone answered.

"Yes."

"I want to see the *social conscience officer* please."

"All in due course."

That was it. The speaker went dead. He pressed the button again. This time the screeching went on for about two minutes, and he actually cupped his hands over his ears, until finally, the same voice answered.

"Yes?"

"I want to discuss with the *social conscience officer* my need to see a solicitor please."

"That has been noted. All in due course."

The speaker went dead again, and Samuel didn't wish to subject himself again to that awful screeching sound. He couldn't know how long they might leave it to torment him, so he sat back down on the bed. A couple of hours later the cell door finally opened. He stood up and saw Shakenhurst standing in the doorway next to one of the custody assistants.

"Come with me please."

As Samuel walked down the corridor with the officers he spoke.

"I've been denied my right to speak with a solicitor."

Shakenhurst replied steadily, "You've not been denied anything. That decision now lies with the social conscience agency. If they think you need to see one, they'll arrange it."

Samuel looked perplexed. "When?"

"After you've been interviewed."

"But aren't they supposed to give me advice on what to say in interview, before the interview?"

"It doesn't work like that anymore."

"Are you a proper police officer?"

Shakenhurst gave him a quick sideways dirty look.

"Mr Shepherd, please don't adopt a disparaging attitude or use pejorative language. We are employed directly as officers of the Community Cohesion and Social Enhancement Agency, and we are not here to become the victims of your verbal abuse. If you try to abuse us in any way whatsoever, you will be charged."

Samuel looked at him astonished. "I was only asking a question that seems pretty relevant to me."

He said no more for fear of what he might be accused of, and because he was afraid that offending this very sensitive man would influence him in a way that would rebound badly on himself. He was led into an interview room where Officer Evans already sat, preparing the recording device that was built into the wall. Its controls were in a touch screen, not unlike an ATM in the street.

He was invited to sit at one end of the table with Shakenhurst to his left and Evans directly opposite him with the recording device to his right and a laptop on the table in front of Evans. There was a camera high on the wall behind Evans pointing straight at him.

He was cautioned, and Evans introduced all parties *for the benefit of the tape.*

"They kept that in then? The caution."

"Do you wish to make a response?"

"I just did." He paused and then added resolutely, "And I'm not happy about not being allowed to seek legal advice."

Evans frowned slightly before getting on with his questioning.

"Mr Shepherd, you have been sharing articles on social media which have been causing people alarm and distress, and it appears that you have been disseminating misinformation contrary to the Community Preservation Act of 2024. What do you have to say about that?"

"I haven't got a clue what you are talking about."

He was genuinely confused. Obviously, he had presumed that his arrest was connected to his scam at the bank, but it now appeared to be something completely different, which he had not anticipated in a month of Sundays, and for that he was immensely relieved. Evans got an image up on his laptop screen and angled it so that they could all see it.

"Do you recognise this image?"

It was a chart, a graph, purporting to show a correlation between the number of viral vaccinations and number of cases of myocarditis in England over the previous year.

"Not particularly. There's loads of stuff like that on social media."

"You shared it to your feed on April the eleventh this year."

"I've honestly got no recollection. I do loads of research and share a lot of it on my page."

"Well, let's have a look at your page then, shall we?"

He clicked on a few buttons and proudly showed Samuel his feed. "Is this your social media account?"

Samuel squinted at it before confirming that it was. Evans then scrolled down the various articles with Samuel watching.

"As you can see, most of what you post contradicts government advice and acceptable information. You post stuff challenging the efficiency of the vaccines. You post allegations of harm caused. You post allegations about ministerial corruption. There's stuff about the unreliability of pharmaceutical research and safety claims. Cover-ups. Claims of doctoring the data, and it looks like we could go on and on."

He stopped scrolling and stared at Samuel. "This is all misinformation. That's an offence."

Samuel looked genuinely astonished. "Who says it is misinformation?"

"The government."

"And you believe them?"

"This stuff is extremely harmful. Vulnerable people might see it and be less likely to avail themselves of medical treatment that is available to them, and that is harmful to them and society as a whole. You're trying to take advantage of vulnerable people, to deceive them and hurt them."

"*I'm* trying to take advantage? What do you think the government has been doing for the past few years? It pumps out propaganda twenty-four seven, year in year out, and it's got all main-stream media in its pocket doing its bidding. They've got an army of psychologists working for them to influence people, to constantly 'nudge' them in the right direction. You can't move without being bombarded with their bullshit propaganda. TV, radio, papers, adverts, texts from the NHS. Phone calls from the GPs. All I do is occasionally share information that has been hidden or censored that shows that the government is lying. I am opposed to censorship. People deserve to have the facts."

"Mr Shepherd, we are definitely not here to have a philosophical argument with you about your misconceptions. We are here to make sure that you are fully aware that to spread information that might contribute to vaccine hesitancy is a criminal offence. We are here to point out the error of your ways. Today we will only give you a warning and ask you to desist. If you carry on in this vein, then you will be charged with spreading misinformation, and the penalties for that, I can assure you, are very high."

"How high?"

Evans gave him a hard direct stare which spoke of intimidating power.

"First conviction, up to two years inside and a fine up to ten thousand pounds. Subsequent convictions, up to ten years in prison and unlimited fines."

He continued the cold, mean stare. Those punishments really were very, very scary.

"It's entirely up to you."

He sat back in his chair looking at Samuel with an air of victorious superiority. Samuel returned his gaze with a stern look of impotent rebellious defeat. The interview was terminated and he was led back to the custody sergeant who was already waiting with a caution form for him to sign. It seemed that the outcome had been a foregone conclusion.

"You can see a solicitor now if you wish."

"A bit late now, don't you think?"

The custody sergeant recorded on his custody record that Samuel had refused the offer of a solicitor. He was given back his things and shown out onto the street. Outside was cool and getting dark. He got out his mobile and called Abi. Thank God, she answered.

"Darling, I need to talk."

"Where are you?"

"Stuck outside the central police station."

"Can you get a cab?"

"Yes, of course. What I'm ringing for is because I want to come home, and to talk to you."

"Okay."

Chapter 18

Charlotte felt much easier about attending her third meeting with Cynthia. She wanted to show her the letter she had written, and was feeling much more positive about being helped to move forwards with her own life. As soon as she found herself sitting in the consultation lounge, she got the letter out of her handbag and handed it to Cynthia, who took it and began reading it in her head. Her face was dispassionate for almost the minute she spent mulling it over, and then it broke into a broad smile.

"That's lovely. I think that if I was in Elsie's shoes with my doubts and confusion, I would love to read this. Well done. I think it is fine as it is. Thank you for sharing it with me."

"Well, it was your idea."

Cynthia smiled some more without saying anything. Charlotte then asked a question.

"How do I get it to her?"

"Perhaps you could ask your police officer friend to pass it on for you?"

"Yes, I suppose so."

"This will be the next step for you restoring Peter's integrity, but now we need to focus on you. Have you engaged with any of those other organisations I told you about?"

"Not yet, but I have researched them and read a lot of their online information."

"Great. Have you found that helpful?"

"Yes, very."

"Oh that's good. I am pleased. And have you seen your GP yet?"

"Yes. She did lots of tests and also referred me to the mental health team like you said she would."

"Good, and have they been in touch yet?"

"Only to make an appointment to visit me, next week."

"Great. I am sure that they will be very helpful. Charlotte, I'd like to work on expanding your social network. As human beings, we're not designed to live in isolation, our only contact with the outside being through a television screen. We are social creatures with real needs for relationship, conversation, and interaction, whether they be romantic, casual friendship, work relationships or whatever. A lack of these basic things makes us much more susceptible to depression and harmful thoughts. Do you agree?"

"Yes, I suppose so, but it's not easy. I've experienced a lot of failure and rejection in the past."

"You're right. It's not easy. Not for anyone. It takes effort and purpose, and sometimes a lot of encouragement. If you've been hurt in the past, you need to learn techniques that help you heal and move forward rather than just recoil and hide. We all do. You are still young and you have your whole life ahead of you. I get the impression that you benefited from being someone that Peter could unload on. Is that right?"

Charlotte laughed. "I don't think 'unload on' sounds quite right. Sounds a bit sexual."

Cynthia laughed too. "Yes, sorry, poor choice of words. You provided him with some support in his hour of need."

"Yes."

"And that made you feel good?"

"Yes. It was nice to feel that I was doing something useful."

"Well, why don't you carry on doing something useful?"

Charlotte looked perplexed. "How? Spend all my time standing on the Brunel Bridge waiting for the next hapless would-be suicider to come along?"

Cynthia chuckled. "I didn't mean in exactly the same way. One of the reasons we have friends is that when we have a problem, we have people we can share that problem with, and vice versa."

"Okay. But getting friends in the first place is not easy."

"Have you thought about getting back into work? The workplace is a great place to find friends."

"Not really. I used to hate the supermarket most of the time."

"But what about some other kind of work?"

"I haven't got any qualifications."

"Well, you have your supermarket experience. That would make you an ideal volunteer for working in a charity shop. They are always looking for volunteers. That could be a first step, and as a volunteer you wouldn't lose any benefits."

Charlotte sat quietly, mulling over her thoughts, and then Cynthia continued, "What about getting some qualifications? You can always go to evening classes."

"Such as?"

"I don't know. That depends on what interests you. Do you like hairdressing? Nail art? Interior design? Gardening? Flower arranging? Carpentry? Painting? Brick-laying?"

Charlotte sat quietly, just thinking.

"And what about getting into sports, just for a hobby and meeting people. Local sports centres offer all kinds of activities and classes where again, you would meet people."

Cynthia looked at Charlotte with her perfected meaningful look. Not quite a stare, but more than a mere gaze. It sought a response.

"I'd like to go to Peter's church."

Cynthia took a moment to consider her answer carefully. "You need closure about Peter, and we'll look at that in our next session if you'd like to, but for now, I don't think going to his church would be a good idea, at least, not until you have a response from Elsie to your letter."

"Do you think I'll get a response?"

"I hope so, but who knows. We can't think for Elsie, can we? We'll just have to wait and see. You've done all that you can do but we are not responsible for how other people choose to react. So, what about hobbies and courses?"

"Okay. I'll give that some thought. I do like the idea of flower arranging."

Cynthia brightened up. "That's great. If you completed a flower arranging course, and you really enjoyed it, I'm sure you could get a job in a florist's shop. Wouldn't that be good?"

Charlotte brightened up at the thought of working with flowers. She suddenly remembered that she loved flowers.

"I particularly like gerberas," she added.

**

Abi was at home cleaning. She had taken a few days off work with stress. This whole situation with Samuel's arrest, and knowing about his scam, was all too much. He'd gone into work though. He was determined to fight his way through all this shite.

Munther was at her shoulder. She was distracting herself with the radio on loudly, but she could still hear that still small voice inside her head.

"Why did you take him back so readily? He has fucked you up and you still let him have sex with you?"

She had warm thoughts about the night before. It had been so good to have him back, cuddling up in bed together. Such a simple pleasure, yet so reassuring. And the sex had been great too. There had been something very raw and atavistic about it last night, like it might have been the last time, or the first time. She thought that maybe she should chuck him out more regularly.

"How is he going to put this right? They will find out that he was the one scamming them. Then what? He'll end up in prison. And now he's getting himself arrested for serious social media abuse as well? Surely, your time with him is up. You deserve so much better."

**

Samuel had a normal day at work. He had told nobody that he had spent a few days away from home, and he certainly didn't mention anything about being arrested, but at about mid-afternoon, he got a call from Mr Mainwaring asking him to go up to his office. This was alarming because normally Mainwaring would slither down stairs and wobble into *his* office. Whatever it was, he had to face the consequences. He stood up and tried to firm his thoughts before slowly and tenderly climbing the stairs to the next storey. He knocked and entered.

"You want to see me, sir?"

"Samuel, please, sit down." They both sat at his desk, but Mainwaring didn't do his usual trick of trying to slide his bulk as far as possible across the desk. In fact, he sat back looking relatively relaxed.

"Samuel, I have some troubling news. We have been contacted by the Community Cohesion and Social Enhancement Agency. They informed us that they arrested you yesterday."

"Why?"

"Why did they arrest you?"

"No, why did they feel the need to inform you?"

"I don't know. I suppose that as they no doubt know that you are head of compliance here that we, Everyday Bank, should know about it. I mean, it does sound a bit incongruous don't you think? Our actual compliance officer getting arrested for disseminating disinformation."

"Is it wrong for me to notice lies and deception when I see it?"

"No, but I suppose it depends on whose opinion you're going on as to what is untrue. Apparently, there are laws about what you can and cannot say on social media these days."

"And you agree with censorship? With people being dictated to as to what they are allowed to say and think by the government?"

"Samuel, you obviously feel very strongly about this subject. It's hard for me to comment as I stay well away from social media. It has proved to be the death trap for many-a-promising career. But I'm not here to debate these issues with you. The point is that you have fallen foul of the CCSEA and now we are being put under pressure to let you go, and that's all there is to it."

"Let me go? You mean sack me because some jumped-up, over-hyped, Mickey Mouse agency tells you to?"

"Samuel, you have put us in an invidious position. We can't be seen to disregard the CCSEA even if you think that you can. That would be tantamount to disregarding ESGs. We are going to have to let you go. We have no choice."

Samuel sat quietly, thinking, planning how to survive.

"And what is my package to be?"

"Package?" He scoffed. "I'm not sure that you will qualify for one under these circumstances."

The thought of a severance package made Mainwaring chuckle. Samuel didn't have any actual dirt on Mainwaring but now was the time to test his intuition and cunning, but he would have to bluff as convincingly as he knew how. He leaned forwards with a steely look in his eye.

"Michael, there's a lot I know about you which you would be very surprised at. I don't waste my time here at this bank. I do a lot of research, a lot of digging, and I find things. I find out bad things about people, but mostly, I keep those things to myself for a rainy day, just like today."

Mainwaring's face reddened. He truly looked worried, but said nothing. A sure sign of guilt. Samuel felt emboldened. His ploy had worked perfectly.

"You work out a nice goodbye package for me, a really good one. I have been here for over ten years after all, so I think you can justify it. Otherwise, it will be you scratching around for dole money I can promise you. Insider trading is far worse than just expressing opinions on social media don't you think?"

Mainwaring stayed silent. A look of disbelief draped over his face. Samuel got up and walked to the door confidently and with poise, where he turned around to announce, "I may as well stay at home for the time being until you either invite me back properly or make me a golden goodbye offer I can't refuse. You don't want to hear about option number three."

With that, he walked out of the office triumphantly and returned to his own office, where he picked up a few things, and promptly left the premises, head held high.

**

Charlotte knocked on the front door. A middle-aged man answered. He had a kindly face, and a ready smile.

"Hi. I answered the advert about a room?"

"Oh yes, great. Please, do come in."

Alexander showed her into the lounge and asked her to sit on the settee. They were both rather nervous. This was new ground for both of them.

"I've got two spare rooms. I thought I'd try renting out one first, and if that works out okay, I might rent the other one too. What are you looking for?"

"Well, I've got a small one-bedroomed flat at the moment, but it's rather expensive, and to be honest, I think I'd benefit from living somewhere that other people are living too."

"You live on your own?"

"Yes. I have done so for quite a few years now."

"That's interesting, because that's partly why I've decided to rent a room out, you know, to have a bit of company about the place."

"Have you lived on your own for a long time too?"

"Oh no. I'm afraid my dear old mother passed away recently, and this old house of hers feels so lonely with just me in it."

"Oh. I'm sorry. Has that been the case all your life?"

"Yes. She was my mother all my life."

Charlotte looked at him with amusement in her eyes. This was no time to laugh, but that statement was actually so stupid, it was unintentionally funny. She struggled to keep a straight face. Alexander noted the amusement on her expression and he suddenly appreciated what a stupid statement he had just made, and he started to giggle himself. That then set her off and she struggled to restrain a laugh. Her giggles set him off. Like yawning, laughter can be incredibly contagious. This was not the time for such merriment of course. This was meant to be a serious conversation, but that seemed to make them uncontrollable and shortly they found themselves inexplicably in hysterics. They were unable to speak, vainly trying to wipe the tears of laughter out of their eyes. Their hysterics were completely disproportionate to one small unintended joke, but it must have been the tension of the situation that exacerbated things. It was like an unintended emotional release for them both, and their shoulders were in competition to see whose could jiggle up and down the most. After a few minutes of this, they both struggled to regain their composure. There was a minute or so of them alternating between pulling serious faces and then releasing uncontrollable giggles again. Finally the composure started to win the battle, and he managed to speak again.

"I'm sorry that was such a stupid thing to say. Obviously, I wasn't thinking straight."

He needed to have some breathing space and decided excusing himself to the kitchen would be the best course of action. She was holding her mouth tightly as if it had been completely out of control. He spoke as little as possible for fear of giggling again.

"Would you like a cup of tea?"

She nodded. She needed him out of her sight to be able to compose herself properly.

Minutes later, he reappeared with a tray with all the tea stuff on, and biscuits. He placed them down on a coffee table and spoke cheerfully.

"Well, that was strange. I really can't explain it. I have barely smiled for weeks, let alone had a good belly-laugh."

"Yes, that was funny. We just got the giggles. I think it's because we're both nervous."

"Yes. I'm sure you're right. I'll be careful not to say anything else that is quite so ridiculous."

A normal conversation followed, covering all the issues they could each think of about her renting a room. He informed her that because of his business as a postie and with his online work, he would appreciate it greatly if she could help with the domestic chores, and particularly cook for him in return for a reduction in her rent. This caught her by surprise. She hadn't expected to be discussing a kind of business deal, and she confessed that she wasn't much of a cook but she was willing to learn. He was more than happy to help her learn. He said that he would help her learn how to cook new meals from online videos and he was quite confident that she could quickly achieve an acceptable level of competency. By the time they had finished chatting, a whole hour had passed, and they shook hands on a deal. She would be moving in a week's time.

**

Amelia found herself sitting in Elsie's lounge again. This time she was the messenger for Charlotte. She noticed that Elsie didn't look too good. Peter's loss had clearly taken its toll on her. She sat rubbing her hands nervously and her face was tight and drawn. Amelia couldn't help noticing the crows-feet around her eyes which she was sure she hadn't noticed before. She was wearing very plain clothes, and no make-up, as if she had lost all interest in her appearance. Her hair could do with a good wash and brush. She spoke with harshness in her voice.

"Did you find her?"

"Yes, Elsie. I did."

"And did you order her to stay away from my church?"

Amelia didn't like the idea of just being there to pass on people's orders.

"I did convey your sentiments, of course, but Elsie, there is more to this than meets the eye."

Elsie's eyes narrowed. "What do you mean?"

Amelia realised that she had to soften her up if she was going to be allowed to say anything on behalf of the enemy.

"I am obviously a police officer, right?"

"Obviously."

"And I am often put in a position where I have to make decisions based on what has happened, but the evidence is not clear. People lie. People see things differently. People have agendas. That can all make my job very hard. So how do I make my decisions?"

Elsie looked surprised at being asked a philosophical question, but she answered.

"I suppose you have to weigh up the evidence as best you see it."

"Exactly. Evidence. Not opinions, but, intuition comes into it a lot. What do you make of intuition?"

Elsie looked perplexed. "I'm not sure what you mean. Do you mean like a sixth sense?"

"Yes, I suppose you could say that, but it's not based on guesswork, or something mysterious. It comes from years of dealing with people. Sifting through lies and truths and learning to read body language. Eventually, you get a feeling for something before the facts establish that your gut feeling was right. That's what I call intuition."

"Yes, okay, but what's this got to do with me?"

She was rubbing her hands nervously again.

"Well, if I may say so, I think that there is a lot more to this situation with the letters than you're giving credit for."

"In what way?" She looked confused.

"Elsie, you have taken them at face value without any real evidence, but it appears that there is another side to this story."

Elsie was starting to look even more worried. "In what way?"

"I have spoken to this other woman. Her name is Charlotte, and she tells me a completely different story, and my intuition tells me that she is telling the truth. I suspect that your letter-writer has been jumping to the wrong conclusions, or maybe they're just being spiteful."

"You don't think that they were having an affair?"

"Absolutely not, and Charlotte is very distraught that you should be thinking this, and she's written you a letter explaining."

She stopped speaking. She needed this to sink in for Elsie, who looked at her lap, processing silently. She waited until Elsie was ready to say something.

"But why would anyone just want to be spiteful?"

Amelia let out a chuckle. "Believe me, Elsie; some people make a career of it. There are a lot of sickos out there. It happens a lot when people can be anonymous, like on the internet, or with anonymous letters."

"But why pick on me?"

"I don't know. Jealousy probably. Jealous of your standing in the community, jealous of your way of life. There could be all sorts of reasons.

You've just suffered a terrible loss. Some people like to kick people when they're down."

"Are some people really like that?"

"Why do some people desecrate the graves of child murder victims?"

Elsie looked at her with a contorted expression of sheer distaste on her face. "Really?"

"Yes, really. For some people, they feel that the only way they can get on in life is by dragging other people down."

Elsie still looked perplexed, and Amelia was beginning to realise that she had probably lived a very sheltered life. Then Elsie stared at her.

"Why would this woman, this Charlotte woman, want to write to me?"

"Elsie, she just wants to put things right."

"How can she possibly put things right? Peter has gone."

"Yes, I'm sorry, Elsie. There is nothing anyone can do about that. She just wants you to know how she met Peter, and why she met him in that cafe."

"She admits meeting him then?"

"Yes, she does, Elsie, but it's because Peter tried to commit suicide once before."

Elsie looked aghast. This was more than she could handle.

"What are you talking about? He killed himself because of our argument. Because I found out about his affair."

"No, Elsie. I really don't think so. There was something else on his mind, and Charlotte can explain this to you."

After a few moments of struggling with shock, Elsie spoke very firmly.

"No. I don't believe her."

She paused, and looked vacantly away. "I don't know what to do."

"Elsie, I wouldn't be here doing this if I didn't think that it would be of great help to you. I am going to leave now. I have read this letter to make sure it's not just another person trying to be spiteful, and it certainly isn't that. I am going to leave it here on the sofa. You can choose to read it or not to read it. It's up to you, but really, Elsie, take my advice, please, and read it."

She stood up and offered Elsie her hand. Elsie stood up too and they shook hands, before Amelia let herself out, with Elsie staring down at the letter on the sofa with hatred etched in her eyes.

Chapter 19

By the time Charlotte attended her next session with Cynthia, she had been visited by a practitioner of the local mental health team, and she had completed or at least started some of the online courses on the I-Talk website. She was very pleased to be able to report that she completed the course on 'wellbeing' and had made a start on 'managing moods', 'dealing with stress' and had even had a look at the course on cognitive behaviour therapy.

Cynthia beamed at her. "My, you have been busy, haven't you?"

Charlotte looked pleased with herself.

"I've also decided to move."

"Oh, that sounds a bit drastic. What are you thinking?"

"I just don't think being stuck in that flat all by myself has done me any good really. I'm looking for a room to rent in a shared house, so at least I might have other people around me at times."

"I think that's a wonderful idea. Will it cost you more than what you pay now?"

"No. If anything it will be cheaper."

"Great. A win-win situation. How are you going to try to find somewhere?"

"I used an online website, and I think I've already found somewhere."

"Wow. That was quick work! Well done you! Do you think it will suit you?"

"I don't know yet, but I'm going to give it a try. The landlord seems really nice. He recently lost his mum and he just doesn't want to live in an empty house, and it's a lovely house. A bit dated but loads of space and a lovely garden."

Cynthia smiled at her with her vibrant broad smile, and then asked, "Well, nothing ventured, nothing gained. I hope that works out for you. Any news on the Elsie letter?"

"Yes. I did manage to have a chat with Amelia on the phone, and I have sent the letter to her for forwarding, but she hasn't got back to me yet."

"Well done. That's great. You have done all that you can do so far."

Charlotte smiled back at her, enjoying the sense of accomplishment.

"Any joy with voluntary work, sports classes or evening classes?"

"No, I've been busy with all that online stuff for now, and researching somewhere else to live, but I have been looking at what's on locally. I rather fancy dance, or maybe even amateur dramatics, you know, spend some time pretending to be someone completely different to me."

"That's great. There's plenty of time. Is there anything in particular you'd like to discuss today, Charlotte?"

Serious look came over her face. "Towards the end of the last session, you said something about closure with Peter. What did you mean?"

"Well, I know you didn't really know Peter, but you did play a very important role in the last week or so of his life, and I think that again, despite the short time you knew him, a significance of some description was built up for you regarding him. Would you agree with that?"

"Yes," she answered quietly, but firmly. "I did something good with him."

"And then he was suddenly taken away. You expected to see him again, but he died under tragic circumstances, and you had no way of saying goodbye. How has that left you feeling?"

Charlotte sat quietly for half a minute, considering her feelings. A few tears trickled down her face. "Well, as you know, it pushed me over the edge."

"What did you feel?"

"Grief, a sense of loss, frustration and of course, guilt, because I couldn't do enough to stop him trying again."

"Charlotte, I don't think you should allow yourself to feel any guilt. You were in no way responsible for what he chose to do. In fact, you did a great job in trying to move him away from destructive thought patterns, but I do think you need to do your own grieving in some way."

Charlotte looked at her mystified. "Doesn't the grief just go in time?"

"Yes, time is a great healer, but there are things you can do to help it along."

Charlotte looked at her, just wondering silently. Cynthia continued, "Do you have anything to remember him by?"

"You mean something physical?"

"Yes."

"No."

"Anything else at all? Particular words, expressions, stories?"

"Well, he's the only person who has ever told me the story of the book of Revelation, but I'm not going to carry a Bible around with me for the rest of my life."

She laughed a bit, realising how odd that was.

"Anything about him, talking about Revelation that sticks out for any reason?"

"Well, at times, I could see the terror in his eyes. Sometimes he actually started crying. I don't particularly want to dwell on those."

"Okay. Maybe you just need to be able to say goodbye to him in your own way. Has the funeral occurred yet?"

"I don't know. It was mentioned I think at that church service I attended, but I was far too distraught to take anything in."

"That's understandable. Well, it's been quite a few weeks now, so it may well have already happened, and even if it hasn't happened yet, I don't think you should go before the situation is resolved between you and Elsie."

Charlotte nodded in agreement.

"I think you should say your own goodbyes to him either at the bridge or at the cafe. Those are the two places that connect you, aren't they?"

"Yes, but I'm not sure I want to face the bridge again."

"I understand that. How about the cafe?"

"What? You mean like wander in one day singing hymns and placing a wreath on one of the tables. Maybe light a few ecclesiastical candles around the place? Scatter a few hymn books onto customer's laps before bursting into eulogy?"

Cynthia couldn't help herself laughing. Charlotte did have a keen sense of humour.

"That's not quite what I meant," she said, still chuckling. "I'm not sure what you could do. I'm just trying to see if you have any ideas."

"I suppose I could go there for a coffee and panini any time I want to remember him."

"Yes, that's true."

"If I did that, you know what would remind me of him the most?"

"No, what?"

"The gerberas."

"What are they?"

181

"A type of flower. They had them in little vases on each table every time we went there. He always remarked upon their brightness and vivid colours, and their flawless formation. He would often pick one up and comment on the wonder of God's creation, but we know what he meant. Evolution, a marvellous thing."

"Oh, that's great. So, you do have something special to remember him by."

"Yes, but I can't go wandering in there and nick their gerberas whenever I feel like it, can I?"

"No, but maybe you could get a tattoo of one."

Charlotte looked shocked. Nothing like that had remotely crossed her mind, but now that Cynthia had suggested it, she couldn't imagine not getting one.

"That's a brilliant idea! I've never felt a reason to get a tattoo before."

"Then that little connection between the two of you would always be with you. No one else need know what it signifies. You could have it anywhere on your body you think would be best. Maybe hidden. Maybe not."

"That's such a great idea! Thank you."

This seemed to stimulate Charlotte's mind because all of a sudden, she burst out with, "He who hath ears to hear, let him hear!"

Cynthia looked at her bemused. "Sorry?"

"That was a little quote from Revelation which he used to suddenly blurt out when he got animated. That will always stick in mind, if only for some of the comically strange looks he got from some of the other customers. To be fair, I picked it up too. It became a bit of an in-joke."

"Well, there you have it. Something else to remember him by. Maybe you could have that phrase tattooed under or around the gerbera."

Charlotte looked astounded. "Yes!" she said loudly. "Yes. What a great idea! Just the thought of it makes me feel better. Thank you. Thank you so much!"

She carried on musing. "Maybe I could have it done in Japanese. That would fox people."

"Or Greek. Wasn't the Bible written in Greek?"

"I really don't know, but I'll find out. Brilliant! Much more significant, and it would still fox people."

**

Samuel cuddled up next to Sky and opened the picture book. It was good to be back in this homely routine. "Where did Mum get up to?"

"She hasn't done any more."

"You mean no more than we last did?"

"Yes."

He looked puzzled. "What have you two been doing at bedtime then?"

Sky sounded very grown up. "Girl talk."

He looked at her with a screwed-up face. "Girl talk?"

"Yes Dad. She just wanted to talk about stuff with me."

She sounded so grown up. He was silent for a moment, and decided that he didn't want to hear about this girl talk stuff.

"Okay. So we'll just carry on where we left off last time then, yeah?"

"Yes please, Dad."

"Okay. I think I prefer talking about rabbits, if that's okay?"

"Yes, Dad."

He studied the pictures. "You remember that Holly and the others were running away from Efrafa but a posse of killer rabbits were in hot pursuit?"

She nodded; thumb now firmly ensconced in mouth.

"Well, just as the patrol were about to catch them, they ran up a man-made embankment. A railway line ran along the top of it, but they didn't know what a train track was, or what a train was. They were just wild rabbits who had never seen a train. Anyway, they ran across the tracks and fell down the other side. Don't forget. It was very dark and they couldn't see anything. Just as the Efrafan rabbits got onto the tracks right behind them, an enormous steam train suddenly hurtled by at exactly the same time, cutting down the killer rabbits before they had a chance to cross. Holly and his fellows thought that this thunderous, fire-spitting, smoking monster had been sent by Frith, the rabbit-God, to save them from their enemies. I suppose they were right really, don't you?"

She nodded certainly.

"It took them another couple of days to get back to their warren because they were ragged and exhausted, and were terrified of being caught by the Efrafans. However, when they did get back safely, they discovered that whilst they had been away, another mission which Hazel had led to get the hutch rabbits from the nearby farm, had only been partially successful, and that Hazel was missing, presumed dead, so all the other rabbits were very sad and downcast."

With a new story, Sky would be constantly interjecting with questions. She had an enquiring mind and would question something as soon as a query entered her mind. It was strange that she was so quiet with this story, but she had no questions because she already knew it word for word.

"They had succeeded in freeing the hutch rabbits, and had managed to get a couple of does back to their warren, but Hazel had been shot by the farmer in the process. Now they all believed that they had lost their leader. However, Fiver had another one of his weird visions, which told him that Hazel was not dead and it even showed him where he was holed up, and he went off on his own and found him. His spooky sixth sense worked again. Hazel was badly wounded, and was holed up in a drain, but Fiver got help and they got him back to the warren where he recovered.

"Hazel was still convinced that their warren would not survive without lots of new does from the Efrafan warren, despite the two new does from the farm hutches, because two was not nearly enough. He tasked Blackberry, who was their cleverest rabbit, to come up with a plan, which involved their ace card, Kehaar. Then one morning, having made a cunning plan, most of the rabbits set off. Hazel was keeping the plan secret, but the rabbits trusted him and Fiver, who had good vibes about it. Only a few rabbits remained behind, particularly Holly who was so terrified of Efrafa, that he couldn't possibly face going near the place again, and he didn't think that Hazel should try to steal their does. He didn't see how on earth they could outsmart the Efrafans, who were so well organised, and highly disciplined."

"Why did they all go, Daddy?"

"I think that Hazel's plan needed them to get as close as possible to Efrafa without being spotted, and then to hide, all except Bigwig, for whom he had other plans, but he was afraid that an Efrafan wide patrol might find them, and then they would need all their numbers to fight the wide patrol, who were such fierce, skilful fighters."

She nodded gently. Of course.

"Anyway, Kehaar caught up with them and Hazel asked him where a good safe place to hide might be. Kehaar was certain that they would have to get to the other side of a big nearby river, but just then, they spotted a fox sauntering along the lower part of the field. Hazel told them all to stay still because it looked like the fox was moving away, but all of a sudden Bigwig broke cover and dashed towards the fox. He led it off towards a thicket further away and disappeared into it with the fox in hot pursuit.

"Moments later, they heard the terrible squeal of a rabbit in its death throes. They all thought the worst, that Bigwig had been caught and killed by the fox, but just a few minutes later, he showed up with them again, hot and panting. 'Wasn't that you squealing?' They asked. He explained that he had happened upon a small bunch of rabbits in the copse. He had charged through them even though they had tried to stop him, but he supposed that the fox had taken one of them. He had inadvertently stumbled upon an Efrafan wide-patrol which was tracking them.

"Hazel told him off for being so reckless, but he explained that he had been so tense because of their mission, he had needed to do something crazy to get his nervous energy out of his system, and that had been his opportunity. Hazel carried on telling him off, but as things turned out, they were all very lucky that the wide-patrol that was following them had now been thwarted.

"Silver realised that they were too close to Efrafa, and despite being exhausted, they travelled through the night until they had crossed the railway line and found somewhere to rest and graze which seemed relatively safe. Kehaar warned them of another approaching patrol, but thankfully, it turned back at the railway line. It seemed that Efrafans weren't keen on crossing the railway track. Kehaar showed them the way to a bridge over the big river, but the rabbits were scared of it. Initially, only Hazel and Fiver were brave enough to cross it, and Fiver had to go back over it to coax the others to follow them. Rabbits are normally very timid creatures. The next day, Hazel had a chat with Blackberry and a few others. They already had a plan to get some does out of Efrafa, and a plan to break up the pursuit using Kehaar, but they still hadn't worked out the last part of their plan which was how to get clean away after that, because they knew the Efrafans would vigorously pursue them.

"Hazel and a few of the rabbits wandered along the river bank, looking for inspiration for the third part of their cunning plan. They found a small plank bridge which they crossed to get to the Efrafan side of the river where they hoped Bigwig would be one day soon with lots of new does, but they still didn't know how they were going to get away from those fierce and determined Efrafans. As they wandered along the river, they came across a strange object in the river, but it wasn't going along the water with the flow like everything else on the river. They didn't know what it was, but luckily, they had Kehaar with them, and as a seagull who spent most of his time out at sea, he knew all about boats, and he explained to them what it was and what it was for, and that it wasn't moving with the flow of the water because it was tied to the bank by a rope. Very slowly its potential dawned on Blackberry, and he explained to the other rabbits that they could get on this small boat and float off down the river if they could bite through the rope holding it in place. That proved to be the final part of the jigsaw puzzle in Hazel's plan. They would use this boat to escape, and he immediately sent Bigwig off to Efrafa to perform the first part of their plan. Bigwig bravely left them to face Efrafa."

"As soon as he got close to Efrafa, he was intercepted by a patrol, and he told them that he wanted to join Efrafa, and he was brought before the mighty Woundwort to explain himself, and that, my dear, is where we will leave it tonight."

"Oh Dad, you're just getting to the good bit."

"Be that as it may, my child, it is past your bedtime, so the rest will have to wait."

He tucked her into bed and kissed her goodnight. He popped in briefly to give Bronson his time-left warning and got barely a scowl back before happily joining Abi downstairs.

**

Munther and Quithel were lying on a cold wet church roof. The wind was howling around them and the rain was lashing down so hard, water droplets were bouncing hard on the black slates next to them. Of course, they couldn't feel a thing. They were pure spirits.

"If only they really knew what was in these droplets these days," Munther mused mysteriously.

Quithel looked at him with his regular quizzical look. "What do you mean?"

"The ministry of poison has become really big lately. Centuries ago, all they did was to encourage people to ridicule those who advocated clean water, general cleanliness, separation of animals from human habitation etcetera. Anything to make sure people were being easily contaminated with nasty germs, but these days, they have so much more to play with."

"You mean because of modern chemicals?"

"Exactly that. Last I heard they've got eighty thousand in use, and hardly any of them are tested for their effects on humans. The ministry encourages a lax attitude towards them and a ready acceptance because they're modern and new. They push humans to be in a hurry, to just think about the money and they've had a great deal of success in making people dependent on them no matter what. I mean, women paste them all over their faces every day, and we're having quite a bit of success lately in making men follow that suit too. They put this stuff in their food, plaster it all over their bodies, swallow copious concentrations of it, and breathe it in all day long. They've even got micro plastics surging through their very blood now as well. They spray chemicals in the sky to change the weather, and now they're even using chemicals to make their actual food. They want to abandon nature's supply altogether."

He laughed, and continued, suddenly serious again.

"The best bit is their using chemicals to make biological weapons. Of course, they have euphemisms for that sort of thing. 'Gain-of-function' they call it or just plain 'scientific research'. They love euphemisms, like when they kill innocent people; they call it 'collateral damage'. I love that one. In these bioweapon labs, they pretend they're looking for antidotes to new viruses which they are actually designing themselves to be more lethal and contagious than naturally occurring ones. In front of their beloved public, they pass resolutions making bioweapons globally illegal, and then behind the scenes, in secret, they develop hundreds of these 'gain-of-function' labs all over the world, mostly in someone else's country of course, just in case something goes disastrously wrong. They even go so far as to preserve deadly agents which have disappeared from nature so that they can still use them in their chemical weapons."

Quithel looked aghast. He was beginning to think that the human race was hell bent on suicide even without their help. Munther looked at him in bemused fashion.

"It's unbelievable!" he agreed quietly.

"Quithel, there are three things you must remember about human beings."

Quithel relaxed, not expecting this revelation to be ground-breaking stuff.

"One-Each generation believes themselves to be highly superior to all previous generations. Two-Humans are intrinsically and thoroughly selfish. We seem to easily be able to get them to turn a blind eye to anything nasty so long it doesn't hurt them directly. They don't genuinely care about other people, or animals, although they happily pay lots of lip-service to it. Three-Most of them happily blindly follow orders from those seen to be in authority, and they are highly vindictive to the minority of free-thinkers who naturally question things."

Quithel was curious. "I wonder why they do that, you know, just blindly follow orders?"

Munther mused on that question momentarily, and then answered.

"I suppose it absolves them of any responsibility. It sounds noble to meekly follow their leaders, and then they can release themselves from having to do any thinking for themselves, or from taking any personal responsibility for the disasters they cause."

"Not being rude, Munther, but what's this got to do with the proliferation of chemicals?"

"Their presumption of their own superiority I suppose. They imagine that all their inventions of new chemicals to be so much better than anything that has gone before. For millennia people have relied on nature—herbs, vegetables, seeds and fruit—for their medicine. This lot, they've chucked all that knowledge out with the bath water because they think they're far cleverer, and so much more sophisticated with their new-fangled chemicals. Moreover, not only do they throw out all the tried and tested solutions of millennia, they seem hell bent on destroying the habitats where such remedies thrive."

He laughed, enjoying his thoughts. He despised humans so much.

"You couldn't make it up. The ministry of poison is having their job done for them!"

Quithel looked perplexed. "But shouldn't we be trying to reduce their use of medicines?"

Munther laughed again. "Quithel, you are so dense sometimes. We need to encourage them to use more. In small doses, some medicines are helpful for them, but in large quantities, they are disastrous to their bodies because their bodies are such complex, finely-tuned chemical factories in themselves, that they simply can't cope with these new foreign influxes in the high concentrations which they are ingesting."

"But aren't they aware of the harms being caused? I mean, they're so sophisticated aren't they? They must know what's going on."

"Yes, in some ways they are sophisticated, yet in other ways, whilst in their pursuit of their dogma and money, they are incredibly ignorant. 'Wilfully blind' is what we often call it. You must always remember rule number one."

"Which is?"

"On earth, money is king. If something makes money it will succeed, no matter how bad it is. Human nature will make sure of that, with a little encouragement from us of course. The people making the money will make sure that any negative aspects to whatever it is that they're pushing get covered up. Medicine is very big money indeed. It's probably even more lucrative than making guns, bullets and bombs. Sometimes I think that *we* can learn lessons from *them*, they can be so devious."

"But don't people resist when these things hurt them?"

"No. Remember once, I told you that all humans have an innate need to worship something. We've twisted that need towards absolute faith in doctors, politicians, and most of all, their media. They love their media so much. Some of them take their bulletins religiously every single day. Others have their electronic devices soaked in their messages all day long. Very few of them would ever question what their beloved media says, even if their advice makes them ill. They even have warm affectionate nicknames for their sources of propaganda, like 'auntie' because they feel so trusting of it. You know, sometimes I actually feel sorry for humans. They are so stupid and so easily deceived."

He burst out laughing, and then gave Quithel more advice, "If you want a really cushy number, join the ministry of poison. They're having a field day at the moment. Come on! Let's go and do a bit of deceiving of our own."

Chapter 20

Charlotte sat at the bistro table which she and Peter had sat on during their second meeting. It was at the far end of the cafe. She chose it because it was close to the toilets and far from the front door and that gave her time and opportunity to disappear into the loos if she lost her nerve or didn't like the look of Elsie. It gave her a strategic advantage, because on entering, Elsie wouldn't know where to look, and that would give her a few moments to make her decision. She stared nervously towards the door. It was just before ten a.m. and the bistro was only half full. She had already purchased a cappuccino but hadn't even started to sip it yet, even though her throat felt as dry as sandpaper. She didn't know exactly what Elsie looked like but she did expect her to walk through the door at 10 am. As it was unusual for a single person to arrive, and those that did so were generally very old, she hoped to recognise her quite easily. Amelia had also given her a description.

Melodic classical music was playing quite softly in the background and a small vase of red, yellow and orange gerberas bedecked the centre of the table, as always. They made her smile briefly. She stared at the lone woman who had just entered. She had medium length brown hair and was aged about forty, and was of medium build. Her face carried a serious and slightly worried expression. Charlotte was pretty sure that this must be Elsie. She stood up and held up one arm. Too late to escape now. Elsie stared at her rather aggressively and walked towards her briskly. She was clutching a tan handbag closely to her stomach. Charlotte suddenly wished that she had possessed the forethought to ask for no accoutrements. Supposing she had a knife in there? Or acid? One read about these things in the papers.

When Elsie reached her table, she seemed unsure as to what to do next. She just stood opposite Charlotte across the table and said nothing. Charlotte managed a weak, nervous smile and stood up.

"Elsie? I'm so glad that you could come. Please, take a seat."

She felt like she was about to conduct an interview, or vice versa. Elsie sat, still clutching her handbag nervously. Her eyes had a slightly glaring appearance.

"If you want something to eat or drink, the waitress will be along shortly. They've very prompt here."

"Yes, well, you'd know all about that, wouldn't you?"

Charlotte sensed the cutting edge to this remark but ignored it. She knew that Elsie was under some painful illusions.

"I haven't been here that often actually, Elsie. Recently, it's only been the three times I met Peter here."

Elsie winced slightly. She didn't like to hear about some other woman talking about meeting her husband. She didn't even like her using his name or hers for that matter.

"And that's what you want to explain to me today?"

"Yes. Amelia told me about the allegations that have been made and I want you to know the truth, Elsie."

Elsie gave her a hard stare. She didn't look like she was in a particularly receptive mood. She looked like she fully believed in the allegations. Just then, the waitress showed up.

"Can I get you ladies anything please?" She enquired gaily.

Elsie didn't look like she was going to respond. She was preoccupied with staring uncomfortably at Charlotte who took it upon herself to respond.

"I'm okay for the time being, thank you. Elsie, would you like something?"

Elsie broke off from her stare and looked at the waitress momentarily.

"Just tea, please."

The waitress moved off and Elsie resumed her hard stare at Charlotte. "Okay, I'm all ears."

Charlotte resisted smiling, but in her head she was saying 'he who has ears, let him hear!'

"Okay, so it started off a few weeks ago with me walking to the Brunel Bridge one evening. It was a cold, wet, miserable, dark evening, and I saw a man standing by the fence at the middle of the bridge. He was just standing there, alone, peering over the edge into the gorge. I could tell instinctively that something was wrong. I tried to speak to him but at first he didn't seem to hear me. I got closer and addressed him more loudly. It was then that he looked at me, and he just started sobbing. His shoulders shook quite violently."

She got a hanky out of her pocket and wiped her eyes. Her eyes were beginning to stream. Emotionally, she was back in that moment, but she could still talk.

"I challenged him—you were going to jump weren't you? He answered 'yes' and carried on crying. I don't know how I did it, but I held myself together. I felt extremely emotional myself, but I felt that I had to be strong for him. I told him that I wasn't going to let him jump. That made him laugh briefly. I mean, that was a stupid thing for me to say. There's no way that I could have restrained a grown man, and then he looked directly at me for the first time and called me an angel."

She had to stop now. She needed a good cry. Elsie was still just staring at her. Her expression hadn't softened. "Then what?"

When Charlotte felt ready to talk again, she carried on, "I asked him if we could talk about it."

"It? What?"

"I don't know. Whatever was bothering him I suppose? He said 'not now' and I started to gently lead him away from the middle of the bridge. We just carried on walking, mostly in silence, but eventually, I insisted on him meeting me another time to talk about what was troubling him. Obviously, I was incredibly worried about him and we agreed to meet here the next day."

"And that's it? That's how you met him?"

Charlotte looked at her with sincerity. "Yes."

She waited for Elsie to respond. "You hadn't arranged to meet him there, on the bridge?"

"No, of course not. I'd never seen him before in my life."

"You didn't meet him online?"

"No. of course not."

"You've never been to our church before?"

"Never. I only went once at the end of the week after I'd met him here."

Elsie looked pensive. She was thinking of how she might catch her out.

"And you think he wanted to jump over the side of the bridge?"

"Without question."

She went quiet. She obviously struggled with that idea, but then after a few moments, she had another question.

"What were you doing there that evening?"

Now Charlotte went quiet. She really didn't want to answer that question, but at the same time she realised that it was best to be frank and honest if she wanted Elsie to believe her.

"Elsie, I've only mentioned this to one other person—Amelia."

Elsie persevered with the cold fixed stare. Charlotte paused, summonsing up courage.

"I was planning to jump that evening too."

She buried her face. She was ashamed and upset, and needed another good cry.

Elsie looked a little perplexed. "So why didn't you? You two could have held hands and jumped together. That would have been really romantic!"

Now Charlotte was the one dishing out the mean stare. "That's a cruel thing to say. We are talking about two people's lives here. As soon as I saw him, any ideas I had about ending my own life evaporated. I simply had to help him."

Elsie didn't appear to be particularly chastened. "So what happened when you met him here?"

"He just told me why he was so depressed."

Elsie looked perplexed. "He never talked to me about feeling depressed."

"Elsie, I can't comment on that. There might be all sorts of reasons why he didn't want to worry you. I did say to him that he should speak to his wife."

She looked at Elsie slightly pitifully. Elsie just looked confused.

"So, did he tell you what was bothering him?"

"Yes."

"Go on!"

"Revelation."

Elsie pulled a very confused face. "Excuse me?"

"He told me that he was a preacher, and that he wanted to cover a subject which wouldn't raise objections amongst the 'woke' community, and so he chose the book of Revelation."

"What do you mean by 'woke' community?"

"You know, people who are easily offended if you stray off their narrow definitions of things like sin, gender identity, the cult of self, same-sex relationships, birth control, etcetera."

"He said that?"

"Yes."

Charlotte was beginning to get the impression that Peter hadn't talked to his wife about quite a lot of things that bothered him.

"And what did he say about Revelation?"

"Well, he basically ran through the entire book from memory. I was very impressed. It took all of three sessions for him to finish it."

"You met him three times, here, just for him to talk about Revelation?"

"Yes. That sounds odd, doesn't it? I suppose I wanted to know what had terrified him so much, and he wanted to get it off his chest."

"He's never talked to me about Revelation."

Charlotte just looked at her, wondering if she was simply a difficult person to talk to.

"So, what happened after three sessions?"

"He had finished his story and said it wouldn't be appropriate to see me again, but that I could attend his church if I wanted to, and so that's what I did."

Elsie was thoughtful. "What was so bad about Revelation?"

"To be honest, Elsie, I can't remember much about it. It was full of strange creatures, with lots of wings and heads and eyes. It was about a guy in heaven being shown what was to come on the earth in the end times. Plagues, the sun going dark, the moon falling out of the sky, wars, famines, earthquakes, mountains being cast into the sea and lots of thunder, fire and brimstone and deaths. Lots of death. And the antichrist of course. I mean it was terrifying if you thought that it was all going to happen, and he seemed to really believe that all this tribulation stuff was going to come to pass during his lifetime, and he couldn't face it. He said that he wouldn't be brave enough to face the traumas and then he wouldn't get to heaven."

Elsie looked stunned and spoke quietly. "Why didn't he talk to me about all that stuff?"

Charlotte could think of an answer or two to that question but knew it was wise to keep quiet. Just treat it as a rhetorical question. She just looked at her silently. Elsie's expression was softening, and Charlotte could tell that she had convinced her of her innocence.

Elsie suddenly stood up. "Thank you," she said simply, and walked towards the door and left the premises. She hadn't touched her tea. Charlotte was gobsmacked by her abrupt departure, but she was feeling so much better now that she had had the opportunity to put matters straight. She was now at peace about her. She had said what she needed to say. She also realised that she also hadn't started her own drink. She sipped it. It was rather tepid now, so she gulped it down quickly and ordered another hot one whilst her mind was swimming with random thoughts about Peter, Elsie, life, death and end times.

**

Samuel was at home doing the laundry. The others were all at school. He had his favourite music blaring out of the sound system and he was feeling pretty good. Then the post arrived and he felt his adrenaline suddenly squirting, as he spotted a letter to him from the bank. He sat down nervously before opening it. He skim-read all the jargon so he could quickly get to the important bit. The bit with the numbers in it; four times his annual salary! They were offering him a golden goodbye severance pay of four times his annual salary! He re-read it several times and smiled. That was a pretty good deal considering that they could just sack him. He couldn't wait for Abi to return from work and to share the good news. He hoped that she would be equally pleased. They hadn't discussed the possibilities yet. They had decided just to wait to see what the bank would say. Now he knew.

**

Later that day, he was snuggled up with Sky on her bed. He hadn't told Abi about the bank proposal. He would broach that subject a little later, after dinner. For now, he allowed his mind to wander no further than Efrafa. He opened the picture where they had left off the last time.

"So, Bigwig was caught by a patrol, but he kind of confused them by stating that he was actually looking for them and wanted to join Efrafa. That was a first for them. All they ever knew was about rabbits trying to escape from Efrafa. They'd never been faced with one trying to actually join them. He was marched off to be interrogated by General Woundwort himself, who found no reason to be particularly suspicious of him, and as he had recently lost three of his captains, one to a fox, another to the giant fire-breathing smoke monster, and the third had been demoted for letting Holly escape, he decided that Bigwig might in fact be Owsla material. He was after all a big strong and bold rabbit.

"So he attached Bigwig to one of the marks to begin his training under that mark's captain. He soon learned that the warren was ruled with an iron fist. Each mark had its own burrow with just one entrance which was always guarded by sentries. The rabbits were not allowed to mix with other marks. This was to make sure that any potential dissent didn't spread. The rabbits were only allowed out for a specific and limited period each day to graze, no matter what the weather, and were always under guard and being watched. The poor rabbits were constantly fearful and subdued.

"Bigwig quickly found the opportunity whilst underground to talk to one of the unhappy, disgruntled does, and risked telling her about his plan to lead them to freedom the following day. The plan was that at sunset the following day, Kehaar would attack the sentries and Bigwig would then lead the escape of as many does as possible from his burrow. She found his story about the big bird attacking the sentries difficult to believe, but she nevertheless trusted him and said that she would spread the word amongst the other unhappy does. Whilst he was out grazing Bigwig got a message to Kehaar when he landed nearby, and everything seemed set for sunset the following day.

"However, the next day, just as Bigwig was about to go above ground to give Kehaar the signal to attack the sentries, none other than General Woundwort himself caught him and kept him back for questioning. Why had he been so close to that big white bird the previous day whilst out grazing? Wasn't that a dangerous thing to do? What was that bird doing in this vicinity at this time of the year anyway? Why had he been talking to the does? Why had he visited another burrow? He also pointed out that another rabbit recognised him as the rabbit that had led a fox onto the patrol where the captain got killed some days earlier, and Woundwort demanded an explanation. Bigwig realised that Woundwort had a tight grip on everything that happened in and around the warren, and that he found out about everything. Nothing seemed to escape his attention.

"All the rabbits had been trained to spy on each other. Everything out of the ordinary was reported to him. Bigwig was beginning to wonder if he could possibly ever outsmart him. By the time the general had finished interrogating him, feeding time was over, and the rest of the mark was led back underground. Now the does were confused. The escape Bigwig had talked about hadn't happened and the big white bird hadn't shown up. Hazel, who was waiting near the railway line for word of the escape, was also confused and was worried that Bigwig had been found out.

"The next day, the doe which Bigwig had confided in told him that one of the younger does, who knew about the plan to escape, had been arrested. It was clear that she would soon talk and the escape plan would be well and truly thwarted. Bigwig knew that he had to act immediately, even though he hadn't arranged new plans with Kehaar. He told his doe friend to get all the other does ready to run. He tricked the sentries into moving off but one of the captains confronted him, and Bigwig had to fight him. He defeated him but in the process got a nasty wound to his shoulder. Then he and all the does made a run for it. The alarm was soon sounded and as they ran towards the area where some of Hazels' rabbits should be waiting for them, they could hear Woundworts sentries already chasing after them. It was an evil afternoon with a dreadful thunderstorm in full blast, with heavy rain soaking them and slowing them down.

"Nevertheless, they reached some of Hazel's scouts and were led towards the river, but the does were rather confused and straggling and before they got there, General Woundwort himself and his posse caught up with them. Just as Woundwort was about to tear into the wounded Bigwig, whom he now hated with a vengeance for betraying his trust, there was a flash of white in the sky and Kehaar showed up just in time, attacking Woundwort and driving him off to nearby cover in a ditch with the rest of his patrol. However, there was no way that Woundwort was going to give up, big bird or no big bird.

"Bigwig and the does were then led quickly to the small tethered boat where Hazel had almost chewed through the rope. They had trouble getting the does to go onto the boat because it was just too strange. Just then Woundwort appeared again with his posse on one side of them as another patrol approached from the other side. The sight of the terrifying Woundwort scared the remaining does onto the boat and Bigwig and the last remaining rabbits leapt aboard just as Hazel finished gnawing through the rope. Then, to Woundwort's astonishment, the boat full of rabbits started to quickly drift along the fast flowing river. He and his own rabbits were dumbfounded. They had never seen anything like this. They had been outsmarted and were soaked and disheartened, and so, for now, they had no options other than to return to their warren where Woundwort would plan his revenge. He wasn't the sort of rabbit who would ever give in to defeat. And that, my dear, is where we must leave them tonight."

"Oh Daddy, you haven't got to the best bit yet!"

"You always say that!" he chuckled.

"Anyway, it's your bedtime! And I've got to go downstairs to speak with Mummy. I have some very important news for her."

Sky looked at him sleepily. "What news?"

"Hey, never-you-mind. Grown-up stuff."

"Is it good news, Daddy?"

"Yes, darling. It is good news."

She discerned that Daddy had something important to do, so she relented in a rather grown-up way.

"Ok, Daddy."

Chapter 21

Munther and Quithel were lying on a church roof quietly contemplating illness, depression and other human attributes. Quithel was curious.

"Munther, do you ever go inside?"

Munther looked at him inquisitively. "Go inside what?"

"Churches."

"You mean when there are people in there?"

"Yes."

"Quithel you're such a weirdo. Why would I want to go in there when they're having one of their worship meetings?"

"Isn't there opportunity to plant doubts in people's minds, you know, when they're listening to a preacher they don't like, or who is really boring?"

Munther pulled a face. "I told you before; we have to pick our time. Approach them when they seem most vulnerable. They're not especially vulnerable in church surrounded by other believers when they're all whooping it up."

"But do you ever go in?"

"I don't make a habit of it, but I have occasionally. Not to try to do any work you understand, just to learn what they believe, you know, stuff from the Bible."

"Is that how you learned the scriptures you recited?"

"Of course, I can't read you know. Can you?"

"No, of course not."

Munther cogitated for a few moments and then asked a question himself, "Did you ever visit earth? You know, when you were a light-rep."

"No I didn't actually. I've told you this before."

"Well, excuse me if I don't remember every word that comes out of the mouth of the mighty Quithel." Munther was worse than sarcastic. He was scathing. Quithel decided just to keep explaining and to avoid winding him up any more.

"There's a huge host of ang…light-reps in heaven, and I got the impression that very few ever visited earth. Some were sent on missions occasionally, usually to deliver messages to individuals I think, or maybe to provide divine intervention in some event. I don't really know."

He thought some more. "Are they usually in churches when they're being used?"

"No, of course not. You wouldn't be able to stand it if they were there. I've heard that they do visit very occasionally though, but none's ever shown up on any of the occasions I've been inside."

"Why do you think they only show up occasionally? What's the reason for it?"

"To be honest with you, I think it's because most churches are little more than social clubs. They don't actually practice what they preach and light-reps have no reason to be there."

He paused and then added, "It's funny that you didn't visit earth before."

"Not really. There's a whole host of ang…Light-reps up there and this planet is acknowledged to be the domain of the Dark One. So they rarely come down here although they are aware of everything that goes on here, but they can only intervene on the express orders of the light one, and he only ever sends his strongest and most powerful servants."

"No wonder he never sent you then!" he scoffed. He was feeling awkward about this conversation and he ended it abruptly.

"Come on, loser. We've got work to do."

**

The kids were both in bed, Samuel and Abi had finished dinner, and everything had been cleared up. Samuel had warned her that they needed to sit down after dinner and have a serious chat. They went into the lounge with two glasses and a bottle of red wine and sat on the sofa together. Samuel put some quiet soothing music on.

"Ooh, are you going to propose to me again?" She asked playfully.

"I hope I don't need to do that, darling," he replied.

He poured the wine and they clinked glasses.

"It's about our future. We're going to have to make some big changes."

"We are?" She queried rather surprised.

"Yes, and it's not just because I've been laid off."

"Oh, is it something I've done?"

"Come on, Abi; don't go all sensitive on me. I don't really know where to start. This is big-picture stuff, and I know that's not your favourite subject."

"You mean I never see things the way you do."

"Yeah, I suppose so. It's difficult, isn't it? But please, just hear me out."

She sat back on the sofa, crossed her legs and said, "I'm all ears."

He sat facing her very directly. "Okay. So, we've got my severance money, and that was probably as good a deal as I could possibly get."

"Oh, that's great! How much?"

"Four times my salary."

"Sweet."

"I've also got that money in the Cayman Islands."

"If you can get it out. You said we might not be able to touch it for a few years, until the investigation at the bank dies down."

"Yes, I did say that, but events are about to overtake us, and I think I'm going to have to risk getting it out sooner rather than later."

"What events?"

She looked worried.

"That is what I want to explain."

"Okay, go on." She sipped very slowly. Now she was feeling really quite nervous.

"If we stay here, I would need to get another job sooner or later, and I think that might be quite hard now."

She interrupted him. "What? Because you've fucked up so much at work and on social media?"

"Yes. Thank you, darling, for being so understanding. That's not quite how I would have put it, but I get your drift."

She smiled at him, all innocence herself. He carried on, not allowing himself to be distracted.

"I think I need to get that offshore money out and we need to sell up and move."

She looked shocked. "Move? Where? Why?"

"There are massive changes in the pipeline for society as a whole, and probably sooner than we think."

She frowned. "You're not going to go off on another of your conspiracy theory rambles are you?"

"Look, darling, I know we don't see eye to eye on politics…"

"Or religion, or the media, or my mother, or the future of this country."

"Yes, I know."

"Or how to eat a bunch of grapes, or hang toilet paper the right way round."

"Yes, I know, dear."

"Or scamming employers."

"Please, let's not get side-tracked with all the usual tr…minor issues."

"You nearly said *trivial* then, didn't you?"

"Sorry, I just mean that we have much more important topics facing us right now. Please, bear with me. This is serious, Abi."

She looked at him sternly. "Things you consider trivial are not necessarily trivial to me. Remember?"

"Yes, darling. I remember."

He paused to gather his thoughts. Then as he looked very directly into her eyes, he continued.

"One thing I am going to ask you though, is to stop using that phrase 'conspiracy theory'. Please. I really mean it."

"Why?"

"Because it's a significant trigger word. As soon as you use it, your brain switches off. It makes you assign whatever subject you are thinking of to the bin inside your head, without really giving it proper consideration."

He gave her his most sincere and serious look. "Abi, I'm being really serious now. Please don't use it anymore."

"You feel that strongly about it?"

"Definitely. People have been programmed to adopt such trigger words by the media to stop them being open to ideas which the media don't like. It's like a type of hypnosis."

"You really think so? That's not just a—what phrase can I use instead?"

"None! I want you to be more open. To think for yourself. Not let them shut your mind down."

"Remind me again, who's programming me?"

"The establishment. They use the media. You *know* the government is big on propaganda. They employ hundreds of psychologists constantly to come up with clever ways of 'nudging' people. That's what they call it. 'Nudging'. Nice little euphemism for trying to brainwash people. They have whole departments devoted to 'influencing' people to think the 'right' way so that they're not seen to be forceful. It's all very subtle. Their messages are seeping out constantly through the TV, radio, adverts, straplines, etcetera, etcetera. It's never-ending. They're probably sticking subliminal messages everywhere they can possibly think of."

"Okay. Go on."

He tried to gain some kudos for himself.

"Remember that in the banking world we are privy to a lot more information than the general public. Some of it we're told about officially, and some of it just inevitably trickles down from the top and is supposed to be on a need-to-know basis. Also, don't forget that the people who run the world's banks run everything else, and I mean everything. Everything revolves around their money. Politics. Business. Wars…"

"Can we get back to the bit about why we need to move please?"

"I'm coming to that, dear. Okay. You know that normal money, *fiat* money, is going to be replaced by Central Bank Digital Currency (CBDC), right?"

She looked a bit unsure.

"Come on, Abi. Our own prime minister has announced it, they're already employing people to introduce and manage it, and I've talked about it before."

"Yes, but won't that run alongside normal money?"

"Not for long, if at all. And it's going to come in soon. The banks are already preparing for it."

He looked at her intently, hoping for signs of understanding or acceptance.

"So, what's wrong with Central Bank Digital Currency?"

"It will be completely electronic. It will be more like an allowance than old-fashioned money. Some faceless, mindless government bureaucrat will decide what you can have in your electronic wallet and what you will be allowed to spend it on. In fact, it probably won't even be a real person. It will be an algorithm. The banks' algorithms will manage your personal allowances. It will all be linked to your carbon footprint. You won't be allowed to spend on whatever you want, like now. And if they have any reason to switch it off, they will."

"Not just me though. Everyone."

"Of course."

"And you really think that's going to happen?"

"Yes, dear, really, without question."

"How could they do that? People wouldn't stand for it."

"What? Like they didn't stand for two-year lockdowns and not being allowed to visit their families? Like they didn't stand against being barred from weddings and funerals? Like they didn't stand for having untested novel drugs forced on them? Like they didn't stand for their mums and dads being left to die alone and in abject confusion?"

She didn't have an answer for that. Anyway, she didn't just want to argue with him. She did want to try to see things from his point of view.

"So, are you saying that we need to get our hands on that money and to use it whilst we can?"

"Yes, darling. Exactly that. We need to put it into something useful and tangible. Soon, money in the bank will be worthless. I suggest we buy a big farm as far from other people as possible."

Abi burst out laughing. "We don't know the first thing about farming. We don't even have a pet hamster, and every plant we bring into the house shrivels and dies almost instantly."

"I'm not envisioning us getting our hands dirty. We can employ others to manage the actual farming."

She looked confused. "You've said before that the government wants to shut down the farms and get people eating synthetic lab-grown food. So what would be the point of having a farm?"

"It would provide us with space and our own food, real food. We wouldn't be allowed to sell any produce, not officially anyway."

"So, how would we pay the workers?"

"I think that because of the severe limitations of CBDC some kind of bartering system will emerge. It's bound to. I think that if we can provide people with somewhere to live, or real food, they would happily work on the farm to help produce it. Food will be the new gold."

"I think you're hoping for a lot."

He looked at her and shrugged his shoulders.

"Where do you get all these crazy ideas from anyway?"

"Abi, they're not crazy ideas. Just like Fiver in Watership Down, there have been people who seem to be able to look into the future."

"Don't tell me that Fiver predicted all of this."

He laughed. "No, he didn't. But what about Aldous Huxley? He wrote *Brave New World* in 1932. George Orwell wrote *1984* in 1948. They both foresaw totalitarian one-world type governments in the future, with the end of democracy, and their visions seem to be coming true right now."

"They were stories. There's nothing to say that these things are actually going to happen, is there?"

He furrowed his brow. "I used to think that a one-world government was an impossibility because I imagined that there would have to be such a huge destructive world war first, to break down the individual nations, and that it couldn't possibly happen, but honestly, Abi, I think it's crept in by the back door without us even noticing."

She looked at him rather blankly. "Explain."

"You know that lot who meet in Davos every year?"

"I am aware of it. The entire world's richest people go for a knees-up once a year."

"Okay. So, who are they? And what do they do?"

"I don't know exactly. Talk about how to make even more money?"

"Yes, that goes without saying, but it's not primarily about money. It's about control. They are the most influential people in the world. Six hundred CEOs of the world's biggest companies. Plus the people who run the organisations that have set themselves up since the Second World War to manage the world's money, health and economies. Plus loads of billionaires just because they are super-rich. None of these people are elected. None! They don't represent the interests of billions of ordinary people, only those of the very wealthy, and believe me, not only are they super-wealthy, they are also super-powerful."

"I thought politicians went too."

"Yes, a few lucky ones do, but only to arse-lick the super-rich, take bribes and get their orders. They're like dogs under the table picking up the crumbs."

"Don't you think you're being a tad cynical?"

"Darling, the more this goes on from year to year, the more I'm convinced of it."

"But what makes you think that they want to change everything?"

"They're delusional. Their wealth and power have gone to their heads. They think they've become Gods. They seem to believe that they can reshape the world in their own image. They want to put microchips inside peoples' brains so they can link them to the internet, and then read them and programme them. They believe that they can help to speed up the evolutionary process to make digital-hybrid humans. 'Trans humanism' is what they call it. They actually post all this shit on their websites, and it seems clear that politicians all over the world are all in their thrall. They treat China as a role model, to be emulated. Can you believe that? A country that imprisons millions of people at a time; a state that crushes all opposition or dissent and imposes its will on the people with an iron fist. These elites, they're also the ones driving the climate crisis hysteria, so that all the draconian actions they want to introduce can be claimed to be saving the planet. That's all they've got to say to get the vast majority of stupid ignorant people to go along with it."

He looked at Abi. She was looking a bit blank. It was all too incredible. He persevered.

"One of their mantras is that by 2030, you will own nothing and you will be happy. I know you've heard of this one."

"Yes, but how could that ever happen?"

"They're going to ban petrol and diesel cars."

"Yes, but by then, we'll all have electric cars."

"Really? And where is all the electricity going to come from? Currently, green energy produces five per cent of our energy needs, and they'll only allow green energy."

"What about houses? We are a proud house-owning nation."

"They'll push interests up so high that nobody will be able to afford their mortgages. Then they'll be repossessed."

"What about people with small or no mortgages?"

"They will be required to upgrade their homes with extortionately expensive environmental upgrades which they won't be able to afford."

"And then their homes will be repossessed too?"

"Exactly."

"So, what's the point of us buying a big farm then?"

He shook his shoulders. "Maybe it will put off the day of reckoning. Maybe buy us time. They'll be working on reconstituting towns and cities first, hopefully for quite a long time, and so it will be some time after that when they try to clear people out of the countryside."

She looked deeply confused. "What do you mean, 'clear people out of the countryside'?"

"They want to *rewild* it. It's all in their plans and published agendas, Abi. You can read it for yourself."

She looked drained. Big-picture thinking was not her forte. She was a details person. The immediate. What she could see in front of her eyes, here and now. But Samuel hadn't finished driving his point home yet. "Abi, you know about fifteen-minute cities, don't you?"

"I've heard the phrase but I don't know what it really means."

"They're preparing for it here, right now, in our very own city. What do you think is going to happen to house prices when people are not allowed to travel more than fifteen minutes from their home?"

"I've got no idea."

"Oh, come on. They're going to plummet. No one will want to move here and everyone will be trying to sell up and go elsewhere. Only a few save-the-plant misguided zealots are willing to be locked up for the rest of their lives. The vast majority will still believe in personal freedom. Being alive is not meant to be a crime for which you deserve incarceration."

Her expression was a strange mixture of perturbation and disbelief.

"We need to sell up before the rush starts. They're already installing barriers and cameras all over the place. We're running out of time."

That did make sense to her.

"But that's only for cars, right?"

"Really? And how exactly do you get from place to place?"

She made no reply. Silent acquiescence.

"And you can bet your bottom dollar that after they've got us all micro chipped, and plugged into facial recognition software, which is another thing they're planning by the way, they won't be just tracking our cars, they will be spying on all of us, all day, every day. Abi, they're planning to control all our movements."

She paused. This was all way too much. Far too crazy.

"What about my job? I love my job."

He sighed. "AI will be taking over your job in the next few years. All that pandemic stay-at-home, work-from-home, teach-your-kids-at-home lark was just conditioning. Getting people ready for when it's permanent."

"How will AI take over my job?"

"Kids will be given an age-appropriate 'toy'. Fluffy ones, animal-like ones, tablets. Whatever appeals to them. Those AI devices will be linked to the internet and will converse with them every waking minute. They will indoctrinate, sorry, *teach* them everything *they* want kids to know and believe. They simply won't need to go to a school. Totally AI. We're only a small step away, even now."

She looked exasperated. He appealed to her earnestly.

"Look, what have we got to lose? If I'm wrong, we'll just end up living in a great big farmhouse in the country with employees managing the farm for us, and you can get a local teaching job if you want one."

"And if you're right?"

"We will enjoy a lot more freedom than our city cousins locked up in their rabbit hutches. We won't be in so much of a virtual prison, and we'll still be eating proper food. It's a long shot, but I'd also try to hack their system. If I could do that, I could possibly make us invisible to the new AI masters, and if we didn't have close neighbours programmed to spy on us, we might be able to live a much more normal life, like proper human beings."

He looked at her very seriously. She didn't look convinced or excited but he had said quite enough to make her think. The seed had been well and truly sown. He had one last point to add.

"Oh, the land would have to adjoin the sea so we can go fishing, for real fish. Fish will definitely form part of the new informal currency."

She looked at him, almost exasperated. "Don't say anything else. You've overloaded me. All I can say right now is that I'll think about it."

Munther whispered in her ear. "He's full of shit! He's just distracting you with his crazy conspiracy theories so that you will forget that he's just completely fucked up his job. He's a complete loser and all he is doing now is clutching at straws and trying to confuse you."

Chapter 22

Charlotte and Alexander were sitting down at a proper dining room table for a proper home-cooked meal of shepherd's pie, and a proper conversation, with some easy-listening music playing fairly quietly in the background. Alexander was very encouraging towards her.

"This is lovely, Charlotte. Your cooking has really come on!"

She blushed a little. "Thank you, Alex. Well, you showed me where to look on the internet to see how it's done. I had no idea how much stuff there is to help. It's far easier than I thought it would be, especially because you've got all the right kit in your kitchen."

"I still think you have some flair for it though."

She was a little embarrassed and changed the subject.

"I don't think I'll ever be as good at cooking as you are on the computer."

He had shown her some of his videos about the human body and they had blown her away, she thought they were so good.

"Give yourself time. Nothing is achieved overnight."

She looked at him curiously.

"What got you interested in the human body in the first place, I mean, unless you're a doctor why would you want to know so much? No disrespect, but you're just a postman, right?"

He put on a serious expression to suit the subject matter.

"Some years ago, I lost two close friends to heart attacks. They weren't particularly old. I don't think they should have died. I couldn't help thinking that for whatever reason, they'd let their bodies down, so I decided to find out more about how the body functions, and how we can help it stay healthy."

"What, because you don't want to die?"

"Of course not. We all die eventually. I just want to live as healthily as possible I suppose, and I think that I need to own that responsibility by knowing how my body actually works. To be honest, the more I look at it, the more amazed I am."

Now, she had got him onto his favourite subject, and he announced proudly.

"I'm starting a new one on the cell, you know."

He looked at her with boyish glee, smiling broadly.

"The cell? What cell?"

"Pretty much all of them. Most of them function in a very similar way. All thirty trillion of them? I'll just focus on one typical cell."

"Won't that be kind of boring? One cell?"

He laughed. "That's exactly why I need to do it. We still have a one hundred and sixty year old Darwinian idea that the cell is a very simple structure that could have been thrown together by a few atoms floating around in the air and being struck by lightning."

He laughed before continuing. "Nothing could be further from the truth. Each microscopic single cell is a whole world of its own with a great deal of inbuilt, intuitive intelligence. We have this idea that our intelligence is in our brain. Only our brain, but that's wrong. Every single cell has its own built-in intelligence which coordinates all the processes going on in that single cell, and there are loads of processes going on in each one of them, twenty-four hours a day, all integrated, focussed and exquisitely coordinated. If any one of those processes fail, we get sick or even die."

She glanced at him as she fed herself another mouthful of pie and noticed the dreamlike fascination in the expression on his face. He carried on.

"A cell looks like a fried egg. The yolk is the nucleus. That is the preserved God-like centre which contains all the DNA, and that's the blueprint for anything and everything that needs to be made in your entire body. I'm not looking at that through, just the albumen."

"So, is the nucleus with the DNA in it the brain?"

"Yes, I suppose so."

"Is albumen egg-white?"

"Yes."

"But if you're only doing a single cell, shouldn't you look at both parts at the same time?"

"No! They're both far too complicated, especially the nucleus. DNA has enough information in it to write five thousand books. Just one strand of DNA has one hundred and forty-four thousand genes in it. Each strand has all the complete information in it about how to make every single part of you. It's unbelievably complex. Maybe one day, I'll try to tackle it, but for now, just the albumen is quite enough."

He stopped to eat a few mouthfuls, but she could tell that he couldn't wait to carry on explaining the wonders of the human cell. As soon as he had swallowed, he continued.

"So, the outer part of the cell is called cytoplasm. There is a skin encompassing the whole cell to keep it together, but it's not completely solid. It has valves or pumps in its surface to regulate minerals inside and outside the cell. How many pumps do you think?"

She looked up, surprised. Was she supposed to have wondered this question before? Should she be expected to know the answer? She hazarded a guess rather hopelessly.

"Two?"

"About a million."

He beamed at her. He was clearly impressed and she thought that she ought to show some amazement too.

"Wow! That's a lot, all squeezed into such a tiny space."

"Yes. Just the valves are incredible, but the really fascinating parts are the main bits of machinery in the cytoplasm."

Before he had a chance to embarrass her with another question to which she would have no idea about, she encouraged him to continue.

"Do tell me!"

"Well, there are two main engines. One is the mitochondria and the other is the ribosome."

She decided to come clean. "To be honest with you, Alex, I've never heard of them. I have trouble remembering the word *albumen*."

He smiled generously. "That's okay. I know that this is all very technical, but with the right vid, I can make this miracle accessible to the masses!"

"So, what does mitochondria do when it's at home?"

"That's the machine that turns glucose and oxygen into energy. I'm not quite sure yet how that happens. I've still got a lot of research to do. It's incredibly complex. There are twenty-three separate and coordinated processes inside the mitochondria just to break down one glucose molecule. Cyanide kills you by blocking just one of those processes."

He looked at her as if expecting a round of applause. She wasn't sure how to respond.

"Okay, so it's a highly sensitive process?"

"Very much so, and so is the ribosome. Do you know what that does?"

"I'll be honest with you, Alex, I haven't got a Scooby. Does it make ribos?"

"You're on the right track. It makes proteins. Every cell in your body has to make proteins in order to survive and it's all down to the ribosomes."

He beamed again. She liked how enthusiastic he was. So many men liked to appear unemotional, but not him. When something took his attention, he wore his heart on his sleeve.

"Actually, ribosomes present a chicken and egg scenario funnily enough. They make proteins, but they are also made up of proteins, so where did the proteins come from that made them?"

He beamed her another rich smile.

"You're asking the wrong person. My mind can't even fathom out infinity in space."

He chuckled, and got back to the subject in hand.

"And how many ribosomes do you think there are in a typical cell?"

She contorted her face. She was way off the mark last time so she aimed higher.

"A dozen?"

"Ten million!"

"Ten million?" She repeated in genuine amazement. "How can that all fit into one microscopic cell?"

"I know. It's incredible how tiny and sophisticated the insides of a cell are. We are only just beginning to learn so much new stuff because we've become so advanced lately with our own modern technology. The most sophisticated electron microscopes today can see down to one ten-millionth of a millimetre!"

He beamed at her in his wonderment again.

"One ten-millionth of a millimetre!" she repeated. "You really know how to impress a girl, Alex!"

His smile disappeared slowly. He wondered what she meant. He wasn't trying to impress her, or was he? She picked up on his confusion.

"It's okay, Alex. I wasn't being sarcastic. You're just funny in your unique way, that's all. I kind of don't know what you're talking about, to be honest."

He still looked unsettled and didn't know what to say next. She was a little perturbed that she had inadvertently unsettled him, so she changed the subject.

"It all sounds incredible, Alex, and I'm sure you'll make a fabulous job of it. On a completely different note, I've been wondering if you'd be willing to help me out with something."

He looked at her with a degree of confidence that indicated that he was sure he could, even though he didn't know what she was going to ask him.

"Of course, fire away!" He replied enthusiastically.

"I've been looking at what dance classes are available around here, and I'd like to try one, but I don't have the confidence to go on my own. Would you come with me?"

That took him aback. He'd never done any dancing in his life. He only had vague memories of being an awkward teenager at discos decades earlier, and being far too embarrassed to actually try anything.

"Oh, you've caught me out. I don't know if I'd be able to actually do that."

She looked clearly disappointed and said nothing.

"Could I just accompany you, without being required to participate as well?"

"I've got no idea. I've never been myself, but it would be nice if you did."

"Oh," he managed thoughtfully. "What kind of dancing is it?"

"Well, there's a surprising variety out there actually. I've checked out the videos too."

Now it was her who was displaying enthusiasm. She was clearly taken with the idea.

"The closest class is Tango, but I'm not sure I fancied the look of that. Too much wrapping your legs around the bloke. I think I'd get embarrassed."

He looked a little surprised at the thought of strange ladies wrapping their legs around him, although the thought did occupy his mind for quite a few moments.

"Then there's one called Bachata. I'd never even heard of that one. I don't think I could do that one, not with strangers anyway. It looks a bit like trying to have sex with your clothes on."

His face reddened slightly. "Oh my goodness. I think we'd better give that one a miss. That sounds a bit embarrassing. Or maybe it's a type of relationship counselling sort of thing."

"I don't know. That leaves modern jive or salsa."

"Could you get pregnant doing either of those?"

She laughed. "Certainly not the jive, it's too fast, even for a bloke! I don't know about the salsa. That still looks quite intimate."

"Maybe the jive then? Sounds the safest. No condom required."

She laughed. "Yeah I'll find out a bit more about it, but would you be willing to escort me?"

"That's a big ask, Charlotte, but maybe I'll be brave. You only live once."

"No, you only die once. You live every day!"

He looked at her with some mock admiration. "Very good."

She laughed. "I don't know where that came from. Must have read it somewhere recently."

He was thinking that she was really rather a lovely girl who had lost her way in life a bit, and that realistically she was far too young for him. The fact that she lived in his house as a lodger meant that he had to be squeaky-clean with his behaviour, but on the other hand, if she was inviting him to do things with her, wouldn't it be rather foolish not to explore possibilities?

She had her head down now, polishing off the last remnants of dinner, but her mind was racing. She had actually been bold enough to ask him to accompany her to something. She really hoped he would accept, because she really liked him. He was quite a bit older than her, but that didn't really matter because he was solid, intelligent and moral. She loved his enthusiasm and his kind nature. Who knew what a small social venture might lead to?

"Alex, I've made a nice cheesecake. Would you like some?"

**

Amelia was in the vicinity of Elsie's house and she could easily sneak in a quick tea break. She knocked on her door. Elsie looked rather startled to see her.

"Oh, Amelia! Is everything okay?"

"Yes, of course. I was passing and just thought I'd stop by to see if you did anything about that letter or if any other issues have arisen since then. I hope you don't mind. Us coppers are a nosey lot!"

"Oh, I see. Yes of course, that's very thoughtful of you. Please come in and have a cuppa."

She provided tea and biscuits and explained about meeting Charlotte in the cafe and that she had satisfied herself that her account was totally plausible. The hardest thing she had to deal with was finding out that Peter had been thinking of taking his own life without sharing it with her. His wife! That was the worst part of it. She actually felt really guilty about that.

"Elsie, I don't think you should feel guilty about that. The people who actually succeed in taking their own lives almost always keep it a very well hidden secret from their loved ones. You did nothing wrong."

Elsie wasn't convinced. She changed tack. "I've sent Charlotte an invite to our church. I think she'd like to come, so I've sent her details of our introductory sessions. I hope she'll come to one of those."

"Oh that's kind of you, Elsie. I am pleased. It would be great if you two get on. Somehow that seems so appropriate."

"Yes, well maybe. Let's just see what happens, shall we?"

**

Munther and Quithel had just finished tormenting some poor sad person who was down on their luck, and had a bit of time to themselves. Munther shot Quithel a mean stare.

"Gronoff says that it's time you went independent now. He'll visit you soon to give you new clients. In the meantime, he wants you to concentrate on that boy Thomas's family and their circle. Since he nearly killed himself, his parents have gone all flaky, wondering about life, death, and the afterlife and all that shit. You need to get in there and cause doubts, confusion and fights. They're actually very vulnerable right now."

Quithel looked very pleased. "So, we say goodbye now?"

"Yes, thankfully. You've been really holding me back with your dim-witted questions and your imbecilic slow grasp of issues. I haven't enjoyed having to nurse you and I will be glad to see the back of you, you thick, stupid tosser. I wish you could go back to heaven and just annoy all the wankers up there like you probably used to."

Munther's face was hard and fixed. He meant what he said. Devils only joked about bad things. Quithel was a little taken aback for a moment, but then his devil-nature kicked in automatically.

"I'm so relieved to be independent now. You are the most crap, incapable mentor one could ever be so unfortunate enough to come across. There's so much I could teach *you*, you ignorant, mother-fucking loser."

"Fuck you!"

"No, fuck you!" and with that Quithel happily departed.